EDE

WITHDRAWN FOR SALE

CHAMOIS

By

Joyce Doré

1663 LIBERTY DRIVE, SUITE 200
BLOOMINGTON, INDIANA 47403
(800) 839-8640
WWW.AUTHORHOUSE.COM

© 2005 Joyce Doré. All Rights Reserved.

No part of this book may be reproduced, stored in a retrieval system, or transmitted by any means without the written permission of the author.

First published by AuthorHouse 01/27/05

ISBN: 1-4208-1962-3 (sc)

Library of Congress Control Number: 2004195083

Printed in the United States of America
Bloomington, Indiana

This book is printed on acid-free paper.

Chapter 1

Impact and certain death! It was the only solution. Chamois made the decision without really thinking.

The Research and Survey vessel Orion would divert the crippled training vessel Excalibur from certain destruction using a manoeuvre like a snooker shot.

Orion and its crew would be sacrificed. However Excalibur and its young, highly achieving officers, including Chamois' own son, Dang, and Stravros' daughter, Melody, would be saved from annihilation.

Oblivion beckoned for Chamois and his crew as Orion headed into the giant red sun, Betelgeuse. Chamois' memory badgered him about the time over thirty years ago, when he was just a kid, struggling through the Star Fleet Academy with old Stonewall as his mentor. Sean and Grant were with him even then; the rest of his crew were like burrs that he collected along the way…

The sand dust drifted across his visor, obstructing his view, causing Charley Stone to lean back even further than his tormented muscles and vertebrae wanted to allow. He felt as though he had been climbing the dark red, sandstone cliff all his life. Sweat, fluid he could not afford to lose, trickled incessantly down his spine as he scaled the almost perpendicular cliff. One exasperating drop snaked past his eye, but with his life support helmet in place, wiping the niggling moisture away was not an option.

In the freezing cold of Mars, normally kept at bay by thermal suits, his sweat could turn quickly to ice on his body. If that happened he would die almost instantly.

He closed his eyes tightly, shook his head in the hope of getting some respite, then he glanced over his shoulder to where Sean Darnley, wearing a regulation space suit with the

Dionysus logo, was struggling to gain a toehold on some loose shale.

Sean's helmeted head was turned towards him, the visor glinting in the harsh sunlight. Charley could not see the look on Sean's face, but he guessed it showed utter exhaustion.

Then, slowly but inexorably, Sean began to drift backwards. His climbing axe and toe spikes were not holding him secure on the sandy slope; he seemed stiff-kneed and off balance.

Charley's heart skipped several beats. There was nothing that he could do to help his friend and valued comrade, and he watched with utter dismay as the loose sand gave way.

Sean's visor was being dragged against the cliff face, causing dust to cascade onto his up turned face. The ineffectual axe and toe spikes were adding to the downward shift of the debris.

As a scream from Charley's throat echoed into the communicators embedded in each helmet, Grant, the third man in the group, lazily heaved his climbing axe in Sean's general direction. The axe looped, and then sank up to its shaft between Sean's thighs, stopping his downward slither.

Straddling Grant's axe, quickly he brought his own axe down into the cliff face to gain purchase. Digging his toes in with all of his waning strength, he managed to give himself a stable hold on the precipice once again.

Charley wanted to call Sean on the com-link to tell him where to place his hands and feet, but his throat felt as dry as the desert.

Even though the red dust marred Sean's facemask, Charley could see that his normally round cheerful face was crimson with exertion and shock.

The greater gravitational pull of Mars was straining Sean's heavy, muscled frame to the limit. Charley's was naturally slim, his body honed by constant unarmed combat sessions with Mito Iwaki. Even so, his shoulder muscles ached; the climb had started to take its toll on his triceps. He felt dizzy and longed to take a rest.

Sean certainly deserved to have won a coveted place as a sublieutenant in Star Fleet, Charley believed, since he had excelled in all the academic tests. It was Grant Geddes, who was the mystery; he had apparently studied cybernetics and gained a Masters degree, yet his gaze seemed vacant and vacuous, and he had only just managed to scrape through the search and destroy test, where dexterity and speed were vital necessities for survival. Yet just now he had executed an impossible throw with his climbing axe to save Sean's life! It didn't make sense. Charley heaved a sigh of resignation; the enigma would have to wait until they were all safely back on board the training space vessel, Dionysus. Then perhaps he would approach Grant about his prowess with the axe… maybe not. To ask Grant outright about the smokescreen that surrounded him would be most unwise. There had to be reasons explaining what the young man was hiding from. Also there may come a day when he would need Grant's aid and abilities. I'll leave it to time to solve this reticence in Grant, he decided and continued his upwards scramble.

Charley was glad that his ash fair-hair was clipped to a regulation shortness that prevented any straying into his eyes, and the life support helmet kept dust from causing even more problems.

He took a deep breath, making a tremendous heave with his tired leg muscles to where he had seen a stable ledge earlier. It would hold all three of them at a squeeze, giving them a chance to sip some water from their rations and relax aching limbs.

Charley waited until the other two were safely seated with him on the ledge before saying, "That was a close call. We were nearly a candidate short for the sub-lieutenant stakes there. I thought you were going to your funeral, Sean. What made you lose your grip?" He glanced at his two companions and asked, "By the way, anyone know who thought up this particular test?" Charley's joke hid the effects of the gut-wrenching trauma of seeing Sean slipping down on his way to certain death.

Sean and Grant grinned at each other. "Come on Charley, you're not that dim," Sean told him. "It was your old pal, Stonewall Jackson himself!" Sean told him. "Stonewall considered the scaling of the cliffs of Moher, County Clare, too simple. Though from what I was told by those who have been given that exercise, it was no funny story climbing up 180 metres of perpendicular limestone sea cliffs with a westerly squall blowing directly off the Atlantic, the temperature no better than that of Mars either; even the emergency rescue dinghies had to run for shelter! As for losing it, I had cramp in my calf muscles fit to murder for."

"It's not surprising you got your legs tied up in knots with the tough climb we've got!" Charley said without rancour. "I think that we've all lost a few pounds in fluid and salt." He then asked, "And I suppose it was Stonewall's idea that we should do it without grav-lift, seeing as how we had no wind and rain to contend with?"

"You got it right first time." Sean quipped, "The Martian gravity must have sharpened your wits, that or the fantastic view from up here." He stretched out his arm to the forbidding harsh landscape of arid barren rocks and dust of the red planet, Mars. "I owe you big time, Grant, and I will not forget; though if that axe had come a fraction closer to my anatomy, I would be singing contralto from now on!"

"Neither will I forget. I can't believe what happened. There was Sean on his way to his own memorial service, then next thing I see, he's sitting on your axe, Grant." Charley added.

"Now, Charley, seeing as you are so clever at spotting that it was your friend Stonewall who devised this physical test, how about finding a nice easy way up the rest of this skyscraper for us steeplejacks?" Grant asked, trying to play down his life saving tactics.

Charley eased himself further into the crevice that made up their perch and grinned at them. These two were at their favourite hobby again, trying to wind him up. "I don't know why you bother. You know that I'm going to get the Clark award." He swung his legs nonchalantly, kicking with his heels against the sandy cliff causing runnels of dead soil to cascade down to the barren ground below.

Every one laughed including Charley. Sean gave him a hearty thump on the chest that should have just knocked him back into the crevice; instead Charley disappeared buttocks over head.

His yell as he vanished out of sight, ended abruptly with a 'grumph'. Grant and Sean looked at each other in disbelief! Then both, as if propelled out of a gun, attempted to dive together into the dark cavern that Charley's swift exit had created.

Grant roughly tugged Sean back by the scruff. "Sean, he's not too far down and it needs only one of us to go get him. I'm that little bit narrower on the shoulders than you are, also you have far more back muscle than I do, it only makes sense that I go after him while you belay the rope," he gasped.

Not waiting for Sean to agree, Grant looped the climbing rope about Sean's waist and testing its security about his own, he then gradually lowered himself through the black hole to where Charley now lay silent.

As the night vision in his helmet came into use, Grant could see Charley's prone form resting on a flat surface. With luck, there would be no protruding rocks that would have caused broken bones.

"What's happening down there?" Sean's disembodied voice cut sharply through the microphone in Grant's helmet. "Is he hurt, can you move him?" The concern that he felt was obvious.

"Wait a minute, can't you?" Grant was bent over Charley and was carefully testing each of his limbs for possible damage. "He seems O K, maybe a bit concussed and knocked himself out. But I don't think we should move him. Anyway the sun is sinking too fast for us to get him out during daylight. I'll stay here with him till he comes to his senses again. I suggest we make ourselves as comfortable as we can and attempt to shift him at sun up."

"You know I'll have a few words to say to old Stonewall about emergency grav-lift. We could have lifted Charley out with no bother," Sean com-linked to Grant. He had started to feel apprehensive about Charley's chances of getting out alive. God knows what mischief he'd got himself into this time! "What does it look like in there?" Sean called.

"To tell the truth from what I can see with the night vision, it looks for all the world like an empty church hall." Grant had lowered his voice as if he was indeed in such a place. "Sean, the floor is smooth and even as if it's been made that way. Know what I mean?" Sean listened and tried to evaluate this new anomaly. "I think I'll send down a flare. This is an emergency so we would be justified in using one. Shut your eyes; I don't want to blind you."

Sean took the flare cartridge from the emergency pack on his back, and carefully pulled the fuse cord and tossed it into the black hole; on its way to the ground, it lit up the stygian darkness, the void now as bright as day, and Grant was right, it did look like a very large room, thought Sean. With his head poking through the fissure, he could even see what seemed to be a doorway in the furthest wall.

"Trust Charley to fall into a genuine Martian hidey-hole! Grant, see if Charley is showing any signs of life yet. He's been out for the count too long. It's about time he surfaced."

Grant checked Charley's life support system. The dials on his wrist showed that the heartbeat was strong and regular. All his life readings were normal; in fact there was no reason why he was not responding. Grant could only conclude that his mate Charley was fast asleep! "Do you know what? He's asleep. Honest, Charley's taking time out for a noddy."

"Okay, let's keep this in perspective. He's safe just as long as he's not cold, so keep an eye on his life signs for temperature drop and so on. You're safe and I'm the only one left out here in the bitter cold! What do you say to you making yourself comfortable, have some water and take nourishment? When it's daylight again, we'll review the situation. I hope that by then sleeping beauty decides to wake up."

Sean felt powerless, yet what else was there for it? He tried to puzzle out if Charley was in worse trouble than usual, but his exhausted brain refused to operate further. He could not really blame Lieutenant Commander Jackson for their predicament. It was a stupid excuse and he had to admit it to himself, if blame there was, then it was his, for slapping Charley so hard.

Daylight, grey and stealthy, crept across the top of the canyon, the sun cast brilliant shards of light of red and orange setting the cliffs ablaze, and depressing shadows of indigo pits where it did not strike.

Sean and Grant had spent a tormented night. Sean asked how Charley was. "Oh, he's great! Slept like a newborn and wants to know where he is. Says he had a weird dream. He seems to think some very anxious people occupy the place. All I can say is they can't be any more anxious than I was when he fell in here."

While he was being discussed, Charley took a mouthful of water and a vitamin tablet, and then stood up to survey his surroundings. The night vision gave a dim outline of a bare room, a doorway, but no windows except for the hole he had made.

"What do you think Grant? What do you think we've stumbled on?" Charley asked as he gazed around the cavern.

"You tell me then we'll both know!" Grant growled. "The problem at this moment is how to get out of here without causing damage. The boffins are going to want to go over this place with a fine toothcomb. Even the dust on the floor will have to be analysed to find out if there is DNA in it."

"You're right. That lot don't miss a trick where possible life forms have existed." Charley thought for a moment. Then linked to Sean. "Say, Buddy, do you by any chance suspect that these helmets are linked to the mainframe? It seems strange to me that us poor unenlightened 'Middies' are set free without old Stonewall peering over our collective shoulders." Sean laughed at the thought of all the desultory and very unflattering things that they had said about the Lieutenant Commander. "I hope not! He'll have us strung up by our cajuns for some of the things we've said. No, I don't think so. If we were linked, surely by now they would have sent in a rescue team, wouldn't they?"

Sean's question had a note of insecurity; he was by no means certain that Star Fleet would be bothered. If there had been a death, then they might…if they were linked… Sean did not wish to think too deeply about the possibility of everything they had said and done being recorded in the main computer. "Why? What were you thinking of?" he eventually asked.

"Well, if we are connected, then they already know the situation, right? Our objective on this test was to scale these cliffs and live to tell all about it, okay? So what do you say to a little exploring, find out where that door leads to?" Charley's voice held a powerful magnet of excitement.

"Noooo, Charley, don't even think it." A concerto of anguish echoed through the com-link. Sean and Grant knew enough about Charley to realise that wherever he went, grief followed like a shadow. "Leave it Charley. We've enough to do to get you out of this hole and back to base. Call us old hens if you want, but count us out of this escapade. I for one want my subby star," Sean yelled at him.

Sean felt the desire to belt Charley once, hard, to knock some common sense into him. Lucky for him he was out of arms' reach.

That skinny idiot could probably break both our necks with one hand tied behind his back, he muttered to himself, but it didn't stop Sean from wanting to thrash the living daylights out of Charley. The sooner they got back to Moon Base the better.

"Come on up. You first Charley, then Grant. We must clear this ravine by mid-day for pick-up." Sean had had enough. They would get back to Moon base then Charley could please himself.

Sean had found Charley a light-hearted extrovert, and his joy of living had made the days at the academy easier to handle, and as much as he enjoyed his subject of astral navigation there were times when he was glad to be cheered up by Charley's company. But there were also times when it seemed as if Charley's adventurous spirit led to all kinds of complications, like now!

Joyce Doré

The pick-up at the top of the ravine was made in a routine orderly manner, and the trip back to the mother vessels made without comment from the shuttlecraft crew that ferried them. In fact the silence felt ominous and the three men felt that there was trouble in store for them from Stonewall. However, once again there was no reception group of 'Snowdrops', the white-capped security guards waiting in Dionysus' docking hall and the group were allowed to go to the mess hall to eat a normal meal instead of the vitamin tablets and water that had been their fare for the climbing test. After a meal, they retired to their cupboard-sized rooms called berths, to rest.

While Dionysus resumed its journey to Moon Base where the rest of the exams were to take place, Charley slept dreamlessly and exhaustedly.

Chapter 2

The sun filtering through the Plexiglas gave her hair a golden nimbus, ranging from honey blond to cinnamon; her shape would have defied Michelangelo, the gifted sculptor of the sixteenth century.

Charley Stone had never seen such exciting curves on a woman; his fingers tingled at the thought that she would be soft and warm to touch.

She was standing talking to Stravros and Sean, who were from the Dionysus, the same Space Training Vessel as himself.

Up in his cabin cum study, on the second floor, Charley resolved there was no way he was going to take his eyes from her by going down the null-grav, and without any thought of how he would land, leapt out of the window and went bounding over toward the trio. It was just as well that Moon gravity was only one sixth of that of Earth.

"Stravros, I've looked all over for you!" Charley lied. "Oh, I hope I'm not intruding," lying even further.

Stravros, the Chief Engineer on the Dionysus, knew his friend was being more than economical with the truth, but then he knew that every man wanted to meet his sister Maria, so he might just as well introduce them and let Maria decide if she wanted to get to know Charley any better.

"Okay, Charley, cut the waffle, this is my sister, Maria." He turned to the girl who was smiling with appreciation of Charley's obvious admiration.

"Maria, I'd like you to meet Charley, he's supposed to be studying for his final exam, before the Space Navy sets him loose as a sub-lieutenant on a Research Vessel, that's if he passes."

Charley's deep blue eyes met Maria's green-hazel ones. Her look penetrated his skull and travelled down through his body igniting explosions of liquid fire as it went and caused perspiration to glisten on his upper lip.

Holding Maria's hand was like holding that of Aphrodite, the goddess of love; the fingers were perfect, soft as a warm kiss, and pink tipped, with little pearly fingernails, oval and with no polish. Charley wanted so desperately to raise the fingertips to his lips.

"Ah-erm" Sean cleared his throat. "Don't mind us, we were just discussing whether or not this contraption needed a new wheel, or if I could get Gabby and Pete in engineering to repair it."

The contraption was an antique bicycle. The trouble was one of the wheels was truly off line.

"I'd give up and start out fresh," Stravros commented. "How about coming over to Beckett's Bar? Maria says that they brought a consignment of citrus fruit up with them. Isn't every day Moon Station gets such luxuries."

"Yeah, why not? I've finished my written work for the exam. You'll have to get a move on though Charley, if you want to meet the deadline!" Sean had completed his training for entry as astro-navigator and would now occupy his time until the final results were published; doing the thing he loved most, tinkering with ancient machines.

Charley looked at Maria, trying to appraise how she felt about him. Her gaze was warm and friendly, just that and no more.

Still holding Maria's hand, he took a chance and said without much conviction, "It'll only take me a few minutes to do the last set of problems. Come on, let's go!" And started to lead the way.

Beckett's Bar, a popular place at any time, was full to overflowing due to a squad of off duty Space Marines. They had just come in after patrolling a cluster of asteroids where platinum had been located. If knowledge of it reached the bandits, and it usually did, then the Marines would be out again before they had drunk Beckett's bar dry.

They were doing their best when Maria, Stravros, Sean and Charley arrived.

Charley noticed furtive movements as illicit alcohol was poured into the innocuous fruit juice. Idiots, he thought. If they get called out, they'll suffer the pangs of hell when they put their life support helmets on.

Maria's entry had not gone unnoticed. Several Marines, who had obviously had more than their fair share of the hard spirit, were leering; then one, with more bravado than the rest, came over and put his arm around her waist. It was an insult that made Charley's ears burn and turn scarlet.

"I don't think the young lady wants your hands on her. Go away, will you?" The sound of his gritty voice was strange even to himself. It was however, the calmest phrase that Charley could utter. He was seething with rage and he gave the Marine the benefit of an icy glare.

With a wide, mocking grin, his teeth like wolf's fangs, the Marine turned his attention on Charley.

"Well, what have we here? Is this lover boy?" The alcoholic slur in his voice spoiled his sneer. Then, turning his back on Charley to face Maria again, he continued to push his luck.

"Come on honey, I can give you a much better time than that freak." The Marine never got to finish his affront to Charley. The man was now flat on his back, and as a mark of loyalty to their fallen comrade, the rest of the Marines joined in. The fight might have been uneven with a whole crowd of Marines against three Spacers but Charley knew how to take care of himself in such situations. He had also shared some of what he had learned from Mito, with his friends, including Sean and Stravros.

The fight was beginning to die down with Marines on the floor or propped up against walls, when the Personnel Control Officers arrived.

Sam Douglas, sergeant-at-arms, surveyed the bar. Then turned to look at the Marines who were still conscious.

Taking in the sight of the three Spacers, standing ready to take on all comers, the girl lounging on a bench, aloof, with an amused smile on her face, told him everything that he needed to know.

"I suppose you leather-necks are going to tell me that this escapee from the church choir started the fight?" Tapping his nightstick lightly on Charley's chest, he choked back the laughter that threatened to spoil his air of command, then he managed to continue, "Next time you start a fight, make certain that you can finish it. You really ought to know better than to pick on someone as skinny as this yard of pump water. Don't you know it's the skinny ones who have learned to take on the likes of you?"

He tapped the table with his nightstick with its punishing electrode switched off and said, "Come on! Clean this mess up and get rid of that booze. I don't want to catch any of you with hard liquor on base again. Understand?"

Turning to Charley and his friends he asked, "Which ship are you from?"

Stravros, Sean and Charley looked at each other; this could cause trouble if their Commanding Officer got to hear about the fight.

Sam's eyes still had a glint of laughter in them. "It's okay! I just don't want to be on the wrong side of any brawl you three get involved in," assuring them that they were not on a charge.

Charley decided to answer for them. "We're from the Training Vessel Dionysus. I'm Charley Stone." Pointing to Sean, he went on, "This is Sean Darnley and that is Stravros Bertolozzte. The young lady is Stravros' sister, Maria."

Charley glanced toward Maria, who was easing herself up off the bench. Her stiletto heels beat a syncopated tattoo on the rock hard Pyrilcite floor, her body keeping to the rhythm, undulated, as her hips swung in an erotic fluid movement. She came toward the group, her magnificent figure declaring her pure female.

Maria's eyes glowed like topaz and emeralds, her eyelids slightly lowered, which partly concealed a glimmer of triumph. They were directly on Sam; she spoke to him in a low, husky voice as if he were the only man in the room.

"I really am sorry if my brother Stravros and his friends have caused you any trouble officer, but they were only putting these lice back in their place." The gesture with her arm took in the fallen Marines, accentuating her voluptuous figure, a pose that made every man in the bar stare at her blatantly.

Stravros wondered at whom the pantomime was aimed; who was his little sister really gunning for? Her curious hazel-green eyes seemed to be only for Sam, yet from time to time, there was a flicker in them towards Charley. The gleam of mischief was there all right!

Sam knew his masculinity was deliberately being got at. If she wanted, this girl could melt the polished steel serving bar. But he just could not afford to get involved. The one called Charley looked as though he had more than a passing interest in her. Tangling with Charley in earnest could prove painful!

"It's fine, Miss Bertolozzte, you can say thank you to these three for sorting out what could have been a nasty incident. No harm done, Miss."

Sam Douglas decided the time had come for him to leave Miss Bertolozzte and her company; he was not entirely immune to her wiles. He would go, and let them enjoy what time they had left before returning to their ship.

Maria now turned her attention to Charley. "That was so brave of you, seeing that slug off. I can't stand being mauled by someone I don't know or like." She was now standing so close to Charley, that the voluptuous feminine figure was caressing him in places; and where she touched was on fire.

Stravros came to Charley's rescue. "Okay little sister, don't give my mate Charley ideas that you have no intention of fulfilling," he admonished her.

"Who said I don't intend to pay my debts? Charley is fantastic. No girl can ignore a man who leaps like a chamois from a window, just to get an introduction then defends her honour from a bunch of Casanovas."

Maria's body was playing hell with Charley's equilibrium as it moved and stroked him. Stravros and Sean glanced at each other. "Do you think my two Leading Hands, Pete and Gabby will still be around? Let's go and find them. They may be able to come up with some ideas about that bent wheel on that thing you call a bicycle." Stravros addressed this suggestion to Sean. Turning to Charley, he asked, "You don't mind staying and looking after my sister, do you?" Stravros had given his friend the best exit lines he could think of. What he did with the opportunity to be alone with his sister was entirely up to him.

"Shall we have a drink Chamois?" Maria was teasing him and enjoying the power she had. "I think that name suits you, gold silky hair, slim hard muscles." She was stroking his biceps, her eyes devouring him.

Chapter 3

"Sure, what would you like, Maria? When you've had that, I'll escort you back to the Rest House. There may still be some Marines about who are three sheets to the wind." He had pounced on the excuse to see Maria home and blessed the drunk Marines for this opportunity.

Later Charley returned to his cabin in the Spacer's blockhouse to join Stravros and Sean. "Hope you didn't *leap* to any conclusions regarding Maria, Chamois," Stravros confronted him, putting an arm across his friend's shoulder. "I know my sister only too well. She don't mean any harm, but then she has never given any man reason to believe that she could ever be serious about him, if you get my meaning."

Sean chipped in. "And how did the lovely Maria say thank you to her brave *Chamois*, hmmm?" The lecherous smirk made his brown eyes crinkle.

Charley Stone knew this was a ribbing from his best mates, yet he was feeling as if he could leap over any obstacle to gain Maria's attention.

"Hmm, yes I like the nickname, a Chamois is just how I feel right now." There was a beatific smile on his face as he made this declaration.

His over active brain would not let him sleep, and after three hours of tossing and turning in his lonely, narrow cot, Chamois got up and worked on the exams that he had to hand in at ten o' clock that morning.

He realised that if he were to stand any chance of making a permanent commitment with

Maria, then he would have to be able to present a solid income so as to be able to share with her some of the good things in life.

Ragged-eyed and grey-faced, he walked to the common room to meet up with Sean, and together they presented themselves and their papers to the examining committee.

After being told they had thirty-six hours stand-easy while their papers were examined, Chamois and Sean went to find Stravros in the engineering quarters.

Moon base relished in having a Plexiglas dome covering an asteroid crater of several square miles and thirty feet high, giving it a perfect balanced ecological unit. The design had been copied from similar ecosystems built to preserve rare and endangered flora on Earth, over small craters left by worked out opencast mines, the first one being built in a small village in England, aptly called, Eden.

With plant and small animal life imported from Earth, tall pillars of moon rock strengthened by carbon fibred steel, held up the geometric shaped panes of Plexiglas, a bye-product of early space exploration when a shatter proof, clear glass was needed.

The low gravity, one sixth of that of the Earth, was ideal for those recuperating from surgery or illness. Also precious crystals were grown, where they could not have formed on Earth.

Tobacco had been outlawed, because it gummed up the air filters and spoilt the oxygen. Alcohol had become a poison; when men were called on duty at a moment's notice, to go "outside" wearing a life support helmet, the effect on those who had been drinking alcohol had been disastrous. The blood vessels had swollen and ruptured causing agonising pain, sometimes death.

Chamois and Sean made their way to Beckett's Bar and were discussing the previous night's punch up, when Maria and Stravros joined them.

"I feel sorry for those leather necks! We took advantage of them," Chamois was saying.

"Don't be daft! They loved it, and are probably looking for a return bout, right now," Sean grinned. "Anyway, what do you plan to do about it, eh?"

Synthetic ale was available as was peach and nectarine juice, and after a hard night's play and even harder morning's work, it was the fruit juice that tasted fresh and clean on Chamois' tongue.

"Maria, Stravros, good to see you. Don't you think those Marines ought to have a chance of a return bout, sober this time?" There was no laughter on Chamois' face. Stravros could see that he was serious.

"They'll be as mad as a flock of wet hens. I'd keep away from them, if I were you!" Stravros said, as he gave a seat to Maria then sat down himself. "I can see nothing but trouble with such an idea."

"Yeah, I know, but it don't seem right. They are trained in unarmed combat and should have been able to stand up to us." Resting his chin in his hands and looking sideways at Stravros, he added, "We've got a stand-easy for thirty six hours. Do you think we could arrange a game of tag with them? They pick three of their best men against us. Come on, what do you think?"

Stravros and Sean were grinning widely, nodding their heads when Maria butted in.

"Fighting again! I suppose you want me to umpire for you?"

"No, you would be considered prejudiced, Admiral Blake is visiting. He likes to think the services are well integrated. We'll tell him that we would like to stage a friendly match, and would he be so kind, et cetera, et cetera."

"Yes! He likes a match and a wager, so it's a certainty he'll agree." Sean was beginning to feel the excitement buzzing from Chamois.

"How about you Stravros? You with us?" Chamois wondered if Stravros, with his rank of Chief Engineer, would want to risk his chances.

"Now how can I let you two squabs show Engineering up? Of course I'll be up there with you!" Taking a deep breath, he asked, "Have you seen anything of them this morning?"

Maria bent her head trying to hide the laughter she knew showed on her face. "Your opponents have just walked in. The only thing is though, they really look as though a dog has dragged them from somewhere rather nasty."

Chamois stood up and made his way slowly to where the Marines were supported by Beckett's Bar. He lowered his voice, so as not to set their jangled nerves screaming, and asked them in all earnestness, "How would you like a fair fight? Last night put you in a bad light with me and my mates." He nodded his head towards Sean and Stravros. "We don't like to think we beat you on unequal terms."

The Marines took a few moments to absorb what Chamois was saying. The skinny little runt was actually asking for a pasting!

"What did you have in mind? We have our good name to consider too. We don't want anyone thinking that we beat up a junior officer that a puff of fresh air would blow away." The man was interested; his friends were all nodding their heads in agreement. "My name is Geoff, by the way."

Stravros, who was heavily muscled, joined in the conversation. "Glad to make your acquaintance, Geoff. We're not all built like Chamois. Sean and I would like to make up a three a-side game of tag. What do you say?" Stravros knew that the Marines would be forced to agree with this suggestion.

"Okay, set it up. You'll have to get the brass to agree though!" Geoff was now looking and feeling far better than when he had arrived at the bar, knowing that at some time the Marines and the Spacers were bound to meet and clash in such a closed community. The loss of the fight to only three Spacers the night before had given them a name worse than cowards.

This way, they could redeem their good name and face the rest of the space personnel. Even if, God forbid, they lost, at least it would be with equal numbers.

A crowd had gathered for the bout, bets placed and taken, favouring the Marines. The three Spacers looked no match for the burly men, commonly called leathernecks, from a far distant custom of having a wide collar of leather around their necks, forcing them to hold their heads high.

Admiral Blake had heard from his old friend of student days, Commodore Gregory, about Charley Stone and his friend, Sean Darnley, and decided to place his money on the Spacers.

Several rounds into the bout, with a display of aerobatics thrown in, due to the low gravity, Admiral Blake decided that enough was enough. One of the trio of Marines was clearly exhausted.

Perspiration sheened his body. He looked like a beaten Adonis. The other two Marines carried on gamely. However, in no way were they anywhere near as nimble as the Spacers.

When Admiral Blake gave the verdict to the Spacers, six points to four, Chamois remembered a word of advice from Mito. "Never take advantage of a fallen man, you will only anger him and take away your own dignity. If he is worthy of combat, then treat him as a friend."

Grabbing the sweating Geoff by the hand, he held it up with his own, and addressing the crowd he shouted, "If anyone out there thinks they can do better than our mates here, then we would be only too glad to oblige them with a little game of tag, anytime, okay?" the response to which, was an even greater roar of approval.

Eventually the crowd of Spacers and Marines went to Beckett's Bar to quench their thirst and celebrate the game, and then they made their way back to their respective billets.

Chamois escorted Maria back to the Rest House as Earth light came over the low horizon.

"We get the results of our exams in ten hours' time, Maria. Sean and I are getting our new orders. As soon as I find out where I am going to be sent, I'll let you know." Words were not coming easy. They were sticking in Chamois' throat. How could he expect a girl as beautiful as Maria to wait for him?

"I would love you to stay on Moon Base and wait for me, Maria, but that would be asking too much. I also long to ask you if you would like to make a permanent commitment, and have our DNAs matched for compatibility." There, he had said it!

"I don't know what to answer, Chamois." Maria was genuinely shocked! She thought this sleek, nimble man a wonderful lover, but to spend years with him? Have his children? This would need very careful thought. None of her previous lovers had ever expressed such a wish. What Chamois was proposing amounted to marriage!

"Let's take this one step at a time, Chamois. We can meet again when you return either to Moon Base or Earth, we can get our DNAs matched. Then if we still feel the same way about each other, in say, one year's time, we could take out an Order of Parental Commitment." The more she considered his proposal, the more she liked it. Gently she wound her arm about his neck. The idea was definitely very appealing.

Chapter 3

No friend or relative watched Chamois pass out to become a sublieutenant, except a medium-tall, lean, black haired man, whose eyes were mysterious as obsidian and ringed with lines and dark smudges. He stood at the edge of the parade ground. His muscular shoulders were completely different from Chamois' whippet frame, pale complexion and almost white hair.

He waited until Chamois had accepted his certificate, and then muttered, "That's my boy! I'll be seeing you later." Then he walked to a sharp-nosed sports flyer and left.

"You are ordered to return to the Training Vessel Dionysus, to take up the post of Sub Lieutenant. Lieutenant Commander Jackson will continue to instruct you. That is all, Sublieutenant Stone. You are dismissed." The duty officer had seen too many young hopefuls pass out in the Space Navy, to be interested in one more. Stone, if he lasted the course, might make it up to Lieutenant, but he doubted it. A few years with pirates and gunrunners to hunt down and weed out would soon blunt this young man's enthusiasm.

Chamois, Sean, Grant and Stravros shared the runabout that took them to where Dionysus floated in space, along with several other Space

Navy vessels within a few kliks of the Moon Base.

The majestic lines of the superannuated 'D' class-fighting vessel, with its logo of the God of Wine holding the Tyhrsus staff, never ceased to enthral any person boarding her, yet to-day Chamois felt at odds with the prospect of serving under the man who had tortured him for the last 3 years, and Dionysus' distinction failed to make an impression on him.

"Wonder what the order of the day is?" Sean asked the other men returning for duty.

"Somebody's nightmare, I bet." Stravros was in fact trying to get through the wall of silence that was surrounding Chamois. He could guess what was on his mind, or rather who. He only hoped that Chamois would get his wits in order before Stonewall Jackson confronted him, asking for the endless chanting of dials and what the readings meant.

Lieutenant Commander Jackson seemed to have it in for Chamois. The senior officer never allowed Chamois to make the slightest mistake; any error on Chamois' part meant a repeat of the same work for an hour or more.

Chamois had tried to keep out of trouble but it seemed to cling to him like tar on a bather's blanket. His affinity for it was sometimes enhanced by the fact he frequently had premonitions about an impending disaster.

Such was the case when at the command console as stand by, with Lieutenant Commander Jackson in charge he closed the fuel control without preamble or asking for permission.

"What do you think you are doing boy?" Puce with fury, eyes bulging, ready to shrivel Chamois, Jackson was the devil incarnate! Chamois pointed to the gauge. "It's stuck sir, sorry sir." Chamois' face was whiter than his hair. He stood shaking like an aspen leaf in the wind.

Then the alarm klaxon sounded its warning.

"Now tell me, young Mr Stone, how did you know the fuel lines were going to cause trouble?"

Jackson was no fool; the young 'subby' had stopped a potential strontium blow out in the engine room.

"I don't know, sir. I think I saw the gauge jump, then sink to zero, then it seemed to go off the screen!" Sweat running down inside the tight fitting collar and a definite desire to visit the 'head' made Chamois' eyes water.

He was not a moral coward, but Jackson could have had him relieved of his post, then he would have been out of the Space Navy.

"Right Mr Stone, if at any time you think you see something, try to tell me first. If you can't, then 'Act for the safety of the vessel', all right? You know the rules."

Lieutenant Commander Jackson had heard stories about old timers who knew when a gun was aimed at them and ducked well before the missile was on its way.

With the defective filter and shield replaced in the fuel system, Training Vessel Dionysus continued to patrol the inner worlds of the solar system.

Chamois worked and studied in the attempt to pass the next grade. He tried out his knowledge with Sean and between them they made slow, positive progress. Stonewall continued to lambaste him for every mistake, no matter how insignificant. There were times when Chamois felt as if the Commanding Officer hated him, yet whenever he reached the end of his patience at Stonewalls' finicky carping about the errors, his common sense told him that when he had completed the work required of him, he was indeed that much wiser.

Some new cadets had joined and as usual the tricks played on them were the same that had been played by new recruits for centuries. Being sent outside to find out which way the wind was blowing was a speciality of the Space Navy.

Chamois could only laugh at some of the sillier ones and remembered his own naivety.

Lieutenant Commander Jackson, known to his face as well as behind his back as Stonewall, had refused a full Commander's star because he would have had to give up the post of training young recruits.

To his way of thinking, it took an experienced man to teach these young people how to fight when the odds were against them. For now he had Mr Stone waiting for the next command.

Chamois stood to attention. He watched the play of thoughts chase across his superior's thunderhead features and speculated about the next flogging he would receive from him. His mind wandered as to what it would be this time.

Stonewall's voice cut across Chamois' meandering mind like a blade of hot Toledo steel. "Set a course for Phobos, Mr Stone. There has been an emergency call come through."

Someone was in trouble, and Chamois could feel the urgency and concern in Stonewall's voice to realise that for once, it wasn't him.

He stood and waited patiently beside Stonewall for his next command. He had not been dismissed and knew instinctively that when the Lieutenant Commander did so, then he was in for a very difficult assignment.

As Lieutenant Commander Jackson finished giving the command to Sean Darnley, the astro-navigator, the ship came about, and headed towards the moons of Mars, Phobos and Deminos.

Chamois could feel the movement of Dionysus under his feet. The engines sounded smooth and in perfect alignment, with no fuzzy vibrations thanks to Stravros and his crew.

Lieutenant Commander Jackson, the senior training officer, was heavily built and stood tall, his shoulders back. In his white tunic and trousers, with its gold collar and cuff stars of gold indicating his twenty years of service and rank, he was an imposing figure to all those on Dionysus. To Chamois he was a terrifying taskmaster who must be obeyed. There was an array of bright medal ribbons on his chest. One had a gold 'sunburst' showing that he had seen battle in the interplanetary smuggling war against drug running.

It involved a most insidious drug, Dream Dust, the first dose of which gave the user hours of sleep that was illuminated with dreams of enthralling sexual activity. The second dose left the user unable to sleep or rest. The third killed.

The narcotic was being smuggled to workers labouring on the terra forming of Mars. This project had been in serious jeopardy and would have had to be abandoned if the smugglers had not been caught. They were demonic in their greed for the rich pickings from these hardworking but bored men.

The battle had claimed many lives on both sides and on Mars itself. No pirates were caught. They had killed themselves, preferring death to being committed to working in the asteroid belt for the rest of their lives for the valuable minerals found there.

It was then that he had acquired the title of 'Stonewall'. Jackson had placed his battle cruiser between the red planet and the smugglers, refusing to let them pass in spite of being out gunned. He had stood his ground and out manoeuvred them until two other Space Fleet Navy cruisers came in from either side of the pirates, bringing about a complete victory for the service and the annihilation of the pirates.

'Stonewall Jackson' was a deserved name and Jackson was secretly proud of it. Smiling to himself as he rubbed his chin, he thought how very close his own life had run to that of Thomas Jonathan Jackson who had stood firm at the first battle of Bull Run and got dubbed 'Stonewall'. That Stonewall also had been a penniless orphan and had risen, through sheer determination and fear of God, to the rank of major, eventually teaching young men how to become soldiers.

Lieutenant Commander Jackson gave a rare humorous grin to himself, thinking hundreds of years may come and go, but it still takes a firm hand and experience, to bring these young gentlemen into line! He shook his head as he assessed the present situation. God help me.... and them, he reflected.

"We will have a rescue team Mr Stone and you will be among them." Lieutenant Commander Jackson's jaw muscles hardened as he gritted his teeth to give the rest of his orders to Chamois. "In fact, Mr Stone, you will be Officer in Charge." He turned to Chamois, his eyes like flint, holding no compassion for the young sublieutenant being sent out on his first dangerous mission.

"I want all the trapped men to be saved. You understand Mr Stone? We will prove Star Fleet Command are wrong in their belief that young gentlemen like yourself are incapable of obeying instructions no matter what the conditions or who is involved, be they other young gentlemen like yourself, or life serving convicts."

"Yes, sir. I understand, sir!" came the expected reply. However, Chamois felt no compunction to give promises he was not certain he could keep.

Jackson wondered if Stone really knew what this mission was all about. It was not only to save these men's lives; it was also to sort the sheep from the goats in Jackson's group of newly enlisted junior officers.

Jackson had already heard of this one's nickname, Chamois. *Let's hope he has got a hard head, tough horns and the balls of an old goat. He'll need them before I'm convinced that he is ready to send to the selection board for his promotion,* he mused!

Standing rigidly to attention, Chamois waited until Lieutenant Commander Jackson was clearly finished giving him his orders and told him he was dismissed. Then, hoping the officer was in a better mood than usual toward him, he requested permission to speak.

"Well, what do you want to say?" Gritty voiced and tight lipped, the Lieutenant Commander gave Chamois a glare, daring him to question his orders. "You have a lot to organise, so say what you have to, then get on with it!" The Lieutenant Commander bellowed.

"Sir, may I choose who comes with me?" In spite of his awe of his mentor, Chamois gave as good as he got from Lieutenant Commander Jackson when it came to out staring.

He remained subservient to authority and rank and accepted the reply, "I chose you Mr Stone, to lead this mission and I will choose who goes with you. You are dismissed, Mr Stone. The rest of the rescue team will meet with you in the small conference cabin at eighteen hundred hours."

"Aye, aye, sir," Chamois replied.

Chamois, with his 'subby's' grey clad back towards the officer as he left the control deck, did not see the softening on Lieutenant Commander Jackson's face. His mind was deep in thought.

Why me? I wonder why he's put me in charge? Sean's a lot better at getting people out of bother than I am. He shook his head in puzzlement as he went to tell Sean his news.

"You know, Chamois, I have often wondered why old Jackson seems to have his knife in your back." Sean sat astride a chair, his arms resting on the back. "I get the feeling that he's driving you toward a specific goal." Sean's head tilted to one side, his eyes half closed. "Yes, I think that's it! Old Stonewall is driving you…"

"Nuts!" Chamois finished for him, flinging himself down on the only easy chair in the cabin, so that he bounced half way back up again.

"No, honestly, I think he's trying to make certain that you come out top in the Commissioning stakes. Think about it for a minute." The wry grin on Sean's face was directed straight at his friend. "When has he ever given you an order that you didn't benefit from in the end, hmm?" The grin became a positive leer. "Do you remember when it took you all day to answer one set of written problems?" Sean pointed his finger at Chamois, "You are a lucky giddy goat. He's booting you up to senior officer status. All you can feel at the moment are the bruises." By now Sean could hardly contain his mirth as he continued, "Stonewall thinks you *really are* officer material!"

"Come on Sean, if you believe that, you'll believe anything." Chamois was exceptionally tired after a gruelling shift, with the Lieutenant Commander watching every move he made, making him repeat graph and dial readings.

The main computer was always switched to manual, so Chamois physically had to type everything, instead of telling the Dionysus what the commands were. Jackson compelled him to repeat every order to him, to ensure he understood the full meaning of that order. Chamois felt he was being victimised and his fatigue made his fogged brain dim. He could not see the sense of what Sean was trying to point out to him. All he felt now was that sleep was vital. He was too exhausted to understand where Stonewall's stinging whiplashes were driving him.

Two hours later, promptly, at eighteen hundred hours, Chamois entered the cabin where they were to discuss the plan of rescue.

Glancing around it was as if old Jackson had read his mind. Stravros stood there, large as life in his dark blue chief engineer's uniform.

"Am I glad you are in on this expedition Stravros. I was hoping that you would be there to hold my hand when the going gets tough!" Chamois shook his friend by the shoulders, laughing.

Most of the men present knew about how Chamois and Stravros had first met in a scuffle in Chamois' cabin. Stravros had thought that he and two other deckhands, Gabby and Peter would help teach young Chamois how to take care of himself. Chamois had changed their minds by beating them with his expert ability in unarmed combat and since then, he and his close friend Sean had been giving them lessons in the gentle art of self-defence, using karate and aikido.

Gabby had been the most apt pupil at learning how to use his hands to deadly effect in the aikido workouts.

Peter had developed flying feet, which made him an excellent sparring partner for either Sean or Chamois. Stravros' heavier build had been honed down to a fighting machine, using hands and feet, slower than Chamois, but just as effective.

"This calls for a jug of coffee and sandwiches all round." Chamois called out to the steward in attendance.

No stimulants of any kind were permitted on any ship of the Space Navy and all serving men were glad of it, knowing that each one was dependent on intelligence and integrity alone, not on alcohol, white powder, or tablets from a bottle.

Chamois and the six chosen to accompany him discussed the problems facing them. They would have to contend with freezing cold, no oxygen, unstable terrain and no water.

"Sounds just like a picnic I went on once," remarked Brad. "We also had mosquitoes!"

The group shared the joke then Chamois brought them to order with a brisk command, "Now let's have some helpful input here." He considered that he needed to let the men know it was a very difficult and dangerous mission to which they had been assigned. In fact, this could be the hardest mission that any of them would encounter in their entire lives in the Space Navy.

"We have been told that the trapped men are running out of oxygen and I think our first priority will be to get it to them." He looked at each person in turn, sizing them up. Some he knew personally, like Stravros, but two of them, such as Brad, he had not encountered before as shipmates. Even on a training vessel, it was not always possible to get to know all the crew and cadets intimately.

"What suggestions do you have Brad, to get the life support to these men underground?" he asked the young man who was a stocky, and definitely unknown quantity except as a well-disciplined and reliable officer. Chamois realised that the sooner he found out what the young man was made of and how his mind worked, the better. He also wanted them to understand that a discussion was one thing. Actually putting into practice what was talked about in the comfort of a classroom was another!

Brad had stopped laughing at his own joke. "It seems we have more than one problem here Chamois!" Reflectively, he raked his hand through his regulation short brown hair and scratched his head, thinking the problem through. "I think we'll have to work sharp like, so as not to freeze to the ground. Make an access to the underground shaft where the miners are, then provide the oxygen, food and heat, in that order." There was still a frown of concentration on Brad's face. "Have I overlooked anything there?" His clear grey eyes were now clouded with concern at the import of the job for which they had been made responsible.

Chamois was pleased with Brad's reply. His brains are also in gear as well as his mouth was the impression he received, and taking a deep breath, he filled in the rest of what he considered necessary.

"There is the minor matter of how we get to them. Also, when we have got them out, what condition will they be in, will they need medical attention?"

He smiled at the group as they absorbed the enormity of the problems. "It won't be like the picnic you went on Brad. Umm, maybe close though!" Chamois shared the joke with the rest of the group with a wide grin that crinkled his eyes.

Chapter 4

The buzz of voices as the equipment requirements were discussed, sounded like a swarm of angry bees. Life support helmets were needed, with the miniature oxygen cylinders that were standard for this kind of rescue, complete with built in thought transceivers and medical assistance by way of analgesics and blood flow controlling drugs.

As soon as a man was fitted with one, he had all that was needed to keep him alive until he reached a medical centre. He was also in contact with other minds that were helping him, no matter what kind of language he spoke.

"We had better find out what the Mars rescue team has attempted in its bid to assist them," Chamois said as he accessed the terminal to the main computer for information. "Hmm, looks as though they have tried a normal laser bore that had to be abandoned because the soil is too dry and crumbles. It shifts too, caving in every few metres."

He turned to Stravros. "Do you remember when that child was trapped in similar conditions in the Australian out-back?" He waited for Stravros to recall. "Oooh yes, I think I do. You mean where they had to use the photon drive that turned the soil to glass with the tremendous high temperature so that the walls were vulcanised so thick that they didn't collapse?"

Stravros' eyes widened with the realisation that they had the answer to the problem. "You've got it! It's amazing what light particles can do. We'll have to use the body heat searcher to locate them though. No sense in cooking them alive instead of rescuing them!" Chamois agreed.

Chamois continued to make a list of appliances that they would need and arrange for them to be loaded in the hold of the Ambulance Rescue Vessel, Saint Raphael.

"Now what I would like to suggest to you…" he looked directly at Stravros, giving him a silent message…" is that we make two teams, Stravros as the oldest and probably the most experienced of us, to take control of back up." In other words, Chamois wanted Stravros to watch his rear for him, if things got a bit difficult, and with two subbies he didn't know, it would be wise to have a friend he could trust with his life, making sure no one made any mistakes that would jeopardise him.

Grant was the name of the other junior officer Chamois had never worked with before. He did know however that he was quick witted and could be relied upon in a dangerous situation. His response to Sean's close encounter with death proved that. Grant had seemed shy and ineffectual, all uncoordinated arms and legs. Chamois wondered though if that wasn't just a façade, especially since Grant had taken control of his rescue when he had fallen through that hole in the cliff face. There was something else too. What place was there for a cybernetics specialist in Star Fleet?

Grant had also got through the university and student stage of Space Fleet training, then been accepted as a cadet on Dionysus and he too had gained a sublieutenant's half ring. Couldn't be too stupid or a wimp. So what was Grant hiding? The puzzle would have to wait until he had more time to work out the common sense of it all.

"When we get to the emergency site, I would like you with me Grant, also Andy and June. Stravros you take Brad and Elsa." Chamois looked at their eager faces; he also felt a thrill of excitement. Yet there was an intuition deep inside him that seemed to warn that by the time they all returned to Dionysus with the miners safely on Mars, they would have learned something about each other and themselves.

The Ambulance Rescue Vessel Saint Raphael, left its mother ship Dionysus, and slid easily through the low gravity and almost non-atmosphere of Phobos. The journey had taken eight hours since the alert had come through, just long enough for the team to rest and gather the vital knowledge and equipment to facilitate the rescue.

The Mars Rescue team had greeted them almost silently. Chamois had his two-way thought exchange facility turned on and a large figure in the red and white uniform of the brigade leader came over to them.

His thoughts were clear and concise. "I sure am pleased to see you men!" tshe thought communicator transmitted. "Who's in charge of you? I'm Sergeant Egmont."

"I'm Sublieutenant Charley Stone, Chamois to friends and those workers, like yourself." The thought process was easy and clear, with no place for lies or deceit of any kind.

"I would like to organise the set up of this photon drive, just off from where they are trapped."

"Brilliant idea!" was Egmont's reply, and he indicated to his team that they should assist

Chamois' men, in setting up and running the drive to bore a hole down to the depth that was needed.

Everyone worked swiftly and carefully. Time was running out. The oxygen tanks on the life support helmets that the miners wore could not be guaranteed to have been full when they were put on, therefore the chances were that they were more likely to be completely empty now.

The heavy machinery was manhandled into position without too much difficulty due to the very low gravitational pull, and Chamois watched to make certain that it stood on even and solid ground.

Stravros the senior engineer, worked as a technician to show the crew how to set up the photon drive to within a few metres of where the miners' echo shadow had been located. Then he adjusted the power to take into account the density of the soil and rocky terrain.

Once he was satisfied that all measurements and the strength of the photon blast were accurate he nodded to Chamois. It's ready Sir. I'll fire it off at your command!" The situation needed respect and so did Chamois. It would help him to master this very difficult job and prove that he was able to comply with any troublesome order that Star Fleet could issue, and Chamois was grateful for his friend Stravros' regard of addressing him as "Sir". It gave him the stature that his position in this traumatic situation called for.

The blast when it came was colourful and violent. A sheet of purple and red tore at the surrounding rounded hills and the ground trembled as if a volcano was about to erupt.

After the heat had dispersed into the ice cold, thin atmosphere of Phobos, the shaft could be seen. It was just over half a metre wide, a smooth glassy tube going down into unrelieved darkness.

"The idea was good, but how can you get a man down there? The cover-alls fill it on their own, never mind about the man inside them. "Egmont's thoughts were concerned and disappointed. "I suppose we can send down a speaker extension just to let them know they have not been deserted."

The germ of an idea began to form in Chamois' mind. He was considering his options when a familiar personality entered his thoughts.

"That is not a choice, Mr Stone. Don't even think it!"

"Who the blue devil was that?" came Egmont's communication.

"Blue devil is right! That was my senior officer, Lieutenant Commander Jackson. My idea didn't please him. Then none of my ideas seem to, but at the moment, I am out of his arm's reach." His grinning face was partially obscured by his helmet.

Chamois' mind told them everything that they wanted to know, and he was inundated with similar retorts that he had received from Stonewall.

"While I'm on my way to get to them with the oxygen, you can start a double bore-hole, then you can send down whatever it is I find that we need to get them out!"

He could sense all the protestations from the group. Chamois clenched his fists. He felt he wanted to hammer his commands home to them. "Stonewall put *me in charge, remember!*" Stravros had never seen Chamois so angry, not even when he, with Peter and Gabby had set a trap for him, to teach him to take care of himself.

"Okay! You've made your point!" Stravros felt the tension too.

"Stravros, what lubricants did you put in?" Chamois felt rather contrite; he knew that Stravros' concern for his safety was making him anxious. He wanted something that was heavy and viscous enough to stick yet would allow easy passage.

"Yes I do have what you want, but please don't…"

"Can you or anyone else think of anything better?"

"No."

"Okay, let's get started before I freeze to death." With that, Chamois stripped off nearly all his protective clothing, leaving on his inner slippers that cushioned his feet from cold, his brief shorts and his life support helmet with a mouthpiece to feed the life giving oxygen to him.

"Get that stuff over me as much as you can but keep it away from my hands," he said, standing with his arms held out so that the willing hands of his friends could carry out his orders. Chamois' long thin legs and torso looked like a two-metre length of string.

The grease, a purified white lubricant that was used for maintaining a smooth running between moving parts of machinery on every Star Fleet vessel, was liberally smoothed over him. The cold was a killer and he was soon shivering uncontrollably. Grant and Andy slapped it on as thickly as it would stick. Shaking and with his teeth chattering, Chamois looked like some fearful waxen creature from a nightmare.

Then, as he let out a long, slow breath, he seemed to stand in a glow of warmth.

"Get the safety line on my waist belt, then fix all the extra helmets on the line after me. I shall need a heat detector to find them and a hand blaster to make the opening." As an afterthought, he added, "A wrist torch would be a good idea too. They may not have any light, and the power is bound to have failed."

Stravros, Brad and Elsa worked as fast as their glove-protected fingers would allow. Even before the extra helmets had been finally attached, Chamois was already easing himself into the still warm shaft with the detector on his wrist and blaster attached to the narrow safety belt. His slender frame just slid down, like an eel through a dewpond, a winch holding the line taut as he disappeared.

Stravros could be heard praying in Latin via the headsets, and what he felt in his heart was known and shared by all the rescuers.

"Just make sure that *idiot* returns to this ship, Chief." Stonewall's anger was so overpowering. Stravros could almost feel the Lieutenant Commander standing right beside him, breathing down his neck. "I'll have a few words to say to him that will certainly take away any chill he may have picked up!"

The interruption was almost a welcome relief as Chamois' lifeline sank the hundreds of metres below ground.

Grant just had time to send a warning message to everyone, when the ground shifted violently, trembled and groaned as if in agony. Then he realised that he was on his knees, holding a loose lifeline. The photon tube had broken somewhere deep underground, and Chamois was entombed in an even worse predicament than the miners. They had each other, but he was alone.

The head-torch and night vision gave enough light to show him that the photon tube was fractured and twisted above him but with use of the phaser to burn hand holds, he could make his way down to where he hoped he would find the miners.

The tube now had rough broken edges in places. Summing up the situation, Chamois decided that everything was as good as it was bad. It would mean watching that he did not cut himself, but the wrecked lining also gave him climbing holds.

He had slid down only a few metres during the quake, and had come to rest on a shelf of petrified rock that had given him time to adjust to the new problem and attempt to come to a working decision. Chamois looked down again to see if he had any other advantages. Suddenly a quiver of fear went through him. He was horrified! His blood was frozen. It trickled like liquid nitrogen through his veins, causing him to lose his grip on the shard of glass that was his life support. It would have been simple to give way to the terror that threatened to engulf him completely.

"Fear is the little death. It is the death of the spirit as well as the body." The voice was soft but authoritative. The glow from where it seemed to emanate, showed the tiny frame of Mito Iwaki, where solid rock should have been!

Chamois could only gape in shock. "Come now, there is much to be done!" It was as if they were back on the training mat. "The way is blocked only at the top. You can reach the miners with little difficulty. An earthworm or snake could do it, therefore so can you!"

So it was with an earthworm and snake like movement, and the use of the powerful hands and feet developed in his karate and Aikido training with Mito, that at last Chamois reached the bottom of the shaft with the vital life preserving helmets. The heat detector on his wrist told him which way to aim his blaster to make the final break-through to where the miners were.

Wriggling and easing his body along the narrow passage that he made, he found the doomed men in a low roofed cavern without room to stand. It was like an etching by Gustave Doré from Dante's "Inferno."

Dejected men lay in their bright orange, "day-glow" work overalls where they could gain some ease. Most had their eyes closed inside their spent helmets. Then a slight movement of one man's leg told him that at least someone was still alive.

Still on hands and knees, he shuffled his way to the nearest and replaced the spent helmet with one from his lifeline, turning on the life saving oxygen.

He went from man to man, until all those that he could see, had a replaced helmet. He sent out encouraging thoughts to them to "Wake up! Take a deep breath; come on! Time to get moving!" The men gradually revived. "What kept you? We thought that you were on a rather long tea break!"

"Whoever that was, welcome to the land of the living," Chamois broadcast his thoughts out to the men. "I'm glad you have a bright sense of humour! Believe me, you're going to need it."

The explanation of what had happened was greeted with resigned fortitude. "We never expected anyone to try to save us. Why should you risk your life for a bunch of losers like us?" A man had made his way over to where Chamois sat with his back against the cave wall.

"I'm Henry Chadwell, at your service, and who might you be young man?" Henry's thoughts were guarded and heavy with sarcasm.

"Me? I'm Charley Stone, Sublieutenant Stone."

"What! They send kids now to do the dirty work. Charley boy, you shouldn't be here. Us lot are a bunch of convicts." Henry was having difficulty coming to terms with what was to him, an innocent child being sent to aid murderers and arsonists, though none had ever harmed a child.

"I am in the Space Navy." Chamois knew that he had to gain the confidence of these hardened men. Convicts they might be, but they were still people to him. "And I am completing part of my training. My Lieutenant Commander ordered me to bring you all out, and that is what I intend to do!" He wanted to add, "So there." He stopped the thought from forming. It would have been childish.

"Well kid, all I can say is, your Lieutenant Commander must think you are ready to join the men's league." A voice had joined in the discussion. "I am Luke Denning, by the way."

"Glad to meet you Luke. How's everyone here? Is anyone hurt or in need of help?"

Yet another joined in the conversation. "Young man, we are just pleased to know that we won't die like snared animals." The agreement came from all the trapped men.

Chapter 5

"We thought that we'd never see the light of day again and along you come, just like the Archangel Gabriel, all glowing and golden!" He chuckled, and then continued, "I'm known as Brookman. Say, young man, don't the Space Navy give you no threads?" The man who was now making himself known, was very heavily built, taller than Stonewall, and his beautifully moulded features told of Nubian origin. His dark skin glistened and his light brown eyes gave Chamois the feeling that this Brookman was a gentle giant who had turned killer because of an injustice. The disgust at what he thought was bad treatment of a youngster made his voice sound as though he would kill the person responsible.

Chamois calmed the man down. "It's okay, Brookman. I had to get my uniform off so that I could get down here, and you wouldn't want me to get grease all over my nice smart outfit would you?" Chamois let them unload themselves and talk. It was one way of passing the time while they waited for the second borehole to be made, and Brookman shuffled on hands and knees to a dim corner of the mine.

Later a scuffling noise from deeper in the cavern made him glance in that direction. Brookman came into sight. He had with him a miner's quilted working overall. He motioned to Chamois to put it on.

"That's just what I needed. I was beginning to feel the coolness down here, and in fact I feel like a slab of beef! Where did you get it?"

"Don't ask! Let's just say that it's spare," came the enigmatic reply, and he helped Chamois to don the warm clothing.

Chamois knew that Stravros would be frantic, organising the re-erection of the photon drive, to make a double shaft down to him and the miners. Mars Rescue team and the group from Dionysus had worked like demons. The tremor had left the photon drive off balance, damaging a support. This made it difficult to manoeuvre to the new site. Sweating and straining the heavy drive into place, then making it stable had taken precious time and effort. Stravros had wanted to tear the ground open with his bare hands. He realised the futility of this and used all his pent-up emotions and anger on helping to move the machine.

Now that it was up and working again, they had to wait until they knew that the action of the photon would not start another shift in the subsoil. Dust and noise added to the scene of urgent activity as every one, including the Ambulance Rescue Service crew with Sergeant Egmont, helped with the realignment of the photon bore.

The lightning flashes once again shimmered to the edge of the close horizon where the horrific noise echoed and reverberated.

Sergeant Egmont and his crew were speechless at the urgency with which the

Spacers' worked to relieve their Officer-in-Charge.

Stravros had made a double shaft and as soon as the sound of groaning of the violated world abated and he considered it safe, he indicated for Grant to take the lead down to the trapped men.

June walked confidently towards the new shaft. She had put on the safety line and buckled it in place with a medical kit as she started to make her way towards the lip of the glass smooth well.

Trying to let her know it was not her courage that was being questioned, Grant said carefully, "I don't want to step on your toes June, but Chamois may need a bit more muscle than you carry. It really would be better for him and the miners if I went down. We know that Chamois is alive only because of the movement of his body heat shadow, but he could be injured." And he stood blocking her way.

Her anger stirred like a scorpion ready to strike. *"You?"* In that one word, June managed to pour scorn mixed with so much derision, it made Grant feel nauseated.

Like a cloak being shed, the round shoulders straightened, the legs and arms lost their aimlessness. The metamorphosis was complete with stern features of hard steely grey eyes and pugnacious jaw.

"June, there's no time for argument. Even you must see the futility of a female trying to lift an unconscious miner in all his gear, even in this low gravity?" His voice was like shards of flint.

June realised that Grant was right and he certainly looked as if he could haul one if not two men from the pit. She had no recourse but to swallow her dignity and help prepare Grant for the descent.

With a new lifeline in place and a cradle to haul every man trapped in the bowels of Phobos to the surface, the rescue was soon completed with the aid of everyone at the scene of the disaster.

Grant tried to stay in the background, but Chamois singled him out for a well-deserved compliment. "Thanks Grant. You were a sight from heaven. Those men are all convicted criminals and had no hope of rescue." Chamois felt that he was looking at the real Grant now.

"You know, I thought there was more to you than what you appeared to be." Chamois still had his mental contact helmet on and could easily have gone into Grant's mind for the answer to the riddle.

"Perhaps one day you will honour me with the reason why you prefer to act like an idiot? Now I have to go and face Lieutenant Commander Jackson."

The emergency cover-alls he had put on were keeping out the cold therefore he could not understand why he was suddenly shivering uncontrollably. The sooner I make myself presentable and get the confrontation with Stonewall over, the better, he thought, He would rather have lain down and slept, a yawn escaping him before he could cover it over.

"Yeah, me too buddy." Sergeant Egmont came and put an arm across the young man's shoulders. "When I saw a bunch of kids come to do men's work, I really thought the Space Navy was having a purge of funds and decided that as we were dealing with criminals, they would be expendable if you didn't get them out." He grinned. "That was mistake number one. Number two was thinking that you were a goner!" With a wry grin, he waved Chamois goodbye and went to join his Life Rescue Craft.

The miners came to say their thanks, and were ready to be transported back to Mars Mining Station. Chamois walked over to where Brookman stood. "That overall, it was spare because the owner was dead, right?"

"Yes, officer, the man had no further use for it. But for you it was a life saver and any time I can help you again, I will." Brookman then nodded his goodbye and waited patiently for the shuttle to take him to his next labour prison camp.

Luke Denning joined them and held his hand out to be taken by Chamois. He held it longer than needed, and then gave him a long hard stare. "I'll be seeing you some time, Chamois!" he had said, as the security officer had led him with the rest of the criminals to their transport back to the Mars settlement.

With the grease cleaned off his body under a very hot shower, Chamois was back in his grey junior officer's uniform, he waited for Lieutenant Commander Jackson to start to bawl him out.

"So the little Billy goat has returned to the fold. Well young man let's see how brave you really are." Jackson went over to the command control chair. "Come on, I've been waiting for you to try this helmet on ever since you came aboard."

Lieutenant Commander Jackson was holding the Command Helmet out to him. Whoever put it on was in complete control of the space vessel!

Chapter 6

Dionysus had been cruising from Phobos, the larger moon of Mars, to the asteroid belt between Mars and Jupiter. The Commanding Officer, Lieutenant Commander Jackson, had received orders to join up with the main fleet. Dionysus' speed had been increased from a mere eight kliks to fifteen hundred kliks an hour. Chamois considered that there would be plenty of time for him to be relieved from the command post before they reached the rendezvous point, time enough for him to learn the fundamentals of the main brain and get out!

Every person on the bridge of Dionysus had ears and eyes for the scene being enacted between Lieutenant Commander Jackson and Sublieutenant Stone. And silence, apart from the gentle hum of the life support machinery, pervaded the control deck of the Training Vessel

Dionysus. Control panels continued to give out information to anyone who was watching them.

Members of the crew stood as if frozen. Everyone on the Control Bridge seemed to be horrified, with people holding their breath. No newly commissioned sublieutenant had ever taken the comm. before! Yet Lieutenant Commander Jackson had ordered Chamois to take the chair at the command centre and seemed to be showing great delight in the younger man's discomfiture.

Chamois' mind was in turmoil. The thought of actually interfacing with Dionysus was both exciting and frightening. He had often wondered what it was like to put the control helmet on. What secrets did it hold? How much of the knowledge contained within the computer banks could a human brain absorb? All these questions had at one time or another gone through his head.

Now he was to start to find out, but why? True he had disobeyed yet another order given him by Lieutenant Commander Jackson by going down the photon shaft, but what else was he to do? The men could have suffocated by the time a larger passageway was made to them. Anyway taking the comm. should not be regarded as a punishment, should it?

There had to be another reason! And while he had briefly thought of *why,* he was being initiated into the mysteries of the mainframe. Chamois shivered as icy cold fingers of mental blackout started to claw their way up his neck and into his brain, threatening him with the ignoble situation of landing flat on his face. The question still gnawed at him like a pack of hungry rats that would not be appeased.

A grunt of determination escaped his clenched jaws. So, I get to play with the big boys now. This really should be interesting! he thought, and on feet made of soft, soapy foam, he made his way to the "comm.."

Lieutenant Commander Jackson's hard grim face was unforgiving, yet there was something about the way he was standing, something that his body stance was saying. Was there a slight crook of the arms and knees? Chamois was too shocked and puzzled by the command to take the comm, to give Jackson's secret body language much consideration.

Sean Darnley, Chamois' closest friend, had been gazing at a holograph of Pele, a rather large lump of rock in the Asteroid belt. He thought he had seen a blink of light on Pele where no light should have been.

He had looked up from the heliograph of the portion of the asteroid belt that he had found interesting. He had wanted so much to study it closer, and so he put the scene on 'save' because the exchange between Lieutenant Commander Jackson and Chamois had him transfixed! Only those with a lieutenant's star came into direct contact with the 'Main Brain' of any ship of the fleet. The apprehension on the flight deck was palpable and Sean could not help but wonder what was Stonewall up to.

Chamois appeared to be completely unmoved by the command. He seemed to walk with a jaunty step toward the comm. chair. Then Sean noticed the purple-red of Chamois' ears. He half expected to see sparks come out of them. The tell tale of Chamois' bright red ears had always been the only give away of the turmoil behind his placid calm exterior.

Eye contact between Jackson and Chamois was as if the older man and the novice were bitter enemies. Both men held an evil glint in their eyes as if they hated each other; Jackson's mocking and daring, Chamois' those of a man who knew he was being pushed to the very limit of his mental endurance. The blue ice in Chamois' eyes would have spellbound a lesser man than Lieutenant Commander Jackson. All the senior officer did was to allow his lips to form a half sneer. Yet still Chamois felt there was no real animosity behind Jackson's attitude. What on earth was happening here? The thought slipped into his mind then out again, without any real judgement being formed. He had reached his objective...the command centre chair with the helmet of control.

He felt for the hand rest of the chair to make certain he did not slide to the floor as he sat down, his breathing physically controlled so as to keep himself from slumping. He was sitting to attention. Then he held his hands beside his ears to accept the Main Brain Crown.

As the helmet came to rest on Chamois' shoulders and cut out all sight of the control room, a feeling of peace and tranquillity flooded his senses. He took a deep breath and waited to find out what Dionysus' contact would be like.

He had closed his eyes to adjust to the helmet screen and opened them to an ultra-violet blue glow and was surprised to realise that he was listening to a low baritone masculine voice, the words beautifully articulated. It was as if he was listening to a very interesting discourse from a close friend.

"Now that you have relaxed your mind a little we can continue to get acquainted." Dionysus did not need to pause for breath; he did however give Chamois a chance to gain his. "You may not have realised, Chamois, that every time you put on a life support helmet, your brain is interfaced with my memory banks!"

"Well, if that isn't "Big Brother" watching, what is?" The thought entered Chamois' head of its own accord.

"Yes! I watched over you because you are in the care of Space Fleet and no harm must come to you, I monitored your every thought and deed. Sometimes you made decisions, and carried them out, which only a very skilled Space Officer would have attempted; even then, he would consider his actions with a lot more care than you have. Lieutenant Commander Jackson was greatly relieved when your companions persuaded you not to explore the labyrinth of caves that you accidentally discovered on Mars!"

Chamois did not know if the computer was capable of anger. One thing he did know was that he was being reprimanded.

The reasoning, comforting and assured voice continued, "Now it is time for you to learn something about the ship and computer that is known as Dionysus." The computer paused again to give Chamois time to calibrate his thoughts.

"As you have already explored the normal layout of the living and working areas, you will now interface with the exterior sensors. You will be given extra time to adjust to this situation." The pacifying voice continued.

"Now, just you hang on there. Wait a moment will you? Are you saying that Stonewall also knows everything that I thought and did too?" Chamois managed to think and not blurt out, his mind going back to the time when the three "Middies" had discussed the Lieutenant Commander's resolve that they should do the difficult climb up the sand stone cliffs of Mars with no anti-grav help. And the Martians knew what Sean and Grant had said and thought only when he had been hors-de-combat? The native Martians, as far as Chamois knew, had not yet given up any clues to who or what they were, let alone share their thoughts with them. They had vacated Mars millenniums ago.

"Yes, your senior officer has noted the opinions of yourself and those of your companions regarding the tests he set you." Dionysus had given him the information as if Stonewall had not made any comment himself, and Chamois tried to imagine how the older man must have felt, being criticised by the young Midshipmen. So that's why he's so quiet, Chamois reasoned.

Contrite, he then understood that they had probably been the cause of a lot of grief for Stonewall and the niggling thought of guilt wormed its way across his heart. The old man had never sent anyone out on a mission he would not, or could not tackle himself.

Holding on to the comm chair tightly to avoid the vertigo, Chamois had closed his eyes again and opened them to a vision that would stay with him for the rest of his life. Looking to the stern of Dionysus, the sky was a panorama of acid sharp pinpoints of light on a frosty night and there, in a backdrop of indigo velvet and scintillating stars, was Earth, being reverently worshipped by her satellite, the Moon.

Chamois' heart ached at the beauty of his home world. A whisper of a white veil of cloud girdled the green land and blue seas, like a bride going to meet her lover. The snowy arctic caps sparkled like diamonds and pearls in a regal tiara. A poem written so long ago came to his mind.

> *"Earth has not anything to show more fair:*
> *Dull would he be of soul who could pass by a sight so touching in its majesty..."*

Earth herself was so majestic. All the videos and lectures had been unable to prepare him for the sight before his eyes. Nothing could compare with the extraordinary tableau seen at this distance. Not even his first sight of Dionysus that had taken the wind out of him with its sweeping classic lines and air of menace.

Then Maria's face swam before his eyes in memory. Would she still be waiting for him? Earth, home and Maria, everything that meant anything to him flooded his memory; but Chamois knew that the Space Patrol would always govern his life, that it would always command his first allegiance.

"We must continue with the viewing sensors. I am pleased you are enjoying this experience, Chamois." Dionysus wasn't going to let him linger too long admiring the entrancing scene, and the spell had been broken.

He continued to control his breathing, remembering that Jackson would be monitoring his every move and reaction. Coming to his senses again and absorbing the vision of the immediate area around Dionysus, Chamois took careful note of the other Space Patrol Vessels and how they were placed in location to Dionysus. The ship was in the cusp of a deep horseshoe formation and now moving at two thousand kliks an hour.

A signal was being relayed to the master computer of Dionysus from the Flagship Victory. As the code was deciphered, Chamois became aware that he knew what was in the signal. "Prepare to take up position of observation in the Jupiter quadrant. No active part to be taken by Training Vessel Dionysus. Repeat, observe only. This is a test operation for the latest weapon of rock molecule disruption. Acknowledge!"

"Message received and understood," was the only acceptable reply.

Chamois had heard about this odd weapon that was capable of causing even the hardest rock, no matter what formation, to disintegrate into powder, yet it left deposits such as metal and carbon complete. The action made no sound, caused no fuel waste. It was perfect for situations where an area had been evacuated and buildings hid traps for the unwary troops.

Expecting Lieutenant Commander Jackson to relieve him of the duty of manning the comm at any moment, Chamois continued to obey instructions coming in from the Flagship Victory, placing Dionysus exactly where they had been ordered. Part of his mind was on the crew going to battle stations, as required by the rules of testing of weapons. The rest was watching the battle fleet deploy themselves to the stations as directed by the Admiral of the Space Fleet.

Alert and watchful, Chamois still waited to be relieved from the command post. Then to his horror, he saw a small private space cruiser emerge from behind Pele. The weapon had been set-up ready for testing with everyone who could observe, doing so.

His breath caught in his throat. Had anyone else seen the tiny mote of light in the line of fire? Dionysus was sending warning signals to Victory as it tried to contact the interloper but no one was answering any of Chamois' signals or distress calls.

He knew by taking Dionysus from its station, was going to put him into deeper trouble with Stonewall, but what other choice did he have? He tried to draw the Victory's attention by skimming across her bows, and then turning towards the intruder, blasting the cosmos with warnings all the time was his only option.

At last there came the response of a very angry voice asking, "What are you about, Dionysus? Clear the area for action!"

"Dionysus to Flagship Victory, civilian craft in the shadow of Pele, repeat civil…"

"Heard you Dionysus. Civilian detected. Return to your station."

Just as Chamois began to draw in a breath of life giving oxygen, he heard Lieutenant Commander Jackson utter the words, "You are relieved of your post, Mr Stone." Then he realised he had held his last breath since spotting the civilian, his brain dizzy. The words were repeated, more firmly. "You are now relieved of your post, Mr Stone." And the control helmet was being disconnected and lifted from Chamois' shoulders.

Getting his bearings back, he blinked his eyes against the change in surroundings and light. He had been "outside" one moment, then on the bridge the next. Chamois gripped the armrests of the chair, gathering his thoughts. He felt damp with perspiration and wondered what he looked like.

Everything had happened so fast once the Victory pinpointed the intruder. Space Patrol Vessels Hebe and Horace went and escorted it back to Moon Base, Dionysus had returned to the Jupiter Quadrant.

Lieutenant Commander Jackson was shaking his head. "I don't believe it; I just can't be expected to believe that as soon as Mr Stone takes the comm, we have someone poking their noses in where they could do a lot of harm and Mr Stone disobeys orders and chases after them!"

The biting sarcasm made Chamois cringe. He felt as if he had run five miles in a Moon Walker's suit. The sweat trickled into his eyes and bathed his body. The whole experience of being in the command chair had been as much as he could have withstood. The civilian had made the situation far too interesting for his liking.

"You may return to your cabin, Mr Stone. I will be discussing your actions with you when I have the time." The dry, insulting voice of Jackson was infuriating!

Chamois' mind was on the intruder. "I wonder what would have happened to the civilian if he hadn't been spotted in time…and who was he?" The puzzled frown was still on his face as he passed Sean on the way out of the control deck.

"Say buddy, what happened out there?" Genuine concern for Chamois' future officer status and promotion made Sean's soft brown eyes as sad as those of a lost, sick dog. He knew that this time Chamois was in real, deep trouble.

Chamois gave his friend a wry grin. "See you after I have been mauled by Stonewall. That's if I remain a sublieutenant in the Space Navy."

It was still a very puzzled young man who showered and shaved, donned a clean uniform and waited for Stonewall Jackson's summons.

His mind went back over all that had occurred while he had been in the comm chair. Whose was the intriguing voice? Chamois wondered. Was he a real person? Then the magnificence of the Earth in all her glory, and thoughts of Maria came back to him. YES!!! It had been worth being demoted to a lower deck swabmaster.

It was the civilian behind Pele's shadow that was the real enigma! Who and what was he doing there? Hmmm. I don't suppose anyone is going to make me any the wiser now.

Chamois could almost feel Jackson's boot on the seat of his tunic trousers. "So this is where you have whipped me. There goes my hide and my career. Yet there is still something I'm missing here." He was talking aloud to himself, when his cabin bell chimed.

Chamois' heart thudded painfully against his ribs. The time had come to face up to charges that amounted to …disobeying an order when under direct orders from the Flagship, reckless control of a ship of the Space Navy and a few other items of insubordination that Jackson would think of.

He was now dressed in his full cadet's uniform of pale grey with silver buttons and the two silver stripes on his epaulette to show for his two years of sublieutenant's training. Chamois' face had taken on the look of someone much older than his twenty-five years. He looked more like thirty-five. The trauma of the miners' rescue and moving Dionysus out of her designated position, had taken their toll. True, some of his actions were of extreme disobedience. He knew he would be told he was not officer material and asked to resign! Yet he could see no other course of action he could have taken. The dulcet tone of the door alarm sounded again.

"Enter." Chamois' voice still held the strong masculine edge of his normal self. He would not let anyone hear or see him as a mass of shimmering jelly.

Two Personnel Control Officers stood there. "Will you come with us please sir?" It was as Brad looked at Chamois, he remembered the courage the sublieutenant had shown when the convict miners had been trapped.

"We are to escort you to the small conference cabin to see Lieutenant Commander Stonewall, Chamois. I hope you can get the scrambled eggs to understand your motives. If it was up to us, you would be decorated with oak leaves." Brad was not the laughing and joking young man of the Phobos rescue mission; he was now a control officer, having to do a job that he had no love for at all.

"Yeah, this job stinks. Whoever it was out there should be in the stocks not you!" Brad's companion agreed.

"Come on, let's get this farce on the road. The sooner I'm kicked out the sooner I can pick up the pieces and start on something else!" Chamois tried to sound nonchalant. The false grin was making his face muscles ache.

"You think we don't know what the Andrew means to you…think again, Chamois; you're like the rest of us. You've got stardust in your eyes and there is no escaping the addiction. You're hooked!"

Brad patted the tall, two striped junior officer on the back. "Perhaps the cost of your training will persuade the Admiral of the Fleet to think twice about drumming you out of the service?"

"Nah, I don't think so. Somehow I feel I've been set up for this. I honestly don't know what it's all about and I don't think those responsible are about to tell me." Chamois turned to his companion and friend from Phobos. "If I get a chance, I'll send back word about what happens."

Chapter 7

The walk to the small conference cabin seemed to go on forever yet it felt as though only a few hours had passed since he had been there planning the rescue of the men on Phobos a few short hours ago.

Brad and the other PCO waited outside the cabin doors. Lieutenant Commander Jackson stood waiting for him inside.

Jackson sighed heavily as Chamois entered. "Looks like you've done it this time young man! Admiral Blake has retired and Admiral of the Fleet is none other than Sir Arthur Pelham." The lieutenant looked tired; his lips were like old parchment, set in a grim line and his eyelids drooped. "You are to attend a board of enquiry at Starbase, Alice Springs, Australia." His eyes met those of Chamois' defiant blue. "This could be the end of your training as an officer, Mr Stone. I can only hope you have learned enough from your experience in the Space Navy for you to get gainful employment elsewhere." Stonewall Jackson looked like a tired old man who had done a very difficult and demanding job.

"Yes, sir." Chamois croaked, his throat dry and cracked. He felt responsible for his senior officer's exhaustion. *What else could I have done?* The question still lingered in his mind.

Jackson raised a shaggy eyebrow. He seemed to ponder over Chamois' situation, and then taking a deep breath he held out his hand to shake that of his subordinate. "I will have to attend the enquiry too, but I doubt if I shall be given the opportunity to wish you well for your future, whatever it may hold!" Lieutenant Commander Jackson rubbed a hand over his strained, bone white face.

"Another piece of information that you may find to your advantage - Sublieutenant Darnley is to attend the enquiry also. Apparently he was studying a holograph of the designated area and had the command on record. It seems that the civilian had been in the area for some time." Jackson now looked resigned. He had given Stone the good news as well as the bad. "Anyway, the times of the incident as it occurred will be down-loaded from Dionysus to the central computer at Alice Springs."

"Yes, sir." Chamois looked around the cabin as if for the last time. "There is also the fact that each time I disobeyed orders, I was interfaced with Dionysus, so everything I experienced, everything I felt will be recorded including some very uncomplimentary things that I have said about you, sir". With a wry, mirthless grin he saluted his Lieutenant Commander. "For this and any other grief that I have caused you, I am deeply sorry and apologise." He looked down at his shoes with the contrition and remorse hidden in his eyes.

"Chamois, maybe the overture has ended and the play is really about to begin. See you in Alice Springs." With that trite rejoinder, the officer left Chamois to get his brain around his last few words.

Chamois screwed his eyes up in wonderment. What on Earth did old Stonewall mean by that? I'm the one about to resign; it's me who has to find new grass, not him. Yet to hear him…I dunno! The young man was as puzzled as ever. Nothing seemed to be making any sense at all. Perhaps he had unwittingly upset someone, but then whoever it was, must be in high places. And I don't know anyone above Stonewall, so who else could it be? Who would benefit from my downfall? No one on the flight deck would want to see me court marshalled, would they? Except…that subby who'd been transferred from the Grafton, Philip Wood. Now there was an unknown quantity if ever there was one. I wonder why the Grafton wanted to off load him?

There was an aura of deceit about Mr Woods, of craftiness and jealousy; could he be envious of me? If so, why for goodness sake, and who was our Mr Wood that he could pull such long strings? Chamois put this idea from his mind; it was leading nowhere logical.

Being confined to his cabin for the journey back to Moon Base, he had plenty of opportunity to ponder the prospects in front of him and how he could have avoided the situation in which he now found himself.

From Moon Base, the shuttle was to take them directly to Alice Springs.

Lieutenant Commander Jackson's transport had left before Chamois' and Sean's, whose escort was only too glad to get some Earth time in, even if it was in the Australian outback. At least the Starbase had brought in a community of traders and amusements. In fact Alice Springs was a thriving city and not just another tourists' attraction.

Beyond the bright garish lights, the deep red earth and scrub bush looked like an alien landscape. Even on the darkest night, the air was warm and the shadows of the bushes and occasional tree were stark black and ghostly silver, creating the feeling that the Aboriginal Dreamtime was the reality and the intrusion of the European, the nightmare was overpowering.

The trip back to Earth was unannounced and no friends or relatives were waiting for Chamois and Sean. Stravros had tried to get a message to his sister, Maria, to tell her that Chamois was on his way to Alice Springs but there had been a clamp down on all communications regarding the enquiry.

"There's something rather odd going on," he told Gabby and Peter. "Anyone would think that our little goat had jeopardised the whole Space Navy instead of averting a disaster that would have called for more than a secret enquiry. The newscasters would have had a field day."

Stravros had made up his mind. "They are going to make our little mate Chamois, a scapegoat!"

"I wonder if we will ever see him again?" Gabby, who had at first distrusted Chamois, had become an expert with aikido and his hands were said to be sharper and faster than the first Lieutenant's tongue, thanks to Chamois' help. "I'll miss him and his lessons, won't you Peter?"

"Sure, I'll miss the streak of lightning, but Stravros is right you know, Chamois has saved the Space Navy's face. That disintegrator would have killed the civilians on that cruiser, but what in the name of Gagarin was it doing there?"

"A good one Peter. Maybe something will surface at the inquiry." Stravros felt as disheartened as his friends at the thought of not seeing Chamois on Dionysus again.

"I'll tell you one thing though, I *will* find out what happens to Chamois, or my name isn't Stravros Bertolozzte!" He thudded his fist into his open hand. "For one thing, the Horace and the

Hebe were the Hunters. Why didn't they find the Civilian?"

"Who do we know on them?" Gabby asked.

"Didn't Bill Carter transfer from the Vic to the Horace? Said he didn't like big ships or something." Stravros was trying to remember. "Yes, I think he'll be our boy! I'll have a word with him when we reach Moon Base. Nearly all Earth leave has been cancelled but there's nothing stopping us from having a drink in the mess together." All three were grinning now like Halloween pumpkins.

Stravros was a tough, experienced chief engineer who had been with the Space Navy since he had left the School for the Orphans of the Armed Forces. He was now in his early thirties and had gathered an intelligence that could not be recorded in an exam test.

A chat with Bill Carter and the chief engineer from the Hebe did not, at first, seem to throw any light on what had happened. Why hadn't anyone spotted the intruder?

Then Bill said, "Well, we did lose power in the main detectors for a second or two, not longer." He shrugged his shoulders. "We still had the heat detectors running though!" He took a gulp of 'free ale.' "I can't see how he could have evaded us really. Doesn't make sense. What about you Jude? Can you give us an idea how the bogie got through our nets?"

Jude Samson, another long serving engineer, breathed deeply through his nose as if it would clear his head and help him think. "It isn't a question how did he slip though our nets. It's who tipped him off as to where to hide and how to disable the detectors for the couple of seconds it took to slip from one barrier of rock to another. I don't like it Stravros! There's more trouble here than what we're seeing." Jude had said more in the last minute than he usually did in a month.

"If you hear anything interesting, let me know will you? A good pal of ours is involved. Gabby, Peter and me, we want to see him treated fair."

Stravros gave the barman the amount of cash credits for the evening's liquid refreshments and wandered over to his cabin quarters with Gabby and Peter in tow.

A message from Maria was waiting for Stravros. She had been unable to get leave from her work with the Marine Biology laboratory. Would she see him and Chamois when they landed maybe? More like, maybe not! Little sister, what can I do? Stravros wondered. He was more deeply disturbed on Chamois' behalf than if he were in trouble himself.

Sitting down to try to puzzle out his next move, he looked at his duty rota. There was a furlough of two weeks due. If he could get to Alice Springs, he could probably learn of Chamois' fate.

"Look here, I've this Long Service time out owing me. No one can cancel that, not even the admiral. I'll take a shufty to Alice Springs and find out what's what, okay?"

Peter and Gabby wanted to give him advice but Stravros' own horse sense told him he would have to play this one as best he could on his own, using his personal intelligence. He said good night to his two friends.

With that, knowing he had made the only wise decision, he lowered the light in his cabin and slept the sleep of the just.

For Chamois and Sean, the trip from Moon Base to Alice Springs was one of mixed feelings. Sean was certain that the new Admiral of the Fleet had wrongly treated Chamois and once the evidence was placed before him and all the other judges at the enquiry, he trusted that Chamois would be allowed to return to Dionysus as a sublieutenant of the Space Navy.

Chamois was in a very different frame of mind; he felt that he was still being tested somehow. What did the top brass want of him? Twice he had been placed in a position of control; first he was in charge of the Phobos rescue, being warned that failure would not be condone. All the miners had to be brought out alive. This he had done, but he had disobeyed an order from Jackson not to go down the first photon hole. He should have waited for the double shaft to be sunk. Hmm, then the men would have been dead though! When he took the comm, Chamois had expected to be out of the chair before the action started, and then lo and behold, there was an intruder hiding in the shadows that the hunters had failed to find! To add to the problem, no one else had seen it either, only him. How come?

Alice Springs at night time was as beautiful as any town or city from a mile or more up in the air. The sparkling lights looked like a coffer of a pirate's hoard, with rubies, sapphires and emeralds along with the diamonds, interlaced with the gold of the ordinary streetlights. On the ground, a slight breeze coming in from the desert barely kept the night air breathable.

As Chamois and Sean parted with Chamois being taken to a secure unit, the friends embraced each other for the first time and the last.

"I tell you Buddy boy, we won't let this muddle upset a good brotherhood like we have. That goes for Stravros and his mates too. We'll be celebrating in Becket's Bar when it's all over!" Sean tried to grin, his face frozen with the deep despair of heartache.

"Yeah, sure! We'll even invite Stonewall!" Chamois agreed. There was no more to be said. Both had beaten their wits in an attempt to find a clue to what this situation was really all about.

Chamois walked into the large room where he was to stay pending the inquiry. The bare Pyrilcite walls of the cell, which even the most violent of prisoners could not mark let alone damage, were a luxury compared with the cabin he had on the Dionysus. The facilities included a video and a computer that would only allow him to study history and other school like subjects. There was no link to the Internet web or any outside activities, so he could learn nothing of what was happening on Dionysus.

There was plenty of warm water for the twice-daily shower that he loved and a reasonable, if limited menu available from the food dispenser.

The harsh odour of a tar-based disinfectant tickled his nose, causing him to wrinkle his face in distaste. The air conditioning did not dispel the scent of the previous occupant. The "Lysol" had barely masked the smell of sweaty fear. But the diamond hard walls bore no other signs, no graffiti or scratches of any kind.

Looking around, he saw that he had everything to make the stay as bearable as possible for a few days. The walls of the cell would emit light or darken when he requested of the room computer.

Although he could entertain himself and keep his mind sharp, he soon realised he could not discover what was happening. All the electronic mailing systems had been cancelled. Not much notice was likely to be taken of a junior officer being penalised for a situation beyond his control or understanding, of that Chamois was certain, and that was all the news that he cared about.

There had never been enough time to watch videos while on Dionysus. Computers had been for the sole use of running the space vessel. This computer had information stored in the software that Chamois found very interesting.

He read a letter that was supposed to have been written by Catherine Howard, Henry the Eighth's fifth wife, to Thomas Culpeper, regarding the Queen's concern for Culpeper's health and her desire to see him and be able to talk to him. It read like a very restrained love letter. Poor Catherine had died because of the letters. She had been accused of adultery and beheaded!

Extraordinary! Today, Chamois thought, if a girl finds herself in need of comfort and love, she has every right to take a lover or companion of her choice. It is only when children are wanted, that the DNA of each partner is examined to make certain that they are compatible. A thorough search is carried out to discover if there are any hereditary broken genes that have not been repaired, or that those applying for parenthood are in no way related…no one has to commit themselves eternally any more, unless they so wish.

He went on to reflect that he and Maria, if they were compatible, would form a bond, get married and have children for which they would both be responsible. As was usually the case, they would stay together for the rest of their lives. Babies were considered a wonderful blessing and were now greatly cherished. For a while he visualised the time when he and Maria would be able to think about making such dreams a reality.

Of course, if they did not pass the stringent test to become parents, then they could still have a very loving relationship and part, if either felt the time was right for a break. Mentally shrugging his shoulders, he decided life must have been very complicated in the year fifteen forty something. Considering the situation of Catherine Howard, Chamois felt a kinship to her. She did not deserve to have her life ended in such a brutal manner, and *he* did not deserve to be under arrest waiting for the outcome of the inquiry.

Eventually his interest and amusement palled. His mind was telling him to be aware… not to be fooled into complacency. Anxiety started to nibble away at his normally calm attitude. Certainly the top brass knew of his coming and should have been prepared to deal with the situation. Perhaps they were making enquiries about the intruder. His common sense was numb, a seething blizzard of snowflakes, with no solid ground for answers.

With new faces appearing every day in the form of guards, he tried to engage them in conversation to attempt to find out whatever he could.

"Say, Buddy, have you heard when I get to go out for a walkabout?" Chamois called to one new guard as he went by the cell. The surly reply was, "Shudup!"

Using the computer to keep tabs on the date, Chamois was aware that he had been in Alice Springs for a week. Abruptly the photoelectric cell that was keeping the door to his room secure was suddenly cut off and he heard the grind of steel as the barrier to freedom was opened.

Chamois glanced up from his study of the last of the Tudor monarchs, Queen Elizabeth the First. Her ability to hold so much power over England, when a woman was considered to be not much more than a chattel, was amazing.

His musings were cut short, when without preamble, he was told to put his full dress uniform on and be ready for the inquiry in an hour!

"What? Don't I get to talk to a Space lawyer?" Chamois asked, fingernails drumming a tattoo on the desk. His patience had been reduced to a thin thread of cotton about to snap.

"Just get ready and don't give us any bother," was the curt reply. The guard's face was not giving away any secrets.

He watched Chamois dress carefully, putting on his number one uniform of grey and silver. When he was ready, Chamois stood tall and straight, looking the guard directly in the eyes. There was no fear in his own deep icy pools, or in the grim straight line of his mouth. Anger maybe, but not fear.

At 10:00 sharp Chamois left the cubicle to be marched along corridors and up flights of stairs. There were no luxuries of a lift or moving pedestrian way in the cellblocks.

The inquiry courtroom had a sophisticated environment-conditioning unit that was set to a temperate climate with a gentle breeze that held a scent of fresh mown hay and clover. After the sweat and antiseptic smell of the cellblock, then the slight whiff of metal and plastics of the Dionysus, Chamois appreciated the ambience even though he knew it would be the odour of dishonour for him and would follow him for the rest of his days.

Shafts of sunlight streamed through the windows, casting pools of brilliance that hurt the eyes, and shadows as dark as black holes.

He was able to see the solitary chair set for him before a long table with a row of chairs behind it, all facing the lone seat that he would be occupying.

As the members of the court of inquiry filed in, led by Sir Arthur Pelham, heads down, not even glancing his way, Chamois felt a sense of disaster. He was baffled. The whole affair was beyond his comprehension. He tried to think again. Who would want to see him in this kind of plight? He felt that he had already been tried and condemned before the hearing and that this inquiry was a farce. Someone wanted him out of the Space Navy, probably right out of the way.

For the first time, he considered his situation with the seriousness that it had now assumed for him. An evil shudder of premonition snaked its way down his spine. Who had he annoyed so much? Not Stonewall. The Lieutenant Commander had proven to be the best mentor any junior officer could wish for. Not the high Lords of the Space Navy. He did not know any of them personally, only by reputation! All his adult life had been spent with his nose firmly to the grindstone. He had never taken time out to get into real trouble. Yet here he was, facing what was obviously a hostile court and not knowing the real reason for it.

All the members of the inquiry had separate video units in order to read and see what Chamois was accused of doing. Film taken from various space vessels showed the Dionysus peeling out of its place into the path of Victory, then heading toward Pele, the target asteroid. No one seemed interested that the Chameleon as it had been registered, the offending vessel, was not to be seen until Dionysus had got close to it!

Lasting only half an hour, the court had come to the conclusion that Chamois was not suitable to be a Space Navy officer, having placed Dionysus and her crew so much at risk, just because he had seen what he had thought were illegal intruders in the weapons testing area near the asteroid Pele.

In fact, the intruder was a Private Survey Vessel, Chameleon, owned by the largest mining company on Earth. It had been in the depths of the asteroid belt and had not received the messages about evacuating the area. Randolph Wood, the owner, had explained everything in a perfectly logical communication of apology. No harm had been done to the good relations the Space Navy had with the biggest taxpayer on Earth. Randolph Wood was also an ardent supporter of the Space Navy. Admiral of the Space Fleet, Sir Arthur Pelham had refused to don the communications helmet that would have explained why Chamois behaved the way he had. Nothing Lieutenant Commander Jackson said altered his mind.

The holograph was dismissed out of hand. The shimmer of light on Pele, long before Chamois spotted an intruder, was considered to be a trick of sunlight on a shelf of rock. The Chameleon had just accidentally strayed into the experimental area at a very bad time!

The exercise had proven successful. Pele had been missed due to Chamois' panic! The 'Dust-maker' had hit some smaller floating debris the size of a private runabout and a cloud of very fine particles was the result.

"Well young man, it is my painful duty to have you dishonourably discharged from The Space Navy and to sentence you to five years' Social Construction Labour." Sir Arthur did not once look at Chamois directly, his face screwed up as if he had just bitten into a particularly sour lemon. He cleared his throat. "I understand that the extension of 'Red Hero', the Space Station Installation at the edge of the Gobi desert in

Mongolia, is short of unskilled labour, so that is where it has been decided that you would be best employed."

Sir Arthur had studiously referred to the communications screen, not taking advice from his subordinates. He had decided Chamois' fate. There was no need for the matter to be referred to a higher court, a complete waste of taxpayers' money! Sir Arthur had considered himself good enough to act as judge and jury in this case. His opinion was, "Stupid panic on the part of a junior officer, who had been placed in a situation of authority beyond his capabilities!" He left with the swirl of dust motes floating like galaxies of stars in the disturbed air as he hurried away in response to an invitation to spend a week on the Randolph Wood Estates in England.

Chapter 8

The Space Fleet had a transport base fifty kliks west of Tennant Creek on the edge of the Great Sandy Desert.

The journey from the court of enquiry in Alice Springs to the small military airstrip was in a closed, armoured prison van with two guards for escort.

As Chamois had been led away to the transport that would take him, he had seen the anguished look on the faces of Stonewall and Sean, and Chamois knew their concern for him. Strangely, Chamois felt light headed as though it was all happening to someone else. He was free from wondering what his fate would be. Now he knew, and heaved a huge sigh of relief.

The guard controlling the van stopped halfway on the journey, on the Tennants Creek road, to give everyone a chance to have a drink and answer the call of nature. The hum of the electro-magnetic motors that kept the vehicle on a steady route and just a foot from the ground was hypnotic, making all three occupants drowsy.

Chamois was fitted with an electronic tag that allowed him limited freedom within a few yards of the van.

His escorts were of a different temperament from the guards in the prison. They chatted to Chamois and wondered what was the real reason for the young man being sent to a wilderness like Gobi. He did not in the least resemble any of the felons they had escorted to other Social Construction Labour camps.

"I'm Spence Melton," the tall raw-boned guard said, extending his hand, "and this is Wes Livingstone. We've been guards for over twenty years or more and we can't help but wonder whose toes you've trodden on. Who have you upset, Stone?" The sunburned face had crinkled up to squint at Chamois with piercing blue eyes that missed nothing.

"That's something I'd like to know too," Chamois replied. "I've given up trying to puzzle it out. I'm hoping some friends will be able to find out something. Still, even if they do, what good will it do?" Chamois was beginning to feel depressed. "I'll be under armed guard, out in the middle of Mongolia, with nowhere to run." He looked at his two guards. "I tell you, that place is at the back of beyond!" The long empty road to Tennants Creek ahead of them seemed to echo his words.

Lignite, the soft brown, coal-like substance had been mined clean and now the local people used electric power supplied free by the governments of Russia and China. Land had been surrendered in a form of recompense, to make way for the Space Fleet development. The Gobi Space station was just over sixty kliks south of Ulaanbaatar, the English interpretation of which being Red Hero. Ulaanbaatar was the capitol of Mongolia. The Space Station Development had been named Red Hero.

It was not right in the sand dune area of Gobi, just close enough to the empty stretch of wilderness for it to be so isolated, so that if there had been an accident to any of the space vehicles, few would get hurt, only those who were actually working at the place. Therefore the vast plains of Mongolia made excellent testing and training grounds for Space development, with plenty of room to expand. The nomadic Mongolians, who still wandered at will over the rolling rough grasslands, were not easily tamed and when troops had been sent to round them up and bring them to Bayanhongor, they had simply disappeared into the mountains.

As the van controller and the extra man for Chamois' escort finished their break, Spence remarked, "Red Hero, that's an odd name. Where did it come from?"

"As far as I can make out, it was the Russians who gave the Mongolians a lot of help building railways and such," Wes volunteered. "Also there was a lot of strife among the different factions trying to gain control and the Russians, who were commonly called "Reds", won, and there ain't nothing as good as a 'Red Hero'. The guard laughed. "Why even the first man in space was a Red you know - Yuri Gagarin, Little Wild Goose, in English!"

Wes thought the whole situation a joke, when he considered how the other Great Power of the time had been beaten by what was considered a backward country. "I think that after the war of nineteen forty-five, the Reds got the cream of German scientists by arriving at the university of Leipzig first. It was of course, the Germans who invented the rocket.... used them in fact, on England in the hope of winning!"

Chamois agreed. "Yes, I do know; we got all that from our classroom studies. A lot of the stuff they tried to cram into us was dull as ditch water." Chamois shook his head in recollection. "We had a good time though when it came to Space History, how it all really started with those German scientists in the Second World War making rockets, and America making the first atomic bomb. How primitive it all seems now. It's fantastic to realise they did not even have the kind of computers that we have today!"

A rustle in the bushes behind them made the three of them spin round and stare in amazement as a man stepped forward. Spence motioned for Wes and Chamois to remain calm.

Squat, black as night, with features straight from the Stone Age, the figure turned and looked back at the three, a slightly mocking glint in his fathomless black on black eyes, as he surveyed them. Then with cold deliberation, he raised his hand, which held a stick of dark brown wood with weird markings and both ends sharpened and pointed it towards Chamois.

"The white Billy goat will sacrifice everything, including himself. He will feel the breath of the Fire God. The Fire God will spit him and all with him, out." A wide grin stretched the ugly features in merriment. " The little goat will no longer be a man. He will not be a god either." The apparition nodded, striking the air with his stick. "You will bring back some of the knowledge of the gods." Coming a step closer he said, in an almost conspiratorial whisper, "Keep your knowledge for those who deserve it, little Billy goat!"

The rustling of the dry leaves as the bushes had parted, was the only indication that the Aborigine had been swallowed up by the sparse trees that edged the Great Sandy Desert, and before Chamois or his guards could collect their wits and move after him, he had disappeared!

"Can anyone tell me what that was all about?" asked Spence, his eyes as wide as dinner plates in amazement.

"Well, my friends call me Chamois. I jumped out of an upper story window to get an introduction to my girl She labelled me 'Chamois' and it stuck."

Chamois gave a wide rueful grin at the recollection. "I was on Moon Base at the time, so it really was no great leap of faith." He hunched his shoulders and spread his hands as he spoke. "It was quite fun, to be honest!"

"So, you're the white Billy goat that Johnny Blackbird was referring to." Spence tipped his wide brimmed bush hat back from his face and looked more closely at Chamois. "And here was I thinking that you were just another snot-nosed, Pommy bastard who had shit in someone else's pants. If what the old man says is true, and I've never known him to be wrong…you won't be spending too much time working at Red Hero at the government's pleasure." The menacing expression on his face spoke volumes. The way Spence spoke, there seemed to be danger in his attitude and Chamois found it difficult to make sense of it. The suppressed anger gave the impression that Spence felt like putting a fist in someone's face. His features were set and grim, hard lines and planes forming on his previously relaxed countenance. Sweat was making rivulets down his neck. Was he angry with him, Chamois wondered, or was the man trying to pay him a backhanded compliment?

Spence stared hard at Chamois for what seemed a decade. "Tell you what, young'un, Wes and me, we run real villains in with pleasure, don't we mate?" He put a large heavy hand on Wes's shoulder and shook it. "Right?" Not waiting for Wes to answer, he went on, "But if by any chance you just happen to be in our piece of the Outback, I hope you'll think to give us a call."

Rubbing the tired muscles in his neck, and making a muddy smear with sweat and dust, he continued, "For the time being though, Wes and me have to get you to Tennants Creek airstrip. We can't afford to lose our jobs when we've only months before retiring by letting you escape now. Anyway, I'm a firm believer in what is to be, will be." As he climbed into the vehicle he turned to Chamois and added, "One bit of advice, if you like, keep a low profile. Don't even make a shadow if you can help it, okay?"

CHAMOIS

With that he climbed back into the van and set the controls for the side road that would take them to the west of Tennants Creek.

From the time that the Aborigine had confronted them to arriving at the airstrip, little or no conversation took place in the van. As it came to a halt, Spence got out, followed by Chamois. Wes stayed in the van feeding the new commands into the controlling computer that would take them back to Alice Springs.

Spence sauntered over to the sentry on duty. "I've got one Community Construction worker for you. Sign here, please!" His words were bitten off as if he hated talking.

Holding out the hand pad, which was linked to the main computer in Alice Springs, Spence waited for the guard to sign it, and then wasting no time, sent it directly by electronic mail. If young Mr Stone was going to escape then he could do it any time from now on. It was no longer his problem!

Spence's eyes crinkled at the corners as he shook Chamois' hand. "Good luck Stone." He added on a cheerful note, "Come and see us when your furlough is up."

"I'd like that. Have a safe journey," Chamois replied, with a wave of his hand.

"Sure, you too. Life is always easier if no one expects anything from you, Stone!"

The small speed craft left the Tennants Creek field in a cloud of dust. Chamois was the only person being taken to the Red Hero station and the bull nosed runabout lifted off and was away with only the members of the ground control to see it leave.

Depression and loneliness kept him silent; the two-man crew seemed uninterested in their charge. As the craft descended, the pilot controlling the main keyboard turned and asked Chamois if he knew anything about Red Hero.

"No, not really, just that it's being extended so as to be able to send more freight out to the

Moon colony. I don't know anything about who or what's there," he replied.

"Well all I can tell you is that after serving in the Space Fleet, you are in for a shock or three!" There was a compassionate grin on the older man's face. "You've heard of the Hilton Astor Hotels? Well, it's nothing like them!" The man's glance was warning Chamois that he was in for a rough ride for the next five years.

The format of handing Chamois over to Red Hero was the same as when Spence and Wes had passed him on to the Tennant Creek guard. This time though, he had an electronic tag fitted before he left the aircraft compound. The tag would cause him to blackout if he went beyond the perimeter of Red Hero and would send a warning signal to the prison control office. Guards were armed only with electric prod batons, which they seemed ready and able to use to maximum affect.

Chamois had lost track of time and felt completely disorientated. He was more exhausted than if he had spent a day with Stonewall Jackson reading computer dials and defining their use and what their intelligence conveyed.

The night air was dry and cold. He shivered in the lightweight overalls he had been given in Alice Springs when he had been taken to the cells to wait for the transport. They were no barriers to the harsh wind that swept over the airfield.

"Come on, I ain't got all night. You can stay in the infirmary until the morning, then you are up for the medical." The guard seemed more impatient than angry at being called out at two in the morning.

Bundled into a narrow white Pyrilcite room, Chamois saw there was a cot that would just about take his length and width. Gratefully he sank down and although there was no turning room, sleep, deep and dreamless came, blacking out all the previous day's happenings.

The rough shaking of his shoulder brought him back to reality. A figure completely covered with a white mask and overall, stood waiting for him to get up and comply with a medical exam that would cover every aspect of his body.

The DNA microchip in his neck was extracted and further information printed on it about his five-year term of Social Community Labour, when it started and when it would end. He was tested for every known disease and drug addiction.

He then became number 1050 'D' on a computer.

Being found completely clear of any medical problem, he was then shown where he would sleep while free from work. Prisoners were given twelve hours free time for sleep, study and exercise.

All the retina and DNA identity tests were completed in time for Chamois to be given a set of thick dark grey overalls, a quick breakfast and then taken out to the overseer and put to work.

Jack Mills had been at Red Hero for six years, graduating from a Social Construction Labourer to his present post. He had nowhere to go, and no family to go home to. The work kept him occupied and gave him a sense of use and belonging.

Space travel was expanding fast with the colonisation of the Moon and Mars, so a lot of freight was needed which meant that he was needed too.

"Listen here Stone, you do your stint, make no trouble and we'll get along all right, understand?" Jack made certain that his fresh labourer knew what he wanted from him. "This is number four Bully. All you have to do is keep it on line with what the screen says. It sucks up loose soil, the bogies follow behind and take the rubbish to the mountains to be tipped away." He coughed and spat as he finished the instructions.

The machine stood there, like a great drooping dinosaur. Chamois could only nod his head and agree with him and climb into the demon beast. The contraption had no air-conditioning. It had a broken window that let in the dust along with the air.

As he directed the machine out to the vast expanse of wilderness that was to be carved up to make the extension for the space station, the noise while the engine was switched on made Chamois' teeth rattle. For someone of Chamois' intelligence, the Bully was a very simple device and required little help from him. It sucked up sand and small stones. If anything large blocked the intake, he had to climb down and dislodge it. Large boulders were scattered all over the plain that stretched before him. Chamois wondered how they were disposed of.

At the midday break Jack Mills said to him, "When you've finished your break, Stone, you can take the dumper and get rid of some of the big stuff. The bogie will follow you. I've keyed it to your number, okay?"

Jack did not expect a negative answer, so Chamois just nodded.

His overalls had his number and name printed on them. The other men barely acknowledged his existence, standing around drinking their coffee or tea and munching on thick slices of dark bread and goats' cheese.

A clanging bell sounded; men replaced cups and plates and made their way to whatever work had been assigned to them. Chamois walked toward the area where most of the large stones lay. At first he found the heavy lifting therapeutic, his mind numb to what had happened to him in the last twenty-four hours. He had lost his post on Dionysus, his identity and most likely Maria as well. Did she know he thought of her constantly?

Sweat and dust in his mouth and eyes made him thirsty and half blind; his muscles started to ache, even though he had always worked out hard in the space ship's gym every day. His body was not used to the prolonged demanding hard labour. Leaning against the dumper, he wiped the sweat from his face with a grimy hand. He was panting for breath and choking on filth.

The sting of the bullwhip galvanised him into action. The man lashing out at him stood with his back to the sun and Chamois could not see who it was. Grabbing the tail of the whip, as it was about to descend again, he tugged so hard that the man on the handle lost his footing and was dragged over the hard stony ground.

His tormentor got up and roared like a wounded animal. He reeled drunkenly toward Chamois, teeth bared and snarling, his hands outstretched as if he were about to grab Chamois by the throat. But Chamois was not there waiting to be slaughtered. He had nimbly stepped aside to allow the madman to strike his head against the unyielding bulk of Bully four.

Dazed, with blood pouring from the gash across his forehead, he turned on Chamois again. Cold and emotionless, Chamois studied him, knowing the man had lost control of himself. Using the art taught him by Mito Iwaki, Chamois allowed his attacker to exhaust himself before tapping him lightly behind the ear, causing the man to collapse.

Chamois then became aware that he had an audience of other prisoners and Jack Mills.

"I see you've met warder Bristow then. Been here half a day and causing trouble already!" Jack looked at Chamois with a cocked eyebrow. "He's alive I suppose?" Jack did not seem at all concerned for this man, Bristow, and Chamois wondered if he disliked the whip-wielding warder.

"Oh, yes, he's okay. In just a couple of seconds he'll be fighting fit again."

Jack was at odds, trying to hide the grin that threatened to spread across his face. The truth was, he hated Bristow, and always had, from the moment he had arrived as a prison labourer himself. "You'd best go and get some more loose stuff out. Get back to number four Bully and try to keep out of Bristow's way for a while. He'll kill you given half a chance." Giving Chamois a friendly shove, Jack turned to the men who had gathered to watch. "I see some people want to work late tonight instead of knocking off at six!" The men vanished as silently as they had appeared.

Bristow was taken to the medical centre by an orderly and was not seen for many days.

Chamois, at six o' clock sharp, headed for what he hoped would be a warm shower, undoing his overalls as he walked into the bathhouse. Suddenly four pairs of vice like hands, two to each wrist and ankle, grabbed him giving him no chance to defend himself.

"Strip everything off him!" The voice came from a swarthy, muscular man, looking more like a Buddha cast in bronze than a Communal Labourer. He commanded every man's attention. The hairless face was as hard as that of every other man working on the extension. He was handsome with evenly modulated features, and his dark amber eyes held a greater intelligence.

Chamois tried to struggle free, but that only made his captors' grip tighter.

"Don't hurt him, you brutes. I want him unmarked, do you understand?" The low guttural voice was almost one of concern.

Oh, dear God! Rape, he's going to rape me! The thought seared its way through Chamois' brain, and he could feel his bones melt with the shock of such an idea as his body being violated.

"Wash him down, carefully mind," the bronze man ordered, when Chamois stood bare of every stitch of clothing.

Four men held him down while two more washed him all over. His platinum, white hair was shampooed clean and his pale, thin torso scrubbed pink.

While still dripping wet, his captors took him toward the godlike devil.

"Put that pail over his head, gently now… lights down," came the next command.

Chapter 9

Screaming inwardly with anger and frustration at his naked helplessness, Chamois gritted his teeth. Then as the cover was taken from his head, he glared his revulsion at this dark skinned man. His deep blue eyes, filled with hatred, were coffin shaped, the ligaments on his neck like strained ropes. He managed to spit out, "If it's the very last thing I do, I'll kill you… I'll get you baldy." His normally pale face was crimson with unadulterated rage and his breath came in short hurried gasps.

A shrewd smile appeared on the extraordinary features of his tormentor who was carefully assessing Chamois and installing him into a niche of which Chamois had no knowledge.

"You did get me Stone, me and a few other men who were doomed to die of asphyxiation. You got us out of a black hole on Phobos. Our demons travel with us wherever we go and the worst demon that any miner has is to be buried alive! You've no idea what that is like, young man."

"Oh no? That's what you think. Have you any idea what it was like for me to be in that narrow hole when the shaft collapsed? I was alone, and before I could get my wrist light working and the night vision came into play, it was blacker than that hell's kitchen that I found you in. I was scared out of my wits," Chamois spat out.

"And how did you manage to conquer your fear and come down and get us out?" his tormentor asked.

"I'd rather not say."

Heavy lids covered the dark eyes as he accepted this answer. "Okay! Now to continue with what I was telling you, and why the charade with the bucket. I just had to make certain it was you and not some little sir echo working for Bristow, though considering that you have today, dented *his* ego, I should have known better. You remember, it was pitch black down that mine, with only your hand torch to give us light to see by. You had your helmet with the night vision on to see us with. We did not have that kind of luxury. Also you were only dressed in a pair of very brief shorts and smothered in grease! I brought you a set of coveralls to help keep out the cold." The voice was now harsh with unshed tears. "That safety helmet that you were wearing made identifying you difficult, too." Brookman Jarvis was openly crying now. Wiping the tears away with the palm of his hand, he said, "I never thought I would see you again, let alone see you in a Community Labour camp."

He wanted to give Stone a hug to let him feel how grateful he was for saving him from a slow and painful death of suffocation, but he walked away toward the benches, knowing that his own emotions would have got completely out of hand and he would have been blubbering like a baby. He indicated with a wave of his hand to Chamois to join him.

"Get this man some decent threads and the best victuals that Cookie can dish up," he ordered the men who had held Chamois captive, whereupon they released him to run to do Brookman's bidding.

Brookman was grinning now as he commented, "I hear you upset that screw Bristow! As soon as someone told me that he had been flattened, I knew there was a man in the camp who warranted my attention." He gave Chamois a sly wink. "Did you really think you were in grief?" Bunching up his fist, he thumped the table. "If anyone so much as stands in your light, I personally will put out his!"

"It's okay, Brookman, I can take care of myself. I hope Bristow keeps his whip to himself though. He is one man with a loose screw," Chamois said, with an easy grin.

"Wait till I get word to Luke Denning. He's still out on Mars." Brookman took a sip of water. The tawny, almond shaped eyes held a mystery.

There was a secret in their depths that Chamois, for all his psychic abilities, could not fathom.

Chamois could not believe his ears. Contact another prisoner! From the depths of one labour camp to another on Mars? Only the flicker of his eyes registered his incredulity. He knew better than to ask questions.

Brookman gave an enigmatic smile, making him look even more like a Buddha, which knew secrets that he would never divulge. "Don't mind me not telling you everything Charley Stone. Sometimes ignorance can save your skin," Brookman said in a low voice. Then he continued to eat his supper, chewing each mouthful slowly and carefully, occasionally taking small sips of water.

Fastidiously wiping his mouth, Brookman glanced over to a man standing by a window, watching for any unwanted visitors, and said, "Peterson, you know what to do." It was not so much an order as a statement.

Peterson went out of the main building to carry out Brookman's wishes with the words, "Okay, I'll be in touch as soon as I have something for you."

Another man took Peterson's place by the window. These men respected Brookman's leadership, Chamois noticed, and wondered what Brookman normally did for his livelihood before he was sentenced to work in a construction labour gang. He would never ask; questions, especially of a personal nature were taboo. He toyed with his food, not feeling really hungry, even though he had not eaten a proper meal for more than a day. The shock of his predicament was slowly melting like a glacier into his bones.

"Stone," Brookman said, after taking yet another sip of water, "if you plan to survive the Social Construction Labour Camp, then I strongly advise you to eat carefully, to get every bit of nourishment from your food, and drink as much fluid as your body needs. The reason for this is that you are now doing labourer's work and need the muscles to do so."

He glanced at Stone to make certain that he realised this was for his benefit. "The cook is a friend of mine, a first class man with food, cooks it to taste good without ruining it." Brookman was now mopping up the gravy with a slice of bread, and grinned as he motioned with the crust, dripping with juice. "Come on, eat up, otherwise Cookie will feel he has let me down!"

Following Brookman's advice, Chamois started to eat everything put in front of him that had been brought by another of Brookman's friends. He suddenly realised that he was, in fact, ravenous.

Charley Stone had decided not to use his nickname that was something which belonged to freedom and happy memories. Until those days returned, Chamois was dead!

Chewing on his food the same way Brookman did, he allowed his mind to consider his situation and his future. As he did so, he ate his way through the excellent meal. From now on, he decided, while working as a Social Construction Labourer, he was Stone. "A good description," he thought. "Hard and keeping as much of myself to myself as possible."

His space career records had stayed on Dionysus and in the Space Navy archives. Only Brookman knew his past and Stone realised he could trust the man with his life.

Then Brookman brought him out of his reverie. "Can you play chess, Stone?" Brookman asked, after they had eaten the substantial meal. "It helps to keep a sharp edge on the mind."

"Well yes, but I haven't had much chance to play for some years," Stone admitted grudgingly, and then added, "I've been kept rather busy, up until now."

As Brookman rose to get the board and chessmen out, he chuckled and agreed, "Yes, I suppose you could say that," and gave Stone a conspiratorial glance.

The board and chessmen were very old and worn by years of use.

Brookman, showing a white pawn, started to set up his pieces. Still smiling he told Stone the history of this set. His father had presented him with it, and he, in turn had been given it by his father, and so on, back for generations.

"I've always managed to keep it with me. Now and again I've had to do a minor repair job on a piece, like when a white pawn became so discoloured it looked black. I had to go over it very gently with a weak abrasive."

Stone could see by the way Brookman handled the pieces that his opponent loved this set, and the game. It was a means of retaining his intelligence. Stone hoped that he could give Brookman a fair game.

The first match was over almost as soon as it had started, Brookman getting Stone's king in check in only five moves. Stone was amazed and decided that he needed to watch Brookman's play very carefully. Gradually,

Stone's game improved. "You're doing fine. By the time you go... to another camp, you should be almost up to my level."

Stone did not altogether miss the slight pause in what Brookman had been saying, but decided not to comment or ask questions...just yet. The man had enjoyed himself and was pleased his young opponent showed so much promise.

"I've got to admit, I never thought that I would ever have the time or motivation to play this kind of game," Stone had to agree.

"Did you play another kind of game, when you had the chance that is? Please don't think I'm being nosy. It just helps to pass the time if you can share another man's interest!" Brookman wondered if he had offended Stone by asking such a question.

Stone gave a huge grin, stretched his aching arms and rubbed his back muscles, as he told Brookman about his practice of unarmed defence. "I don't think Bristow knew what he started when he came at me. I hardly touched him. He did most of his damage himself."

"Now, tell me truthfully," Brookman's head was close to his, "can you teach this gentle art of self defence to another person? Me for instance." Brookman's mind was racing. His muscles were stronger than Stone's, having done so much hard labour, but he knew he lacked the magical knowledge of how to use this particular art.

"Why not? I'll give you a trial bout and show you some of the basic moves. Then if you don't mind I must get into my cot!" Stone's eyes were bloodshot and gritty through lack of sleep. Brookman was shocked to realise that he had kept Stone up playing chess and talking when, of course, the young man was bound to be exhausted, first day here, making a fool of Bristow and doing labour that found muscles which the poor guy didn't know he had.

"How stupid can I be? Sorry Stone! Look, I've set it up so that you can share a dorm with me and three of my most trusted friends. You have a corner cubicle so that you won't be disturbed, and you only have to ask any one of us for anything you need." With a disarming smile he added, "We can discuss a practice match tomorrow after work." Brookman's embarrassment made Stone grin. The man was a heap of contradictions. He was so obviously in control of a group of men; he was also very powerfully built, yet in no way could he be called a bully. The men he called friends did as he asked, because they wanted to.

His sleeping cubicle had the usual Pyrilcite walls, floor and ceiling, a cot just big enough to accommodate his long frame, a chair, a small locker, and a toilet. Home from home! Charley Stone felt comfortable in the Spartan cubicle, it was almost the same as the space he had called a cabin on Dionysus.

Taking off the clean overalls he had been given by Brookman, after he had established that he was the one who had come to his aid on Phobos, Stone draped them over the chair, fell into the cot and was asleep. There was no time for worry about Bristow, or anything. Slumber claimed him as his head touched the pillow.

Meanwhile, in the communal room men were gathered around Brookman, the murmur of conversation low.

"Do you think Luke can orchestrate something?" Brookman was being asked.

"From what I've learned about that man, he could fix the Space Navy with his hands tied," came Brookman's voice. "You sure he got the message?"

"Yeah, sure. No doubt he's sorting things and making contacts."

"Do you think Stone needs wising up how to survive here?" another man asked. "I mean, he should never have let Bristow get so close without being aware that grief was on his back. True, the creep was on a flitter-bug and didn't make any noise, but still… he just doesn't seem to have any cred!"

"Well, I'll tell you this much about our new friend, he's a long way from being stupid or a snivelling coward, so all he needs is to be made aware that in the nick, not everyone is on the side of the Angels, and he should be extra careful of Bristow's dummies. We'll just have to keep an eye on him and make sure he and trouble stay apart." Having said that, Brookman looked at the timepiece on the wall. 21:55, lock up time. Brookman bade all the men good night and made his way to the small, five-man dormitory.

The massive electrical charge that secured the open portals in order to stop anyone from taking an unscheduled walk had not yet been switched on. Once it was on, he would not have been able to reach the safety of his cubicle. At 22:00 hours, he would have been recorded as being out of bounds. Then the electrode in his neck would have been activated, sending a charge to his brain. Most likely he would have died. The least that would have happened, he would have ended up a madman. He had seen the results of a mistimed walk.

As he prepared for sleep, Brookman made a mental inventory of what he knew about his new dorm-mate, which was considerably more than that young man would ever realise. More than he knew himself! Charley Stone was twenty-five years old, was the son of Ingrid and…a friend of Luke Denning, born just after the devastating meteor storm and volcanic eruptions in the Pacific. "I wonder how you survived, Sunshine?" he murmured to himself. Educated at the university of astro-dynamics and space physics, had difficulties with the written word. "Now that must have been one hell of a problem to beat." Stone had also acquired a nickname of 'Chamois!' "Interesting! I wonder if he will ever talk about his life in the Space Navy?" He'd got into a fight with some drunken marines over a girl, and then challenged them to another fight the next day when they were sober. "What a boy!" He would have considered Stone to be too good to be true if it wasn't for the fact that he had an affinity with trouble and the temper of a scalded cat that only the Space Navy training had kept in check, until now!

If my guess is right, this young man is going to cause quite a stir in this stew pot. Secretly, Brookman was pleased, pleased that he had something to do that required a lot of careful thought, which would stretch his intelligence to its limit and thereby bring his intellect back into gear again and stop the rot. Also it gave him a chance to help a man who had saved his life. Then there was Luke's friend, a brilliantly clever man to be reckoned with if ever there was one.

Luke Denning thought the world of this person and trusted him implicitly. He was a link to Luke's life before he saw the inside of a labour camp. Anything at all that he could do that would be a benefit to *him*, he Brookman Jarvis would do. Charley Stone was the only child of this friend of Luke Denning. Therefore he had a double reason to be pleased at the prospect of being able to help the young man. "But first *you* have to be eliminated," he said, holding the black king from his chess set, in his massive fist.

At 06:00 sharp, all labourers were outside and ready to be told by Jack Mills where they were to work for the day. After two hours, they would take time off for breakfast.

Stone was told to continue where he had been working before Bristow came on the scene, picking up the larger rocks.

The dumper followed him like a huge puppy dog, and as one became full, another took its place, the weight of the load telling the built-in computer the container was full.

By breakfast time, Stone felt he had been doing the job all his life. There seemed to be no end of large rocks to be shifted. The sun had risen and hunger was gnawing at his stomach. When he returned to the base for his breakfast, men stood around in groups near the trestle table that faced the rolling plains and desert. This outside arrangement was used for breakfast and the midday meal. The men from Brookman's dorm greeted him like an old friend and handed him a mug of coffee and a rough-cut sandwich.

"Don't ever put your cup or wad down! Keep them in your hands so no one can doctor them. Anyone can slip you a Mickey when you're not looking, then before you know it, you've got a double dose of Dream Dust inside you and death rattling your brains." Stone turned to see Peterson standing near enough to speak in a low but clear voice. "So watch where your food is all the time, if you want to stay alive, that is!" Peterson nodded his head and wandered off, for the entire world as if he had just said, 'Good morning' to Stone. Instead, he had started the steady life-saving education, which Stone was now receiving.

The wind blowing in off the plains was chill and the sweat on the men soon turned to ice. Stone lifted his face to the breeze and actually felt at peace. Whatever happened, he reckoned that this period in his life was to be used to its full advantage. The men with whom he worked and spent his free time were just ordinary people. Whatever dark deeds or secrets their past lives held, they were no part of them now.

Chapter 10

He had been in line for a post on a Deep Space Patrol Vessel and had worked so hard. And thanks to Lieutenant Commander Jackson, he had succeeded. Stone felt that he could have operated the Dionysus blindfolded.

Instead he was working with a group of criminals to help extend the take-off strip in Mongolia, a place so remote, that with only the implanted electronic tags and electrode in their necks, plus a hundred or so warders and overseers like Jack Mills, thousands of men were kept under control.

Jack Mills came to him when he had finished his breakfast, and directed him to take Bully four and sweep the top end of the perimeter of loose sand and pebbles. "It's a long way out I know, but the architects want us to begin laying the outer perimeter foundations in a couple of weeks' time, before the hard frosts start, so get a move on."

"Okay, Jack, I'll see if I can't get this can of pebbles called a Bully to work a bit better, then it might get the job done that much quicker." Switching on the solar drive and computer, Stone eased the Bully out of the line of machines and rattled off toward the distant edge of the proposed extension. With a dumper following, Stone still thought of the dumper as a puppy.

Whenever he stopped to unblock the intake on the Bully, he also cleaned off a lot of dirt and dust that gathered over the solar panels. There were a few tools in a metal trunk under the seat, which he used to tighten up several loose bolts on the engine housing case. The Bully still made a bone-shaking rattle. Stone decided to listen and feel the drive cover to see if he could locate the source. He was rewarded with a distinct tremor from the drive! "Bad," he thought. Turning off the drive engine and removing the cover, he discovered that several moving parts had worked completely out of line and almost worn away. Adjusting and tightening up what he could, Stone then continued to patrol the perimeter, sucking up sand and stones.

Towards midday, a particularly large chunk of rock was caught in the nozzle. He switched off the intake drive, prised the rock loose and found it to be what looked like a lump of dark brown glass. He could see there was something embedded in it as he wiped away dirt and dust. To his Spacer's eyes, it looked like nothing other than a chunk of gears from a motor, just like the one he had been tinkering with on the Bully. The glass was like the process of a blast from a photon drive!

It now came as second nature to him to cast a furtive glance around to see if anyone was watching. Heaving a sigh of relief when he observed that the likes of warder Bristow were nowhere in sight or sound, he placed the anomaly in the tool box, then looked around for evidence of more glass. The strange stuff seemed to start where he had worked up to the edge of the perimeter, and then went southwest. Casually he brushed aside the loose debris covering glass. He could see more bits of machinery were encased. It must have been the mother of all barbies; glad I wasn't around to join in, he mused!

With his eyes, ears and nose tuned to the slightest change of sight, scent or sound indicating inquisitive warders, Stone continued to sweep the area of loose sand and small rocks until the lunch break by which time his stomach was already rumbling in anticipation, even though it would only be a hunk of bread, a bowl of mixed vegetable soup and a mug of water. Looking around for Brookman, Stone manoeuvred the Bully to where he could see it while he was eating.

Brookman was squatting in the protection of an outhouse, out of the constant icy wind that sliced in from the north. "That Bully seems to be running a lot quieter now, Stone." He gestured with his mug of water for Stone to join him. "No unexpected visitors this morning?"

"No!" he replied. "Just as well too. I've something I would like you to have a look at, Brookman." Stone nodded toward the Bully. "There's a lump of what looks like glass in the locker under the seat. I'd like your opinion about it."

"Sounds interesting. We don't have much time to talk now but I'll get Peterson to rescue it and we'll discuss it over supper." Looking toward Peterson to catch his eye, he beckoned with his head for him to join them, whispered what Stone had told him then added, "Bury it in a sand bucket in the kitchen. Tell Cookie we'll pick it up later."

Peterson eased his way towards the Bully, rested his soup dish and mug on the step, sat down beside them and seemed to lean back to rest his aching limbs. The toolbox was opened and closed, the lump of glass hidden in Peterson's overalls so stealthily that Stone could not believe he actually saw what happened. Brookman had continued to eat as he usually did, slowly and thoroughly.

Stone dipped his bread in the soup and savoured each bite. As he did so, he came to the conclusion that, whatever these men were convicted of, some of their talents were obviously very useful.

After wiping his dish with a crust of bread to extract the last of the soup, Stone took the drooping dinosaur, as he thought of Bully four, out to where the perimeter was to be laid, careful to avoid disturbing any more glass.

By late afternoon, he had filled so many dumpers he had lost count. The sun had started to sink and the burning glare made his eyes water. He squinted to try to ease the blinding agony. As he did so, the rays caught an up thrust of rock about thirty metres from the perimeter, westward, away from the camp. The lowering sun seemed to burn right through it, like translucent amber. He wondered what it was. He had no chance to go and investigate, not unless he wanted to have his head fried with an electrode charge.

At 16.00, during the tea break, he got word to Brookman about the semi transparent rock. "It could be part of what I have already found, but what the hell it is, I have no idea!" The chagrin in Stone's voice was loud and clear.

"Don't think any more about it, Stone; we'll discuss your rocks tonight, as I promised. I may also contact a friend who knows about such things, okay?"

The last thing Brookman wanted was for Stone to get too interested in the local legends and mysteries. The stories about what was known hundreds of years ago as The Silk Road, which was supposed to have run right across the place where they were excavating, would probably make young Stone want to investigate further. "God help me!" Brookman whispered to himself. "How am I going to keep Stone and mischief apart? Well if the Space Navy finally lost the battle, I guess I'm going to have my work cut out."

Giving a deep sigh and mentally shaking his head, Brookman returned to his labour for the last two hours of the working day, heaving large boulders onto a dumper. His broad, brawny back and shoulder muscles marred with dusty sweat, rippled in the dying rays of the sinking sun.

The siren clarion call for 18:00 and the end of the day's toil was welcome to all who heard it.

A shower, a change of overalls and a meal, were the top priorities. After appeasing the body's needs, men could then think about what subjects they were studying or what videos they wanted to watch, whatever it was that kept them sane in the confines of the prison camp.

There were no surprise parties waiting for Stone this time as he entered the blockhouse of showers. Instead a clean set of overalls lay neatly folded on a chair, the name 'Stone' and the number 1050, imprinted on the breast.

A shower cubicle with a hot air dryer was empty, waiting for him. A broad grin, the merriment of which reached his eyes, wreathed his face, as he tore open the fastenings of the overalls he had worn all day and let them drop into the chute provided, then stepped into the soothing water. He lathered his face and scrubbed his chin with the hair removing cream, shampooed his hair and washed his body clean, giving an extra scouring to his hands and fingernails. Stone realised that as he erased the day's dirt and scrubbed himself clean, he really felt at peace, cheerful even! And why not, he asked himself. The company's good, the food is far better than that delivered from the food dispensers, the work is boring, but at least I get to breathe air that hasn't been through the scrubbers a dozen times. The only fly in this ointment is the people like Bristow. Also I've lost so many great friends! Or have I?

Stone's mind continued to dwell on Dionysus and her crew; did they ever think about him, or did they have too many problems of their own to worry about him? Whatever was happening in the outside world, there was nothing he could do about it. Take the ball and run with it was all he could, and would do.

He threw back his head, and the laughter welled up from his belly. The Lords of the Space Navy had wanted to punish him. Instead they had delivered him right into the hands of people who only had his welfare at heart, because by some freak stroke of justice, one of them was a man he had helped to safety.

As he entered the food hall, Peterson nodded to where Brookman was sitting. "Your supper is on the table next to Brookman. He'll be pleased to see you looking so cheerful."

"Thanks, Peterson. Yeah, I've just been counting my blessings and came up with the fact that I've hit pay dirt being sent to Red Hero." Stone placed a firm and friendly hand on Peterson's arm and looked at him directly in the eyes, nodding his head, confirming what he said.

"Now that's what I call smart! If you can't beat grief, then make the most of it." Peterson felt that his efforts to 'educate' Stone were going to be worthwhile.

Stone made his way to where Brookman was waiting for him. As usual, he was eating his supper with studied care, taking the occasional sips of water.

"Sit down and fill up. Don't let your food get cold."

Brookman sounds exactly like an anxious parent, thought Stone. "It's getting to be just like home here, only I never really did have a home, unless you can call a Home for Foundlings, home!" The voluntary piece of personal information had slipped out before Stone had realised.

"Join our club, Stone. A good half of us don't know who our parents were. We make the best of anyone who does us a good turn. It's going to take a while for you to understand fully what I mean. But you never know what might happen." Brookman tapped Stone's plate with the plastic spoon. "You, for instance, will find very few people wishing to harm you, except Bristow and his mates. Word is out to those who can be trusted, that you are the young man who risked his neck to save a few convicts. All those who are in the know will try to make your life bearable here." He carried on eating his meal for a while and let Stone eat his. Brookman's mind was on the fact that Charley didn't know that he had a father! Not my place to interfere. There's usually a good reason when a man doesn't claim his son. Though for the life of me, I can't see this one, he thought to himself.

As the plates were being changed by a friend of Brookman, the big coloured man continued to explain to Stone the possibility of Bristow taking revenge for the humiliation he had suffered at Stone's hands. "The man's a killer. He'll have a go at you when you're not expecting anything. All the men in this dining room are okay, you understand?" He held Stone's hand to stop eating and forced him to look at him, to make certain that Stone was getting this message and understood its importance. "There's a couple of heavies in another section though, who Bristow has blackmailed into spying for him, and there's one who is as bad, if not worse than he is, at being a spiteful, vindictive cuss."

Stone gazed at Brookman as he savoured the fruit pudding.

"I see." Stone digested this piece of information as he devoured his own food. "What you are saying here is that Bristow may get another man to do me a permanent favour, eh?" This could be bad, if he didn't know who to watch out for. He would have to use all the knowledge that his Japanese friend and mentor had taught him. Stone summed up the situation. "Okay, thanks for the warning. So, I'm safe enough when I have our dining room guards about. It'll be when I'm among strangers that I'll need eyes on stalks." Taking a sip of water, he continued, "I don't suppose Bristow would do anything as simple as reporting me for my misdemeanours?"

"No, oh no! He'd be the laughing stock for the rest of his service here at Red Hero. I'm not being personal Stone, but if you look at yourself and compare Bristow's build to yours, well, you'll see what I mean. Chances are though, that if you eat all you can, together with the daily grind of field work, that situation will soon alter."

Finishing the last of his coffee, Brookman then motioned for Stone to follow him to a corner of the common room where there were no other prisoners. "I've had a word with Crispin Avery, and he's very interested in the piece of rock you brought in. Avery, by the way, knows more about space drives and nul-grav than those who claim to have discovered them." Brookman's face had lost its usual cheerful bonhomie. "I don't suppose you have ever heard of Crispin Avery?"

Stone was raking around in his memory. The name meant something, but what?

"I'll tell you, it's only fair that you should know who you are dealing with. Avery had all the maths for the nul-grav in his computer. He e-mailed it to Aerospace Development for their opinion. Avery put an identity tag on it to prove he was the owner. He had received a message back to say that this equation had already been evolved by A.S.D. and had been found defective. The next thing he knew, an agent for World Security had arrested him on grounds of hacking into the A.S.D. computer and stealing the nul-grav formula. Incredible as it may seem, Avery was found guilty and given fifteen years Social Construction Labour." Brookman paused to think about what he had told Charley. "He was an old man then, and time spent here has hastened his ageing. We don't get any youth pills here; when you're starting to lose your marbles, all you can do is watch them roll away!" he said regretfully.

"Yes, I remember now, I read something about his trial in the history library, but that was more than fifteen years ago. More like twenty-five surely?" Stone was frowning, trying to pin down the elusive memory about Crispin Avery.

"Yes, well as I have already told you, too much knowledge can do you harm, and Avery knows too much!" To emphasise what he was saying Brookman tapped Stone on the chest with his pointed finger. "He has more qualifications than any other person I know!"

Stone could feel the bile start to build up in the pit of his stomach. A rumble of anger escaped his clenched jaws, as he remembered Avery 's list of achievements in the academic world.

"Now calm down." Brookman gave Charley a placatory grin. "We take care of Crispin. He's safer here than anywhere else with us to look after his back. He's given all the more interesting jobs to do, and your piece of rock is a gift from heaven. It'll keep him happy for months to come. He wants to meet you and on Sunday, when we're allowed to go the swimming pool and football pitch. He'll walk with us around the pitch perimeter. A lot of us take a Sunday afternoon stroll."

Stone knew that he was being given an excuse to keep him under control, but there was nothing he could do to help. Finding the bit of brown glass would alleviate Doctor Crispin Avery's boredom. He would have to tell him also about the large chunk that had caught his eye as the sun shone through it. Muttering to himself, Stone realised that he was not the only person who had no right to be in S C L.

"Come on Brookman, it's time I gave you your first lesson in unarmed combat," he said, feeling he had to get away from the injustice of Avery's incarceration. It was choking him. "This mat will do, and these prison overalls are well suited for the job." Stone proceeded to show Brookman how to honour his partner, before he tried to dislocate his arms. Brookman was astonished that someone with Stone's slight build could lift and throw him over his back. After half an hour, Stone called a halt to the lesson. "We stop now, while I tell you a little of what else you need to know to help save your skin."

He guided Brookman to a seat. "You have the speed, suppleness, stamina, and of course the strength, and I don't think you'll have much trouble with the skill or psychology." He told Brookman, who avidly absorbed everything Stone was telling him, how to listen and smell for the signs that would tell him if there were an unfriendly person about.

"When you have had the type of training that Mito Iwaki has given me, you begin to realise how vulnerable a man with just a knife in his hand, really is."

"I'm beginning to understand what you're saying, but I think it's going to be a long time before I've got the kind of skill I've heard that you have." Brookman kneaded a shoulder muscle, which he had fallen on rather heavily.

"If you like, I'll give you a trial bout every evening, until I feel you could hold your own with some other friends I've given a few lessons to," offered Stone. " What do you say?"

"Okay, it's a deal. In return the boys and me will give you the benefit of our not inconsiderable skill in taking care of yourself while you are a member of the S C L." Then Brookman's sense of self-preservation made him glance at the clock. "Come on, it's lock up time. Peterson and the rest will come looking for us if we're not in the dorm by 21:55."

"I didn't realise the time. I don't want to give any of Bristow's friends a reason to switch the electrodes on." Stone's long legs took him to the dorm at double speed, with Brookman in pursuit.

The walk with Crispin Avery that Sunday was informative and interesting for Stone. Crispin told him how the facility for nul-grav was developed from some experiments over a hundred years ago that were not wholly successful.

"They had the right idea. It was the application that let them down, and of course they were being pushed to find an alternative from the liquid fuel used in the boosters. It was so volatile, a shuttlecraft exploded with a crew on board. Dear God, can you imagine the pressure to find a safer way? Man was reaching for the stars, cooped up in a tomb of metal and plastic that could blow up, without any hope of getting out alive!" Crispin gave a wry smile. "In a way, I'm glad the A.S.D. developed the nul-grav as quickly as they did. It has saved so many lives and made space travel a safer reality. Just look what has happened since they installed it in the Moon shuttles. The Moon has become the landing stage for exploration of this solar system and there are already plans for a leap out to other stars. No, I'm not all that sorry. I don't care a fish's tit for the kudos, but I should not have been handed this can of worms to carry home."

The three men walked in silence for a while, each with his thoughts about what Avery had said. Brookman was the first to speak. " Luke has been alerted about Charley's presence here. I think the person who is responsible for you being here is the same one who has done the identical thing to Charley, and for the same reasons. I have good reason to think that he was the mastermind behind the drug run to Mars that your friend Jackson put paid to. Luke is going to arrange for this particular felon to be taken out of play… permanently!" Brookman's expression made Charley shiver. Whoever Brookman was referring to sounded as if he deserved what was on its way to him; but who was he and what had a junior officer done to deserve his attentions? He knew that one day he would find out, but it was no use asking Brookman now. He would only tell him what he wanted him to know and it seemed that Brookman was keeping him ignorant for a specific purpose. Brookman continued talking while Charley let these observations trickle through his mind.

"Have you been able to come to any conclusions about that piece of rock that Charley picked up on the outer perimeter, Crispin?"

"Hmmm, a right mystery there. It's of incredible age! Not less than several thousands of years old. I can't give a precise dating without the right equipment, but I'd venture a guess that it was caused by an explosion, possibly atomic. The cogs and wheels inside will take some time to reach without damaging them. I'm wondering if I can use a vibe gun to shatter the glass without destroying the metallic bits."

Crispin Avery's mind was on what Charley had found as he walked with his head down, seeing his feet and the ground in front of them, but little else.

The chill of late afternoon brought him back to his surroundings and company. "Sorry, I was miles away. It looks as though we'd better say goodbye for now, until we meet again next week.

That is if you can spare me the time and let me know what Luke has done about our mutual enemy, will you?"

"Certainly! Luke has more strings to pull than an octopus has arms. It will be interesting to watch that devil's spawn's destruction. And nothing would give Charley and me greater pleasure than to share our news with you. You may have more to tell us about the rock by then." Brookman's smile was kind-hearted and concerned for the old man.

"Yeah, it's been a pleasure to meet you, Doctor Avery," Stone declared.

"Please young man, don't stand on ceremony. Call me Crispin or Avery, and the pleasure is all mine, believe me. If it would not be too much of an intrusion into your privacy, I would like you to tell me something of yourself, if you don't consider I'm being too nosy?" The old man had a yearning smile on his tired features that Charley could not ignore.

"Sir, it would be an honour to have you to talk to, and if my life story is of any interest to you, then I promise you I'll chew your ears off with it!"

As Stone and Brookman walked back to their own common room to wait for dinner, they talked over what Avery had said. "Somehow, I don't think we'll ever know for certain what that bit of rock you found is all about." Brookman kicked at some loose gravel, causing the dust to rise and settle on his boots. "This place is old, Stone, and we are scraping away at the cover of dirt that has hidden its secrets for centuries. I wonder if it's right?" Brookman asked.

"There's not a lot that we can do about it. We're only the robots who drive the machines, Brookman. For the Social Construction Labour, we're a cheap way to get the slogging work the World Development want done." Stone had realised the practical use that felons had been put to. He also felt that there must have been many times when there had been a miscarriage of justice, but at least people were no longer put to death for the transgressions they committed, like that of the Tudor Queen!

The working periods and those of relaxation took on a regular rhythm for Stone, the time passing incredibly fast. He was surprised when Brookman informed him that Bristow was again in charge of their section after he had been away from duty for six weeks sick leave.

"Now we wait and see just what plans he has in store for you, Stone. Someone will be able to keep an eye on him for most of the time. It'll be those occasions when you are alone and beyond our reach that you'll have to fend for yourself, though from what you've shown me so far, it'll be Bristow who is going to need the help."

"I don't intend to stir him up. He's not fully responsible for what he does! In fact I honestly believe the man is schizophrenic." Stone knew he would be dealing with a man who would lose control of himself all too easily, and was therefore very dangerous to himself as well as to anyone he attacked.

"Okay, you're probably right, my friend." Brookman's experience of the likes of Bristow made him feel fearful for Stone's life. "All the more reason to be extra careful of the brute." From then on, Stone used all of Mito's training to keep himself aware of danger from any quarter.

The evening of a game of chess, followed by a set of exercises that would give Brookman greater mobility, and a friendly bout of aikido, had become the normal way to spend their spare time. There were Sunday walks with Avery, the three of them chatting about Stone's previous life in the Space Navy, which Avery found fascinating. He asked more and more questions regarding the running of Dionysus, and because of the training given him by Lieutenant-Commander Jackson, Stone was able to satisfy the old man's thirst for knowledge.

When Stone and the rest of those in the dormitory where he slept, went to their cots, it was to sleep undisturbed believing the electric charge over the portals protected them.

One night, dreaming of being on the flight deck of Dionysus, Stone turned in his sleep. He was obeying Stonewall's order to take the comm again... the helmet slowly going over his head, the tightening of the collar...

Noooooo! Heaving his body through the air, Stone lashed out. There was no tight collar on the comm helmet. In fighting mode, Stone reacted violently, all restraint removed by his will to survive death. Someone was trying to strangle him. Then there was an electric prod on his bare flesh which made him half-mad with pain.

Whoever it was, stood no real chance of gaining their ends. Stone had let slip the bridle that held his killer instinct in check, and the intruder was now bent over backwards on Stone's knee. A sharp thrust of forearms on thorax and pelvis would have broken the back of whoever it was who wanted him dead.

"All right, Chamois, you can give the bastard back his life." The words had been spoken by a tall, well built man, dressed all in black, including a facemask.

Chamois stared in disbelief. He had been addressed by his old nickname and realised there were, in fact, four men standing in the shadows. The voice was familiar. The touch of the helping hand that raised him to his feet, he knew from…where?

"Lights," ordered Brookman, who had woken at the sound of the voice, and was leaping from his cot, ready to come to Stone's aid.

The four strangers stood relaxed, yet ready for action should they need to defend themselves.

"It's okay Brookman. I'm not sure who all of them are, but one thing I'm certain of, they're friends."

Chapter 11

The low chuckle confirmed what Chamois had suspected. He had heard it many times aboard Dionysus, also when he had been stood down from duty. The animal smell of three of them was so familiar to him that if they had stood there in full dress uniform, their identity could not have been plainer.

The fourth man he did not know, but he had come with known friends, therefore he must also be considered a trusted friend too, Chamois reasoned. Moreover the stranger's body carried an aura of honesty and strength. It was something that could not be faked or false in any way. Chamois felt good-humoured and with a conspiratorial glance said, "As you once told me Brookman, sometimes it's best if you don't know everything!"

"Yes, he's right, but confirm with Luke Denning. Tell him, 'Swan came for his Signet,' okay?" It was the unknown, short, thickset man who had spoken; Chamois did not know his smell, or the voice that had an accent, which he could not recognise.

Brookman came forward and held out his hand to be shaken by the man who called himself Swan. "Sir, this is a great pleasure and honour to meet you. I am glad that you are attempting to get this young man away from here. That nasty piece of work asleep over there," pointing to Bristow who had collapsed into a stupor, "would have caused him more grief than even he could handle for the rest of his stay here." Brookman wanted to tell him so much more, but he knew that for the time being he would have to bite his tongue and say nothing. Charley was going back to the free world, and that was compensation enough.

Meanwhile Swan had turned his masked face directly toward Chamois. "We've a lot of ground to cover tonight before you get reported missing."

Turning back to speak to Brookman he said, " By the way Brookman, there was someone keeping watch outside this block. He was wearing prison garb, but I think he was in league with that one over there," nodding toward Bristow. "Anyway, word of warning, he's dead.

Came at one of us with intent to murder, and he had to be stopped. We'll take that one...."

Brookman intervened, pointing to the man who was now coughing and struggling to regain consciousness. "That's Bristow, and the one keeping watch was Shar Chi. Loosely translated into English, it means, ill wind or bad breath. Death couldn't happen to a more deserving corpse! He was one of the most evil people that I have ever had the misfortune to meet. You've done the world a favour. Not only that, the Federated States of China are just going to love it, when they find out that their favourite spy and hatchet man in this prison colony is dead." Brookman's joy at such a prospect glowed all over his face, like warm sunshine.

"As I was saying, we'll take Bristow and put him near Shar Chi. Make it look as if Bristow was trying to stop his friend from escaping, making it seem as though three men attempted a breakout together, and only Avery and Chamois succeeded. Bristow isn't going to argue with that, seeing as how he intended to murder Chamois, and it was Bristow himself who shut off the power in the first place!"

With that, as Bristow fought for consciousness, the man who called himself Swan landed a stunning blow to Bristow's head and another to his ribs. Then, continuing in an almost conversational manner, he said, "He'll sleep till sun-up. When he's found, you know nothing. You slept till reveille, all of you; and most important of all, you know nothing about this young man's disappearance." The voice was hard and ruthless. It was the voice of a man who was used to being obeyed without question.

The tall well-built man, who also had a hard gritty voice, interjected, "The electrical power to this block will be resumed. There will be absolutely no trace of anything occurring out of place coming from here. A dose of 'Wide-awake' will keep the duty watch-keeper at the security controls from worrying about the time lapse of an hour. His eyes will still be wide open, with his brain dead to the world." Chamois could just imagine the wolfish grin on old Stonewall's face! This was going to be even more interesting than the brawl in Beckett's Bar with that platoon of 'off duty' marines.

Sleep had left the other three men with slightly fuddled wits and they were trying to work out how the intruders had got in without setting off the alarms. As if reading their thoughts, Stonewall continued, "Your overseer, what's he like?"

Peterson spoke up for the rest of the men. "Jack Mills is one of us. Done his time and stayed on. He isn't going to ask what happened."

Stonewall was enjoying himself. He was having difficulty controlling his laughter as he visualised the scene when a screw like Bristow was caught with one dead prisoner, plus two escaped prisoners to account for.

He strangled his mirth as he concluded, "So Jack Mills won't want to know how a couple of prisoners were spirited away at the same time that Bristow and his friend are found in a most uncompromising situation, eh. Let Bristow carry this can of muck, including the death of Shar Chi." The laughter, as it bubbled up from deep within his throat, was as sinister and mean as his black, light absorbing, skin-tight clothes. It was enough to make the prisoners shudder, and they wondered if their dorm buddy really was safe with these men.

Meanwhile Chamois and Brookman were looking at each other in absolute amazement. Didn't this 'Swan' know about the implants that were not only a trace, but also a deterrent, giving an electrical shock that was enough to stun, if not kill, anyone going beyond the confines of the prison perimeter? It was a mystery how these men got in, but no one with a tag in his neck could get out.

"I'd like to come with you, but there is something you should know." As Chamois spoke he held his neck toward the light where the tiny scar hid the DNA and coded microdot implants.

"That says I'm going nowhere for the next five years, except where the Social Construction Labour Committee decrees."

"We're prepared for that…here, put this suit on, quickly…. I developed an extra blanketing insulation to protect the guidance systems in my new vessel from stray electrical impulses. I'll wrap your neck with an extra layer of it, then you won't even exist inside or outside this compound."

As he spoke, Swan helped Chamois into the all black outfit, aided by the three men with him. The hands pulling on the light absorbing, skin-hugging outfit were as familiar to him as were his own. They had helped and given him assurance many times.

"I must say, a few weeks in this environment hasn't done you any harm. You're carrying twice as much muscle as you did." The tall lanky man helping him was Grant. Trust him to be in on a scam like this. It was Grant who had come to his aid when he had fallen into the hole on Mars and again when he had entered the photon shaft on Phobos, coming down the second and larger shaft to help him with the men trapped there.

Chamois considered that Brookman was entitled to know that the other man who had laid his life on the line, in the pit on Phobos, was in the room.

"Brookman…hey! Don't worry man. I'm in the safest hands possible. They've even helped in your rescue too, okay?" He held Brookman in his arms as he was about to leave, and said, "I'm sorry I've got to leave you and the rest of the men who made my life quite bearable here; you've been like an older brother to me. Thanks!"

Brookman knew he would miss this young man, intelligent, resourceful and kind, yet he had a temper that would surely bring disaster to whoever upset him and to Chamois himself. He had come to mean so much to all who had shared his work and play. The news that the same man who had come down the double photon shaft to assist Stone on Phobos in the rescue was here as well did not really surprise him. His rescuers had been two of a kind.

"I'll miss you Stone, or can I call you Chamois?" With his head held down to hide the gaunt shadows of loneliness, he turned away.

"Avery is coming with us. Swan decided that if he didn't get away from the labour camp now, he never would. Also he needed him to help with his research program. You will be seeing more of us as well Brookman, as soon as your term of office is up." This was Stravros Bertolozzte's voice. Chamois knew it all too well. Charley Stone was about to become Chamois all over again. His cup was full and running over.

The four men who had come for Chamois were carefully making their way out of the sleeping block, guiding him along a wall, keeping to the shadows. Stravros had slung Bristow over his shoulder in a fireman's lift and was waiting for Swan. Then they scurried to where the prone form of Shar Chi lay. Stravros laid the unconscious man down carefully, placing one hand on the dead Shar Chi's collar, the other with the electric probe in it, aimed at his neck. Then just to make certain that Bristow did not waken until well after reveille, Swan gave his arm a shot of 'Sleeptight'.

Swan and Stravros ran silently to catch up with Stonewall, Grant, Avery and Chamois as they made their way through the sleeping camp into the freezing night, where stars were glistening points of light in the midnight sky. Puffs of vapour burst from their mouths as they made their way to the western parameter, Avery being assisted by Chamois to help him over the uneven frozen ground. Winter had come to the Gobi.

"Won't our footprints leave a trail?" Avery asked anyone who would know the answer.

"Not in the outfits we're wearing." Swan was running alongside Avery now. "We won't show up on any search attempt. Even our body heat is absorbed by these suits."

"What body heat?" Grant trotted with them. "I don't think I've ever felt so cold."

"It's colder than a witch's tit," Stonewall said, as he gave Avery extra help over a large boulder.

"That's the lump of rock I told you about Avery," Chamois said, as they kept up the killing pace.

"Perhaps it is, but I don't seem to have the time to stop and examine it. Next time round, perhaps." Avery was doing his utmost to keep pace with the rest of the group. He knew his running days were long over but he was determined to make this bid for freedom even if it did cost him his life. At least he would die a free man.

Eventually, it was with Chamois and Grant on either side of him, with his arms around their necks, that Avery was able to make it to where Swan had some Bactrian camels hidden in a ruined village.

Dawn gave the sky its first cold, grey shafts of light as the six men staggered into the shelter of some ruined walls and out of wind that had the bite of a sabre toothed tiger.

"You'll call me Swan, until I tell you otherwise Chamois. I don't plan on getting caught, but until we are in a friendlier environment, we'll all keep our identities to ourselves. We rest here until dusk then we must head for Hami. I've hidden the shuttle near there," Swan said. He was unloading some blankets from the camels as he spoke.

You might just as well know now," Stravros told Swan, "Chamois knew who we were the moment we entered the dorm; we didn't even have to speak." Stravros knew Chamois' abilities only too well. His introduction had been through a 'lesson' that he and two of his friends wanted to teach Chamois, only to be caught out themselves. Chamois had felt the warmth of their breath and the smell of strangers in his cabin, and before they knew what was happening they were all either on their backs or knocked unconscious.

"Chamois would know us a couple of kliks off, even if we were wrapped up in lead thermal coveralls!" Grant added. "The only one he doesn't know is you, and he has probably sussed you out by now to be on his side, so for the time being you are as safe with him as we are." This enigmatic statement was not lost on Swan.

He knew everything anyone could, without actually meeting Chamois, and now having had him in his direct company, his assessment of the young man had not been misplaced. Yes! Chamois would fit the job he had in mind for him, perfectly!

As bitterly cold as it was, no fires were lit. The possibility of the heat being noticed on the Earth scan satellite high in the heavens was too great. This was the same reason Swan had hidden the shuttle as far away as possible from the prison camp. Its drive signature would be logged and identified. By parking it among other shuttles at Hami and lifting off at the busiest time, keeping pace with another shuttle, Swan would be able to outwit the police and Personnel Control Office searchers. He felt sure that the Federation of World Safety would be out for Chamois' blood. As far as they were concerned, Chamois was a felon who had jeopardised the safety of the Space Navy.

As dusk drew the shadows purple fingers across the sky, Chamois fed the camels and gave them a drink from the precious water supplies that were kept from freezing by a tiny graphite battery that gave off just enough heat to stop the fluid from turning solid.

Grant noticed that as Chamois offered the fodder to the beasts, he chatted. At first he thought Chamois was talking to the animals, because he was grinning and nodding his head as if he was answering and agreeing with someone, yet the rest of the camp were still dozing in their battery warmed, sleeping bags.

"Who's your friend, Chamois?" asked Grant.

"Oh, this is Ogodei. He says his army came through here, but now he is on his way to the

Chaghatai khanate, wherever that is. He was saying that the old gods from heaven fought here too, using their lightning fists to strike each other from the sky, and one of them fell burning to his death here." Chamois' face was quite straight and innocent as he spoke.

He means this, thought Grant. I wonder if his prison sentence taken him over the edge?

"Umm, errr, this friend of yours, will you introduce him?"

"Sure, but he says that you are not able to see into his heart, therefore you won't be able to see him like I do." The grin on Chamois' face was like a split melon. "Say buddy, did you think I'd taken time out, talking to myself? I tell you, this is a very interesting situation here. Ogodei is from the days before the Great Khans. He has been describing one or two things that a lot of people are dying to know… literally!"

"Oh, come on, give me credit for some sense, Chamois! Next you'll be saying that the lump of rock we dragged Avery away from is the god that was struck down by lightning." Grant's attitude was rather disparaging, and to Chamois it felt good to be back with his old friends who would tear him to pieces when he seemed to behave differently from what they considered the norm.

Swan and Avery had edged their way closer to where the two younger men were arguing. "Would you mind if we joined in this conversation? It may help us to understand a mystery that surrounds the question of how did Chamois here know the Chameleon was hovering in the region of Pele while no one else saw it. Sean only had a flash of light on the holograph, not a full sized space vessel!"

Swan stood with his black mask still in place; the steely dark eyes were demanding an answer to the problem.

"Yes, that might be a good idea, Chamois. Don't forget you owe me an explanation too. When you came off the command chair, you didn't say a word about how you spotted the Chameleon," Stonewall chipped in. He already had some experience of Chamois' peculiar behaviour. Was there a possible connection between knowing about a faulty shield, seeing the Chameleon and now talking to this Ogodei fellow?

Huh! Chance would have been a fine thing. I couldn't get a word in edgewise."

Chamois held his hands up in surrender to the protests. "Okay! Okay! I'll tell you what Ogodei said, and as I am the only one who can hear and see him, you will have to take my word for it. First thing he did though, was to fall about laughing. He says that you have all grown fish scales over your eyes and can't see further than your pointy noses. I can see him and other things, because no one has ever told me I can't! Anyway *I* really don't know why you can't see him too."

As Chamois stood with his hands on his hips, his head tilted to one side, it was obvious that he was still listening to his invisible companion. "He said that he would lead us to a path that would take us to Hami by a short route, and also tell us if we are being followed. He finds our company intriguing."

Chamois nodded to the apparently thin air, then turned and helped load the Bactrian camels. As he did so, he looked back at the man he knew to be Lieutenant-Commander (Stonewall) Jackson. "Stonewall, you don't mind if I call you by that name to your face, do you?" Without waiting for a reply, he continued, "I'd like to say something while I have the chance. I owe you an apology and I hardly know where to begin." He felt so sheepish his ears had started to burn. "I've had time to think over the times when I thought that I was being hard done by. I couldn't have got it more wrong if I'd had tried, could I? I'm sorry! My thoughts about you at times would not bear saying out loud; I've cursed you time and again. Yet here you are helping to get me out of trouble once again." Chamois' smile was wry; his eyes were pain wracked. He felt that he had betrayed a good man who only wanted to pass on to him his hard earned experience and give him the best training possible.

Chapter 12

Stonewall's laughter rocketed around the empty landscape. "I'll tell you this young Chamois, you've been quite a tonic for me. I've had to stay alert when you were awake and out of your cabin. I never knew what you would do next. And if you want to know why I pushed you as hard as I did, you can partly blame that man who calls himself Swan, and since you are no longer an officer in the Space navy, Stonewall is just fine!"

Stonewall looked to see if Swan was taking any notice of their conversation, and continued when he could see that Swan was busy. Nodding his head in Swan's general direction, he continued, "He and I go back a long way and I know that I can trust him; when he asked if I would make certain that you got the best tuition that I could give, then I was only too happy to comply. On the other hand I came to realise that you would one day make a good Space Captain. You were already showing signs of being a good leader with power of command. With your innovative idea about the photon shaft, you displayed original thought, a rare gift in anyone. You were worth the extra needling I gave you!" The laughter had stayed in his voice as he spoke. "It's been my pleasure to give you the benefit of my wisdom, even if it did land us both in embarrassing situations. I had to explain what you were doing at the comm to the Lords of the Star Fleet!" Stonewall continued to chuckle as he slapped Chamois' back. "Let's get going to wherever Swan is leading and we'll use our past to make our future."

Swan had given Crispin Avery and Chamois a thick felt coat and leggings each to put on over the black coveralls. Then he indicated who should ride which animal. Chamois was to mount a female that had the salubrious name of Sapphire; she seemed docile enough with her long eyelashes over melting brown eyes, and soft rubbery lips. Sitting between the two humps, Chamois felt at ease and very comfortable. It was pleasant and quickly he got used to the rhythm of her gait.

He now had time to consider what was happening to him and his friends. Everything seemed to be Swan's responsibility. Swan was the one who gave orders. Chamois wondered where it was all going to lead, and why this man should be so interested in him as to spring him out of the construction camp, putting his own life in jeopardy. He wants something, that's for sure, he decided silently. And somewhere in his life there is a devil chewing him to pieces and somehow it's connected to me. I'll have to find a way to make him laugh again; it's the only way he's going to untie the tangled knot that he's in. He glanced at Swan's back. It was straight with his head held high. There was such an air of utter loneliness and dejection about him that Chamois wondered if he would ever be able to break through the barrier of pride that had been in place for untold years.

He then gazed up at the night sky; the moon was at its second quarter, shedding enough light for him to see the barren landscape that resembled parts of the Moon in Earthlight. The steep hills and valleys were covered with white snow and purple shadows, but unlike the Moon, ferocious animals were among the shadows. Then he spotted a wild goat silhouetted against the milky skyline, with its massive horns piercing the still air.

The slight swaying movement almost rocked him to sleep as his companions and he headed into the freezing cold night on the road to Hami, led by Ogodei. Eventually he must have dozed off.

He came to his senses with a jerk. It was raining! How could that be, in the middle of one of the most arid areas on Earth on a freezing cold night?

"Hey, Stonewall, it's raining! Can you believe that?" His voice rose in pitch, with incredulity.

Swan laughed for the first time since Stonewall had known him, which was for many years, and said, "Chamois, it isn't rain. You have a female camel! Think about it."

Swan's laugh was deep and held a hint of release from pent-up misery and despair. Without meaning to, Chamois had broken the chains of melancholy in Swan's heart. He glanced over his shoulder to see Sapphire flicking her tail from side to side in the moon glow. The 'rain' fell over Chamois' back and everything else in range of the spraying urine.

"Is this the mysterious perfume of Arabia I've heard so much about?" Chamois asked the group, as they recovered from their laughter.

"You'll find out when you take your coat off and get a whiff of it!" replied Swan. His once bleak eyes were now as full of the happiness of living as were those of his companions.

"Ogodei tells me that only a rich man rides a female camel," Chamois said, smiling wryly as the rest of the party continued to chaff him about the terrible odour. "She gives milk, produces wool to keep us warm when the snows come and gives birth to young to swell the herds." Then he added, "Ogodei preferred to ride his pony. It's faster and not so fussy about food or shelter and was more faithful. He keeps his pony with him for company, so he says, for now he needs only to think where he would like to be and he finds himself there. I know where I would wish myself to be, but I guess the patrols are out looking for me, and Dionysus is a ship I will never be able to serve on again!" he finished, and raised his eyes to the sky, to the aura of the Moon, where he thought the space ship to be.

The man who called himself Swan sidled up to him on his camel and spoke in an earnest and powerful tone. "Young man, your life is only just beginning. Once we reach our destination, I will place a proposition before you and your friends which I think you will find more than compensates you for your dismissal from the Space Navy." With that, Swan urged his camel forward at a faster pace as if to get to Hami, where he could unburden his ideas to them and ask for their help and allegiance. He had secrets that tore his heart to shreds. At least now he might yet get an opportunity to unburden the horrors that tormented his dreams.

Stravros mused to himself as his camel swayed and lurched its way over the unending tundra. I'll bet a month's pay to a pinch of salt, that this Swan is, or has been, a Chief Engineer in the Space Navy. No one, but no one could get so much done with so little said! He let that idea percolate through his practical brain. He needs our Chamois, that's obvious, but what in the name of Gagarin does he want the rest of us for? Hmmm...it seems to me young Grant is keeping a few aces up his sleeve too. Stravros looked about him, to make certain that he hadn't spoken his thoughts out loud.

The group was travelling much in the same order as they had set out, except Swan's camel was now in the lead. Crispin Avery had used the front hump of his camel as a cushion on which to lay his head, with his hands buried deep inside the thick fur of the animal and the heavy coat that Swan had put on him, keeping him warm.

Crispin seemed to have slept for most of the time they had been riding, as if the camel's gentle movement had rocked him into deep relaxation.

Stravros wondered if Chamois' conviction that there was someone called Ogodei leading them, could be true, and Swan's camel was following a path that he, Stravros, couldn't see. Mentally shrugging, he decided that at times like this the only thing to do was to follow where fate or an invisible friend led. With that, he copied Crispin, hunched his shoulders down into the felt coat, and let himself relax between the two humps of the camel. The steady gait and rocking made him drowsy, and he too slept for the rest of the night.

Meanwhile, Stonewall's eyes were wide open. Chamois always had been a strange one. He had joined the cadet group straight from college having won a full scholarship; a wide blue eyed, fresh faced, innocent boy, who seemed to live in a world of his own in spite of attracting a varied bunch of close friends. He had graduated to sublieutenant and was re-assigned to the Dionysus. And now, he'd just stopped him from murdering that screw Bristow. Bristow deserved to have his back broken. He'd stopped Chamois from killing him because it was his opinion that Chamois was not the kind of man to have the stain of murder on his hands without feeling guilty later when he had calmed down. A lot must have happened to Chamois to make him change so dramatically.

Stonewall continued to go over in his mind his knowledge of the younger man. He'd seen a space ship where no one else would have thought of looking for one. He'd used a photon shaft to get criminals out of grief. Now he told them to trust someone they couldn't see! He glanced at the compass strapped to his wrist. By his reckoning they were travelling south by southwest.

"That's about right," he conceded. "As for making sure of our safety regarding being followed, who'd want to follow us in this God forsaken place?"

The answer came in the form of an eerie plaintive cry, a long way off. Stonewall tried to think where he had heard such a blood chilling sound before, but the high pitched wail defied his memory.

"You'd better go and tell the stragglers to keep up. The wolves have got wind of the camels and in this wilderness anything edible gets eaten, especially unwary travellers." Swan had addressed Chamois, in a manner that suggested Chamois would see the good sense of his words and not argue.

Urging his camel to go as fast as its legs would carry it, Chamois raced back to where Stonewall and Stravros' camels were in the rearguard.

"I would say those wolves are still about half a klik away, but take Stravros' camel's lead, and make it keep up with the rest of us, otherwise he'll end up on the menu. I'll get Grant to keep an eye on Crispin's camel." So saying, Chamois handed the trace lead to Stonewall. Stravros was dead to the world and just nodded his head loosely as the camel was made to walk that little bit faster than it had been, then, as if realising that the wolves would like a nice piece of tender camel as well as man, it altered its gait almost to overtake Swan in its desire not to be at the top of the bill of fare.

Stonewall held the animal in check, realising that Swan needed thinking space. Not knowing all of the man's plans, he was still prepared to go along with him as far as resigning his commission in the Space Navy.

It had been time to give some of the younger men a chance to find out what it was really like to be in sole charge of a class of green cadets and junior officers, and keep them alive and out of trouble, while teaching them to become leaders.

He had volunteered for this post when he had realised that his own training had been sadly lacking in experience. The officer who had been in charge of his cadet years, was too young himself to have known what a mineral claim jumper, or drug runner, would do when caught in a tight corner. Gold and silver, as well as some of the rare earths, had been located in the asteroids and planetoids, rich pickings for the bandits and pirates stealing from space vessels as well as from the mines.

By the time he had earned the title of Stonewall, he knew he was in a position to teach a novice how to stay alive in the land of the living when his opponent was determined to put an end to it.

Stonewall grinned to himself, as he thought of how he had unloaded just about all he had learned by firsthand experience onto the young shoulders of Chamois. At Swan's instructions, of course! Swan had made it clear when he had first approached Stonewall that Charley Stone was to be taught everything Stonewall knew about space piloting and the running of a ship as well as all the mechanics; a tall order. The poor kid didn't know his left hand from his right when he had first come on board, only a lot of theory. He'd a good head on his shoulders; otherwise he wouldn't have got as far as the Dionysus in the first place.

However it had taken Stonewall's brand of teaching to make the boy into a man to be reckoned with. Chamois was no longer an ignorant, callow, fresh faced youth.

Stonewall had witnessed the arrival of the lines that furrowed their way across Chamois' forehead, the dark rings of exhaustion, the eyes once a crystal clear, cyan blue, that had crinkled most of the time with laughter, were now steely grey, and as grim and forbidding as Swan's, and that was where the superficial likeness began and ended.

It was the character where the two men really became as one. The harder Swan had been hit, the tougher his resolve. This had emerged in Chamois' behaviour too. Chamois was the same age as Swan had been when he was first brought to his knees, only to rise quietly and stealthily, ready to reclaim what had been snatched from him so long ago. He was ready now to strike back at those who had brought him down. Chamois no doubt, was to be his sword arm. Stonewall said a silent prayer, thanking God for allowing him to be part of this event.

Grant continued to carry out the instructions that Swan had given him when they had first struck an agreement, many years ago.

The Saturnine looking man had introduced himself as Swan. There had been a group of young people, all like himself, cramming studies that would enable them to take their places in the halls of higher learning. Grant knew his chances of getting a full scholarship were pretty thin, and so it was that he worked at a food preparation depot during the day to buy his food and pay for his room where he lodged. He studied most of the night to get that coveted certificate which proved that he had useful intelligence that would allow him to enrol in the Academy of the Space Navy.

Grant was on his way back home from a night class at a nearby college. He had said goodnight to the last of his friends and had continued to walk towards the place he called home. It was no different from any other night. He had no cares about being assailed by those less fortunate than himself. His well worn, paper thin jacket, down at heel shoes, trousers that barely reached the ankles of his two metre frame, were a dead give-away that he was a poor man among the very poor. Then he had become aware that he was being followed and had quickened his steps. When the shadow kept pace with him he had turned and confronted it.

"If it's money or credits you're after, then all I can say is, your judgement is way off line!" The shadow had become a short, thickset man, the distorted light from the street lamps made black empty holes for his eyes.

Anger had started to bubble up inside Grant. The man was well dressed, a thick dark blue coat, well polished boots that protected his feet from the bitter cold of the pavements, a wool scarf about his neck to keep out the evening chill, all contributed to the air of being a person of money. He was undoubtedly better off than Grant with more credits in the bank than he would earn in a decade.

"You don't look as though you need a handout so what do you want from me? If it's a fight you're looking for, then okay!" He had prepared himself at least to give as good as he thought he was going to get.

Instead the man had asked him in a deep, yet soft voice, "Do you want to earn enough credits to release you from your daytime work, then you could study full-time as well as at night college, making certain of a place at the Space Academy?"

"How come you know so much about me?" Grant remembered demanding.

"I know enough about you to trust you with a very important job. Are you interested?" the man had persisted.

Grant was feeling the result of working and studying for sixteen hours and was just about ready to collapse into bed. "I'll take a chance with you mister, I'm just about all in. Suppose we carry on with this conversation in my room." Grant's feet were chilled and aching after standing in a freezing cold room, cutting up slabs of meat all day.

"Fine! And you can call me Swan. I'll explain myself to you once we've had a cup of coffee."

He had taken Swan back to the shabby room, given him a cup of ersatz coffee. In the dim light of the low wattage bulb, Grant could be seen as a pale-faced young man, thin to emaciation, with intense grey eyes.

They discussed Swan's scheme, which seemed to Grant a gift from the gods. They came to an agreement. Grant would be given a bank account that he could draw on to pay for his necessities so that he could study full time. A warm comfortable room and food in the fridge were luxuries beyond Grant's dreams. Soon the two men were shaking hands in friendship on the deal.

Once he was at the Academy, he was to keep a protective eye on a young man named Charley Stone. At no time was Grant to let Charley know that he was under surveillance or being cared for in any way.

"You've got to understand, at no time must he ever know about me!" Swan had been most emphatic. "I want him to develop as his nature would have him. He can take care of himself under normal situations. He's had training from the same guy who has taught me how to watch my back while defending my chin, Mito Iwaki, and I want you to spend some useful time with him too." Swan dug his fists deep into his overcoat pockets, his mind on whether Grant would be strong enough to carry out everything that would be required of him?

"There's something else. I know that you are interested in pure maths and would like to study cybernetics if you had the opportunity. This is what you will do. Once you have gained the qualifications to get into the Space Navy, it is a subject that I too am interested in. Your workouts with Mito will be quite strenuous. How do you feel about that?"

Grant had felt like a million credits! "Mr Swan, the thought of being able to tackle trouble with only my hands and feet is something that I have often dreamed about, I can't believe what you are offering me, money so that I can study full time and have the best mentor there is to teach me un-armed combat, and it all being legal?"

Chapter 13

Grant remembered being puzzled. "Why me?" The question had to be asked, no matter how tempting the proposition was, there were plenty of other men in exactly the same situation as he was, so why him, Grant?

"Oh, the answer to that one is simple; you've got the right personality for a start. You're determined to get to the top the hard way, by sheer hard work, you haven't asked for any handouts and your friends are a good bunch. You've heard the old saying…. birds of a feather flock together. Well I think Charley and you will see eye to eye, without getting in each other's way."

"How do you know I won't take your money and run?" Grant remembered he had asked. The knowing wry grin had made his eyes dance with devilment.

"If that was part of your character, you wouldn't be slogging your way through college to study in the world's top academy. No, my money's safe!"

There had been no humour in Swan's voice or on his face, only a slight relaxing of the bitter line of his mouth.

Grant had kept his side of the bargain. He had not interfered when Charley had got into some brutal fights at the academy, and as a cadet in the Space Navy, the fights had continued even after he had been promoted to sublieutenant, until a squad of Space Marines had made the usual mistake of taking Charley for a pushover. Now that had been a beaut! Marines all over the place knocked out of this world by Charley and Stravros.

The skinny little runt had even had the gall to give the Marine sergeant a chance to clear his name, saying the 'poor' man was drunk, and the outcome had been yet another man and his squad to guard Charley's back; or Chamois, as he had come to be called. The only occasion when he thought it was time to exercise his prerogative was when Chamois had slid down the shaft to rescue the trapped criminals. Grant had decided that enough was enough and had taken the next, and wider shaft down, to haul the stupid idiot back up to the surface by his toenails if he had to.

It was thanks to those rescued criminals that Chamois had come out of prison in one piece and smelling of roses…. well almost. Stonewall had barely stopped him from murdering a screw. What Bristow had done to get Chamois in such a murderous rage, God only knew, he thought, but he bet he had it coming to him.

There was a feeling of deep contentment in Grant. A feeling of having done a good job keeping an eye on Chamois, without stifling him, and he hadn't let Swan down.

Swan had let the camel have its way. It seemed to know where to go and where to put its feet with a surety that he would have found difficult even in this starry night.

The pendulum had gone almost full swing and was about to swerve in his favour. He had the men he needed to help him. Grant and Stonewall had aided him in the past. Stravros Bertolozzte had proven to be a great man to have around when the atmosphere got a bit thick. Also Chamois trusted him. There were other men who had become close associates of Chamois, all prepared to back him up when the going got extra rough. In fact, he seemed to have acquired quite a following of useful friends.

Chamois?... A deep sigh escaped Swan as he thought about the younger man. Dear God,

I've got to play this one carefully; otherwise it will all be for nothing.

About twenty-five years before, he had left his pregnant and beautiful, loving wife, Astrid, to go off to the rings of Saturn to rescue his best friend, Jacob. Jacob's fuel control was off line; his life support was down to a couple of weeks on starvation diet, and half the needs of breathable air. As only a best friend would do, Swan had gone out and brought him back alive. His space vessel at that time had been 'The Black Swan' that skimmed the space lanes like the thoroughbred she was.

The cost of saving Jacob Avery had been everything he loved. When they had returned to Earth, Astrid had vanished; her parents' home had been destroyed by one of the first impacts of the Trojan asteroids propelled out of Jupiter's orbit when the planetoid Chiron had thrown a wobbly. The three hundred and twenty kilos of Chiron had sent the clusters of asteroids in every direction. A few had fallen on the Moon causing minor damage. Some had come to Earth. The impacts had devastated most of the North Americas and nearly all of Europe. The Low Countries had disappeared. The small island of Britain had become even smaller.

Japan had slipped into the sea as earthquake followed earthquake, and volcanoes such as Fujiyama that had slumbered since the dawn of time had awakened with ferocity unknown in man's history. The Pacific Ocean was now known as The Dragons' Nest, with seething volcanoes where beautiful islands had once languished under the tropical sun.

Australia seemed to have been spared up to a point, but in the vast wastes, fissures had opened and mountains had toppled. The beautiful Blue Mountains with their forests of gum trees had once again caught fire, leaving blackened tree trunks like ugly decaying teeth. Once again nature had restored the trees, which burst back to life as the first drops of rain quenched the inferno.

China had struck and had annexed every country that was still reeling with the trauma, concentrating on the countries that still had intelligent manpower and technology, taking them for her own to become the Federated States of China. Unlike the very early Communist China, the mantle of ownership lay very lightly over the acquired countries, leaving them free to govern themselves as they had before the devastation.

The presence of Chinese rule was obvious only through empty jails. Everyone worked and the unemployed had been given jobs mending roads and buildings. It was only the very old who were given the benefits of free credits without any strings.

The Federated States were not loved by anyone who loved freedom, but even those who hated the system most, like Swan, had to admit the Chinese had got the world back on its feet again, mended and turning on its axis. He had come to respect them, wondering, nevertheless, how much they knew about the battle he fought for his rights. Were they keeping him under surveillance? He wanted to laugh. Suppose they knew and were even now tracking him and his party through the Gobi desert? He most certainly wouldn't put it past them!

His knowledge about Chamois was thorough. He had traced the young man's life from the time he had been picked up by the patrol searching for survivors. His DNA had matched Astrid's and his own. His attitude towards life was the same as his had been at Chamois' age, but physically he had come to resemble the mother. This had at first caused him to resent the child's escape from death. He had reminded him of everything else he had lost. The boy had been given the name from a list held in a computer. No one had the time or inclination to check out who he really was from the DNA databank - until Swan, searching for any trace of his wife at her parents' home where she had gone to deliver her baby, had been told that Astrid had borne a son. He had also the date of the birth. The baby had miraculously survived in his crib when the rest of the house and everyone and everyone in it had been destroyed.

As time had gone by, Swan had started to visit the orphanage where Charley Stone had been taken. He should have claimed Charley then, but the laughing infant, so much like his beloved Astrid, was too much for him to handle just at that time.

Trouble had struck almost as hard again when Jacob's father, Crispin, had been accused of fraud. Jacob had sprung to his father's defence with proof of his innocence. Then Jacob had been found dead from an overdose of Dream Dust, the first dose of which gave exquisite pleasure of sexually active dreams, the second gave the user a sleepless night, the third was responsible for dead addicts with a mask of horror and agony. The poison had been injected into Jacob's lymph glands, spreading throughout his body and prolonging the process.

The anguish Swan felt for his friend's torment was equal to what he had felt when he had to face the fact that he would never again see the woman he loved more than life.

Swan knew his friend had never touched drugs in any form. It was murder, but he and Crispin could provide no proof, only the certain knowledge that whoever had framed Crispin for the computer fraud, had also been responsible for Jacob's death.

Then had come another soul tearing time when everything Crispin Avery owned had been awarded to the plaintiff as compensation. This had included his spacecraft that he had designed and built himself, The Black Swan! Swan had visited Crispin while he was held for investigation and had tried to find out who was the shadow behind all this aggression. Why had they picked on Crispin Avery?

They were stunned to think that after losing so much, anyone would want to take away the Black Swan and it was while they had discussed this, that another man held for inquiries into fraud, came and spoke to them in the visitors' room.

"The name is Denning, Luke Denning. You don't have to rack your intelligence to know the Black Swan's destination or who stole it. I can tell you. The same man, who framed me for fraud and embezzlement, is at the bottom of it all. Randolph Wood is setting himself up a nice little empire in the world of avionics and rare metals. He's at the bottom of it all." Luke went on to tell them, "I had a company that was prospecting on that little planetoid, Miranda, and we had discovered a seam of crystals, not diamonds. They were harder than diamonds, and were all colours of the spectrum and had a peculiar way of glowing. No one had ever seen anything like them before. They didn't even need cutting to display the fireworks in them." He paused, as his memory reminded him of this magical mineral.

"I don't mind telling you, when those devil's spawn, spies of Randolph Wood, got news to him about my good luck, I was as good as in the coop; but two can be as sharp as he is. Here's a com link number, sound only. It's dubious as to whether I'll get out of this place alive. Take it; tell the people who answer that you've come for the Lucanite. Leave the rest to them. They'll see to it that you get whatever you need to start up again." The chagrin he felt was making his voice harsh.

"I had a very large piece of Miranda, a small planetoid, shipped into the asteroid belt. There are credits stashed away that the Federation know nothing about, let alone the law courts. Make me a happy man and get even with Mr Woods!"

Luke had sat down; he had been determined to use the space jockey to get his own back on Randolph as soon as he had set eyes on him. Luke Denning had seen the worth of the man when he had shown Crispin Avery so much compassion.

"You'd do me a favour if you could straighten up a crook like that corkscrew, Randolph!"

Crispin and his visitor looked at each other. Both were giving Luke's proposition careful consideration. The visitor, who came to be known as Swan, shook hands with Luke and the number was palmed to him. As he put his coat on to leave, he turned. "You haven't seen the last of me, Denning! I've a few scores to settle, and I always pay my debts, good as well as bad!"

The long climb back had begun then, and now he had Crispin out of prison. He could only hope that the time spent in such dreadful confines had not addled the old man's head.

The next manoeuvre was to get Denning. Chamois had already saved Denning's life once; and Chamois would be the best member of the group to augment the chances of Denning's successful rescue from Mars, and of getting him back to the homestead that he had in the outback of New South Wales. Swan had run it as a stud farm for horses; while he taught mathematics at the University of Victoria, it had proven to be a wonderful cover for his operations - a city man all week, who went home to his country home at weekends to play at being a farmer.

The huge barns had been the birthplace of his brainchild, and he had secretly hauled it, piece by piece, to the asteroid that Denning had owned, there to be assembled to become the successor of the Black Swan, Swan's heart had ached for the feel of the fantastic machine that Crispin, Jacob Avery, and he, had designed and built; a forerunner of the direct link between man and machine. But that was the past and now he had no time to concern himself with what had been.

Now it would be a good test for "Orion" to see if the computer-cum-spaceship was as good as he hoped it would be, to rescue Denning and find out if Orion and Chamois were compatible.

Chapter 14

The gentle motion of the camel's gait had soothed Crispin's spirit. He had slept in snatches with his memory of the past coming and going in brief flashes. He wished he could recollect where he had met Swan before. He knew the man from somewhere, but where? The voice and attitude were familiar; he knew by the way Swan walked that he had, at some time watched him walk before. He knew it was shortly after Jacob had died, but remembering Jacob only brought pain, and he shied away from the heartache. His memory had other ideas though.

The wonderful days when he and….who was it? Days of laughter, and testing the computer intelligence of The Black Swan. Jacob' s slow methodical thinking through a problem and….. come on! Come on! You *do* know his name…he saved Jacob's life for God's sake! Oh, if only Brian was here! But Brian was here. It was Brian,

Brian…keep saying the name then you won't forget it again.

Brian Dangerfield. Hold on to that, don't let it slide out again, he admonished himself. He had recalled Jacob's friend at last. The shock of remembering was like a blast of air from the frozen Arctic. He shivered as he asked himself how could he have forgotten Brian Dangerfield. The tears of helplessness trickled from under his closed eyelids. I'm old, and no use to anyone, least of all the man who needs my help most, he told himself.

Slowly Crispin pieced together the fragments of memory. The loss of The Black Swan had been a bitter pill to swallow. He had hoped to give it to Brian as a thank you gift for all his help in saving Jacob, but the courts had decreed that the plaintiff had grounds for repatriation, and The Black Swan was forfeited. It had ended up in Randolph Wood's fleet of private space yachts.

Crispin wondered if the rest of the group knew Swan's true identity. He thought not. The man had good reason to trust no one!

Everyone seems to have an alias, Crispin mused. They've left old lives behind them to go where the new lives would take them. Charley Stone, if that was his real name, had become Chamois. The good Lieutenant Commander Jackson was now Stonewall and who was this Grant? Swan used him as his personal aide de camp.

Only Stravros Bertolozzte was what he appeared to be, an honest Spacer, again, if there ever were such an animal.

Slowly, Crispin Avery regained his confidence. He cursed the memory that was letting him down from time to time. However he had something none of the others had, a more complete picture of what had happened and he also had a good idea of what the future held. He must hold on to that memory! The bitter cold was eating its way through the felt coat and insulated overalls that Brian had given him, and his lungs felt as though they were on fire with every breath he took. I've too much to live for now, to give up, he told his flagging spirit. I must go on until the last of the jigsaw falls into place, life is getting far too interesting; and with that thought, he allowed himself to be lulled again into somnolence.

Chamois watched the group as they followed their invisible guide. I wonder what they would think if I told them everything I know, and can see? He grinned inwardly at the thought. No, perhaps that would not be such a good idea; they already suspect me of being slightly nutty!

He tried to trace the time when he had become aware of his extra 'Gifts'. The years had gone by so quickly, he had hardly noticed their passing. He pushed his powers of recall back as far as he could. Orphanage, school, taking martial arts as an extra study and meeting Mito Iwaki; college, Space Academy, then special training in astro-physics, graduation and passing out as a sublieutenant, for more training on

Dionysus, and coming up against old Stonewall Jackson himself, yet again! The man had taught him what every nut, bolt, button and coloured touch-light was for. Chamois knew his way around Dionysus blindfold and could tell if the old ship was happy or had a sore seam anywhere. The note of the driving core to the vibration of deck under his feet, had told Chamois the full story of the spaceship's well-being.

Being able to keep out of some of the trouble had been the first indication that he had something extra. He had known that the marines in the bar were looking for trouble even as he had walked in with Stravros and Maria; he had also known the outcome. It was as if everything had already been planned. I might just as well go along with this situation and see where it all leads. He laughed under his breath. Can't do much else anyway. The thought had come unbidden into his active mind. It amused him to think that for most of his life he had been led almost blindfold to this.

His one and only personal decision had been to join the Space Navy. "And look where that has led me!" Chamois had spoken his thoughts aloud.

Swan came, and pulled on his camel reins, to ride by his side. "We're all free agents to do whatever we think best," he said. "It's just that some of us get guided into situations in which we had no intention of participating. One day I'll tell you the whole sorry tale, but for the time being, I'll have to ask a lot of you, and that is for you to trust me implicitly, no matter what you learn from anyone else. The only clue I can give you is, that I have the best reason in the world to interfere in your life and keep you as safe as it is humanly possible."

The more Chamois thought about what Swan had said, the more convinced he became they had met before the breakout from the labour camp.

"Tell me sir, have you and I ever met before you came to Red Hero?" Chamois was certain this man had played an important role in his life, yet if they had actually met, he was equally certain he would never have forgotten.

Brian looked intently at his son and the temptation to get all his hidden heartaches out into the open was very strong, almost overpowering, but not entirely!

"I'll answer all your questions when I consider the time is right, but for now be content with the knowledge that you can trust me."

The look on Swan's face was enough to prevent Chamois from questioning the man further. "Okay! I get the message. But perhaps there is something you should know right now." Chamois would not be put off by Swan's forbidding expression. "I get the impression that you and I have a score to settle, and one day, as you say, you will explain yourself. I'll go along with that; meanwhile whatever it is that's bugging you, and making you keep your cards so close to your chest, don't matter to me! I accept you for what you are, the man who came and got Avery and me out of the brimstone. For that alone, I'm prepared to give you my word, that if, or when, you need a friend, I'll be there, no matter what!" Chamois snapped his lips together, tight; he had said what he wanted to say. The rest was up to Swan.

Chamois could see that Swan was fighting some inner emotion, and the younger man spurred his camel on, to give Swan the privacy he obviously needed.

Ogodei had stopped at what appeared to be a dead end in a valley of rocks. "If you move those smaller rocks aside, you will find a cave behind them. You and your camels can go in and shelter. I'll also show you where to light a cooking fire." The old Mongol was one of the most obliging men Chamois had met.

"You will need some firewood, and you will find some a little way back there." Ogodei pointed in the pale light of dawn, to some low growing bushes that were white with hoarfrost.

"They are quite dead, and will burn brightly once the frost is knocked from them."

As Chamois told them about the cave, the little old man grinned at the travellers in their disbelief. "You will find drinking water in the cave too. Just let one of the camels loose and it will find the spring."

Chamois looked curiously at Ogodei, who sat on his little pony watching the faint, milky light of dawn start to creep into the sky. "Thank you for your kind help Ogodei. I get the impression that you were considered as strange too, when you were in mortal form," was Chamois' reply to his spirit companion. Ogodei turned and smiled at him, and nodded his head.

Passing the messages on to Swan and Stonewall who gathered up the fuel, Chamois joined Stravros and Grant, and the three younger men set about clearing the entrance to a labyrinth of caves.

A harsh blizzard had sprung up and the wind-chill was a killer, scorching everyone's lungs as they laboured. Once within the cave, the men had the impression of being inside a vast, old cathedral that had never felt wind or rain.

"Well, well, who'd have believed it? Your mate has come up trumps this time. Not only do we get to have something hot to eat, we also sleep out of that perishing cold!" Stravros said as he dismounted his camel.

"As usual, Stravros, you got it right first time!" agreed Stonewall.

Meantime, Ogodei had guided Chamois to a place where there had been a fire many times in the distant past, with ash and a path of soot on the rocky wall, snaking away up into the gloom, to be lost in the darkness. Then Grant and Chamois helped Crispin Avery from his kneeling camel; they laid him gently onto a pile of camel blankets and covered him over with Grant's felt coat.

"I suggest you put your coat outside, as far away as possible, Chamois, otherwise the cave will soon become a gas chamber!" Grant had not minced his words about the stench coming from Chamois' coat.

"Stravros, can you get a fire going?" With the light of his wrist torch, Chamois had shown Stravros where Ogodei had indicated a fire would burn best in the cave.

Soon the glow of blaze reflected back onto the little group of men as they sat at ease, casting long bizarre black shadows behind them onto the rocky walls, stalactites and floor of the gigantic cave. The atmosphere was so primeval they whispered their conversations.

Swan was bending over Crispin; he no longer had the facemask on and his concern for Crispin showed in the gentle warmth in his eyes. "Come on old friend, I have something to take away all those aches and pains. You'll feel better once you get this inside you."

The rejuvenating drugs that had been denied Crispin for years would improve his memory as well as give him back a youthful body. "Chances are you won't recognise yourself in a couple of days time. Here, wash it down with some hot tea that Stravros has just made," Swan encouraged Crispin, and with a deep sigh, Crispin sipped the proffered beverage and gradually felt the warmth seep though his tired old body.

"If what you say is true, then I will be even more in your debt, Swan." Rheumy, pale eyes looked deep into the depths of Swan's dark brown ones, and let the message of his recognition and a promise of silence go to him also.

It was an inadequate price to pay for all that he had done for him and his son Jacob, but when Swan needed him to help, then if he did have the intelligence and vitality to assist his rescuer, he would use them to the very limit of his capabilities.

After a hot meal made from the reconstituted meat and vegetables, washed down with the tea, which had made a lot of difference to everyone, Swan asked for their attention. "This has been something of a blind man's buff, for all of you. You have trusted me, some of you for years, and some," looking at Chamois, "for a few hours only. I have made it my business to know what I needed to about all of you, yet you have known nothing about me. Well, for your loyalty, I am prepared to tell you now, that if we get caught before I can execute my plans fully, then we will all end up facing a much worse situation than Crispin and Chamois were in." He gave a desultory chuckle and then continued. "However, I think I can trust you enough with the information that we will be splitting up shortly."

Turning to Grant Geddes, he said, "Grant, I would like you to escort Doctor Crispin Avery, to Camber Park, the stud farm in Australia. You will use the small flit-about to get there. Take care of him, and start the workout for his recovery. I need him in good shape, physically as well as mentally. Do you understand?"

Grant nodded as he answered, "Yes, sir."

"The rest of us will use a shuttle I have hidden at Hami, to take us to where I have the successor to The Black Swan hidden on an asteroid." Swan turned once more to face Chamois. "You, young man, are to be its pilot. It already has your DNA in its databanks, and will recognise only you as its commander."

Chapter 15

The bombshell caused Chamois to choke on a mouthful of hot tea. Once he had finished coughing and spluttering, he looked at Swan, dumbstruck! "Whaa...." Chamois gazed at the rest of the company, hoping for understanding and help.

"This decision was made many years ago, so don't let me down by refusing." Swan gave Chamois a chance to recover his breath and thoughts to think clearly again. "The Orion has taken years of hard work and a couple of fortunes to build. If you are prepared to take the command, you will have the crew you want. I have already singled out your number one…Stonewall, what do you say to the job of being Chamois' 'Buffer'. You are, to my mind, most suitable for the post." Swan had allowed his eyes to glitter with suppressed amusement as he watched Stonewall's reaction to the prospect of going into space again, and on a ship that he had never even heard of before, let alone been on!

"If you don't think I've gone past my sell-by date, I'd give the rest of my lifetime just to walk the decks!" Stonewall shook his head in disbelief, as he sat with the canine grin on his face that had terrified so many young trainees assigned to his tender mercies.

"Now Stravros, if Chamois agrees to command the Orion, he is going to need a first class 'Engines'. As you seem to have an affinity with motors and all things that make machines do what you want them to, I can't think of anyone better than you, so would you like to help your friends to take this bird on its maiden flight?"

Stravros, like Chamois, was speechless, and could only nod his head vigorously, and utter a strangled, "Yeah, sure."

"Well, Chamois, you can either leave us at Hami, and go with Grant to Camber Park, or join us on the Orion." Swan stood with his hands on his hips. His face gave nothing away; it was like a shuttered house, waiting for someone to light a candle in the darkened windows of his eyes.

"Sir, there are others with a lot more knowledge and experience than I have. Are you sure I'm the man for the job? Sean, my friend on Dionysus, he's brilliant at maths. Have you thought of him?" Chamois was indeed having difficulty coming to terms with the prospect of being put in control of a multimillion credit spacecraft.

"A while ago, I asked you personally to trust me to know what will be the best for your advantage, which also happens to be the best for all of us. Everyone, including my spaceship, Orion! I chose you for this post. Right from the start of your training with Stonewall here, you showed a spirit of adventure. Remember when you suggested that the three of you investigated the doorway on that cliff climb on Mars? The courage that it took to descend the photon shaft alone, to rescue some miscreants, your power of command when everyone challenged you not to do so, even Stonewall? All these instances and more proved to Stonewall and me that my decision to have you skipper this vessel is the right one. So don't mess me about. Say yes, or no. Though if it's no, then believe me, everyone is going to have a hell of a job getting everything about Orion reorganised, from the mainframe to the size of the comm helmet." Swan knew this young man all too well and had realised that his reluctance to take the command had been not so much fear, as a slight lack of confidence at such a responsible undertaking.

He continued with his reasoning. "I'll come clean. Stonewall had my instructions before you joined the Dionysus. You were to be taught how to run a ship from the moment you stepped on board. Stonewall didn't let me down. The way you've handled yourself in some of the situations that he put you in, would have done credit to a long-term serviceman. Mind you, don't go down any more mine shafts. Our nerves won't stand for it!"

The ensuing laughter broke the tension that had started to grow when Chamois had been confronted by the proposition of command the Orion. He was now nodding his head, with his hands covering his face, feeling somewhat overwhelmed by the opportunity of taking control of a new and fantastic spacecraft. The very name, Orion, conjured up other galaxies, other star systems.

That seemed to end the conversation regarding the flight of the Orion, for the rest of the time they spent in the caves.

As evening came and they prepared to leave the cave, Ogodei appeared to Chamois. "When you go, replace the rocks over the mouth of cave. Those who need to know where it is will always find it," the Mongol told him. Then he waited by the track that only he could see to escort his self-imposed charges to Hami.

Crispin Avery had wakened with a clear head and without the usual stiff joints; the promise of a day's riding a camel was no longer so daunting as it had been.

The group travelled ever south-by-south west towards Hami. At one point Chamois held up his arm to indicate that they should halt. He told them that Ogodei had suggested that they wait for a caravan of Mongol nomads who would give them food and shelter.

Swan looked about him. There seemed to be no end to the vast plain that stretched for miles in every direction, with the wind singing a dirge of destruction and certainly no sign of any other travellers. "In this God forsaken place there are people moving? Nah don't be daft!"

"Yes there are. Can't you smell them and their camels?" Chamois asked. "Listen! You can hear the sound of the bells around the sheep's necks." And faintly there came to the weary voyagers the tinkle of bells, then the sound of people and animals moving. The fugitives were greeted as old friends and made welcome.

The felt yurts put up by the wandering tribe of Mongolians were a relief to Chamois and his companions. The friendly people gave them warm milk from the mares, some dark, but edible bread and a place to sleep in their homes.

As Chamois stood outside the yurt that he was to sleep in that night, his spirit guide and helper Ogodei came and told him that later, the journey would be in a more mountainous area where this tribe did not wander. They were plains people. Those who dwelt in the mountains would also feed and shelter them as long as they posed no threat to their freedom.

Chamois thanked him for his advice and was about to bid him farewell for the time being, when an old man came and joined him. "You talk to the spirit of Ogodei. He is a good companion and will care for you along your way. He has often warned us of the approach of those who would imprison us inside walls. You are most fortunate and you are more than welcome in our homes." He smiled at Ogodei and bowed in salutation as he left to go to his own yurt. Chamois was speechless to think that someone else could see Ogodei.

True to his word, wandering bands of nomads in the hills, assisted the group and they were afforded unstinting hospitality by these simple-living, uncomplicated Mongol nomads of the Gobi desert.

Eventually, after many days of weary travelling, they reached the summit of the crest that overlooked Hami. The group was surprised to see the whole area lit up. There was a glow of golden light illuminating the city.

"It must be Chinese New Year, and what's more it must be the year of the Fire Dragon!" Swan remarked. "They've got the Dragon lights burning everywhere and they are doing the Fire

Dragon dance! But even so, there seem to be an awful lot of people about." He paused for a moment to consider. "Look! There are guards all over the place! I wonder if they've got a senior Federation member visiting this God-forsaken spot?"

"Could be to our advantage," Stonewall suggested. "All the time they're kow-towing to their visitor, they won't be watching for us!"

"Let's hope that's true. We've come too far now to be stopped. Another hour and we'll be out of here." Swan was feeling uneasy, even as he spoke. There was the inevitable sense of dread of being caught at the gateway to space and freedom.

Ogodei looked at Chamois. It was time for him to resume his own journey to the Chaghatai Khanate. "Goodbye and the luck of the gods go with you. We will not meet again for many years for you have a very long and interesting road to travel." So saying, the little Mongol turned his horse back toward the north and the place that had once been his earthly home, and was soon lost in the air frost and fog.

No one stopped the five men as they drew closer to their goal in the bustling city. The stench of camel urine from Chamois' coat began to make its presence felt as they entered the warmer area, and brought a look of shock to many faces as they made their way to the lift-off zone.

Grant and Crispin had said goodbye to Swan and the rest of the men who were to go out to the Orion, and Swan led the way through the crowded streets to where he had hidden his shuttle in a huge silo, with several other craft of similar shape and design.

It was while they were passing a rather dark shadowy place in a back street that they found themselves surrounded.

"Please, do not fight. You are safe." The officer in charge of the guards was actually bowing to them.

"Perhaps he's mistaken us for one of the V I Ps," suggested Stravros.

But Chamois knew these men had been waiting for them. Yes, they were safe; no one intended any harm, yet if they put up a struggle, then one way or another, they would overpower them.

"Do as they say," Swan ordered. He too knew that to fight would be to invite trouble, which they could well do without.

"Please, to come this way. Would you, Mr Chamois, mind removing your coat, please? I have a sealed container for it," the taller of the guards invited. "It was one of the ways we were told we would be able to identify you…the smell of camel. I had no idea what that was like until now! So please, sir, your coat!"

Stonewall was cursing Chamois. "Once again we have Mr Stone to thank for our troubles! Swan, the day you gave me the job of teaching him a few things, you forgot to tell me what a flaming nuisance he could be!" he said, in mock anger.

"Please, there is no trouble." Again the officer was emphasising there was no need to be afraid. "This carrier is to take you to your destination." He was pointing to a land shuttle with blank windows. "Please, get in."

"Well, whatever I've landed us all in, at least it's being done with the greatest of respect," Chamois commented, defending himself as he gave the offending coat to another of the guards, and saw it hastily locked away.

"You know we could take these boys out, and they wouldn't know what hit them," Stravros whispered quietly in Swan's ear. But Swan knew better. They had been under surveillance for a very long time; of this he was certain. They knew too much to be here just by chance, or even from a tip-off. They knew about the camel's urine, so what else did these guards know?

"No! Make a fuss and we'll have no chance at all of getting out of this fix in one piece. Do as the man says and we'll go with dignity, fight, and we'll go with null burns!" Swan had seen the result of the stunning effect of the null-nerve gloves, a charge of electricity sent through the body that nullified all the motor nerves. The victim was left without any control of his body, yet still aware.

Entering the vehicle indicated, the four men sat in stony silence, the eyes of each one asking the others the question, how were they betrayed? When the vehicle slid gently to a halt, they were ushered into a long low building. Their footsteps were silent on the soft plastic floor of the corridor that led them to the door of a room, guarded by yet another man in uniform. Their escort tapped gently, and was answered by a low voice bidding them to enter.

Chamois had never seen a room like it before in his life. There were soft wool rugs on the wooden floor that had been polished with loving care for centuries; soft, golden-yellow lights glowed from globes on walls and ceiling, the walls themselves, a living golden colour. Chamois could not resist the urge to touch; it was smooth and felt warm, almost alive. There was also a living fire to heat the room that added to its luxury. The leather chairs were deep enough to make even his long body welcome.

The room was dominated by a huge, carved wooden desk and the man who sat at it. He rose as Swan, Chamois, Stonewall and Stravros entered. The guards had not followed them in.

Chamois gasped in amazement; his eyes opened wide at what he could see. He knew that he alone saw the panorama that spread before him as the Chinese man came towards them; he seemed to float in an aura of emerald green suffused with shafts of blue and gold. Swan and the rest of his companions, were blind to such scenes.

He came from behind his desk and surveyed them. "You have not disappointed me," the soft voice said, with only a very slight oriental accent. "I have been looking forward to meeting you for several months. Please make yourselves comfortable," he said, pointing to the inviting chairs.

Coming towards them a few paces more to look closely at his guests, he held out a small hand as if to show them he was without weapons of any kind, and introduced himself. "I am Wong. You may know me as The President. I preside over the committee of the Federated States."

With this bombshell, Wong bowed slightly, from the hips. Chamois, jumped to attention and in his turn, gave him the acknowledgement reserved for the grand master of martial arts, bowing, and covering his clenched fist with his other hand.

Gravely Wong returned the gesture, giving all his attention to Chamois. For a few moments, the only sound in the room was the crackling of the burning coals in the fire-grate, the travellers hardly daring to breathe.

"I wanted to meet you before you disappeared into the dark reaches of the universe. I have known about you and your activities since your adversary, Randolph Wood, made the mistake of becoming too greedy, and tried to steal whatever mineral deposits there may have been in the debris of Pele. We have learned so much about his corruption, and that of his associates.

"It was his greed that led my emissaries to you. Mining on Phobos had been outlawed because of its unstable terrain and had no real wealth to offer, therefore the questions asked were why and who would benefit most? And who gave the order to mine? Everything led back to Randolph Wood, including the explanation for one of the men incarcerated in the collapsed mine being Luke Denning.

"Randolph Wood had swindled him out of a fortune in valuable minerals; his trumped up charge was beginning to show signs of weakening and the last thing that Mr Wood wanted was for Luke Denning to be released, a free man to wreak his vengeance."

The President seemed to be enjoying his cunning knowledge and continued, "I reviewed the complete situation - which were the men trapped, and who was responsible for their rescue, and there again there was a link to Randolph Wood." The smile became devious. "I soon realised that it would be only a matter of time before you would attempt the rescue, sir, of this young man who made the rescue of Luke Denning and the other miners and whom you would choose for I have documented evidence of this fact. Your other companions have been known to be in your company frequently many for years and you trust them. "Therefore I arranged for you to arrive at Red Hero and leave, without obstruction!" Your escape to say the least, was executed as only people of your calibre could do so. Now we come to why you so desperately need this particular young man."

The gimlet eyes of President Wong alighted on Swan. "I will not complete this exposure at this time. I will leave that for those concerned.

And you may be pleased to know that all of Randolph Wood's acquired wealth is to be returned to those from whom it was stolen." Wong allowed the impact of this statement to filter through their startled minds.

"This Randolph Wood wouldn't by any chance have a relative in the Space Navy, sir?" Chamois asked of the president.

"He would indeed, young man, a son; and since he did not complete the physical requirements and test, he was asked to resign."

Chamois tilted his head to one side, his right eyebrow cocked; he wanted to ask which test had given Philip Wood. A glimmer of a smile crossed the president's face and disappeared. "If you are interested what the test was that caused Mr Philip Wood to depart from the Space Navy, you need only to ask Lieutenant Commander Jackson. He set the examination."

All eyes were now on Stonewall. "I only gave the young gentleman the same set of exams that I had already given Mr Sean Darnley, Mr Grant

Geddes and you, Chamois!" Without a hint of amusement, he continued, "It seems that young Mr Wood got as far as the climbing site on Mars, almost in the same spot as yourself, Chamois, when he developed a feeling of intense nausea, and decided that he no longer wished to be a Spaceman!"

Stonewall, unable to contain his mirth, laughed aloud. Chamois grinned at the thought of the obnoxious young man's discomfiture. It seemed that they were indeed father and son.

"Randolph Wood and his associates are exactly the type of men the Federation were looking for. We needed men to go to Mercury to start mining the liquid iron. We could not send the normal criminal; we needed highly resourceful people who would survive no matter what the odds, and Mr Wood and his friends fit the job description perfectly. Come to that, sir, so do you and your companions. However, we have other plans for you."

Chapter 16

The dark brown eyes held the glint of inscrutability. Swan was still at a loss as to how much the Federation knew.

"I think you should know, sir, your identity is no longer a secret to the Federation, therefore I suggest you stop this charade of calling yourself Swan, and use the name you have and deserve, Professor Brian Dangerfield. Our DNA research had told us why you find this young man," nodding to Chamois, he continued, "as interesting as you do, and I further suggest that you tell him why, now, as I told you earlier, I do have precise evidence!"

Wong, a grand master of chess, knew how to manipulate the chessmen into place to the best advantage. Now he was forcing Brian to break his silence.

The atmosphere in the room was charged with expectancy. Brian was being unmasked for the first time in twenty-five years. He had got used to the cloak and its anonymity but he would be glad to come out into the daylight of the truth. As for telling Chamois that he was his father, the idea still made his blood freeze.

"Mr President, sir, if only I could, but what you ask of me is probably the hardest thing I have done in the whole of my life." His torment was such that Chamois went and placed his hand on his shoulder.

"What did I tell you a couple of days ago? Have you forgotten?" Chamois sensed the anguish that racked Brian. "So whatever it is, and no matter how bad you think it is, it's time for you to trust me and the rest of us who are your friends, as we have trusted you."

Brian realised that still thinking of Chamois, his son, as a boy, was a mistake. The boy was now a man. He had lost the wide, innocent blue eyes. They had become grey and as ruthless as that of a man sorely tried. His pale complexion was now tanned and ruddy with freezing cold windburn and oxygen rich air. The slender shoulders that were once able to squirm down a narrow shaft were wide and muscular; and now he had a man's way of dealing with the vagaries of life. He was not about to throw a tantrum on receiving the knowledge that had been withheld from him since his birth.

"Okay. Here goes. Chamois, I'm your father!" The bald statement left everyone waiting for Chamois' reaction. No one dared make a sound.

The only noise was the ticking of an ancient clock, as it creaked and whirred to strike the hour of midnight.

The room spun about Chamois' head. The phantoms he had witnessed upon entering the timeless chamber had increased in number. President Wong appeared to be in several places at once, with Mito Iwaki for company. They were mouthing words at him that he could not hear or understand.

Then his eyes were drawn to a tall, slender, beautiful woman, standing beside his father. Her hair was as white as the breast of a swan. She was gazing at Chamois with untold love and compassion, as if her heart were breaking. He tried to look away, but her magnificent eyes drew him to her.

The ethereal apparition had placed an arm on Brian's shoulder and gestured to Chamois to take her other hand.

The experience was all too much for Chamois, who had been on the run from the labour camp for days, hardly sleeping or eating. The floor started to come up and greet him. Stravros leaped forwards and wrapped his strong arms around his friend to give him support.

"It is time everyone had a good night's rest. The guard is instructed to take you to your sleeping quarters. You will find food and a hot bath have been provided." Wong dismissed them as he returned to his desk.

Stravros guided Chamois where the guard led them to a bathhouse. The door was held open for them; the steamy room was redolent of a perfume of spice and wild flowers.

Brian and Stonewall helped Stravros take off Chamois' filthy, sweaty clothes, before they wrestled themselves out of the felt coats and black coveralls that they had worn for days.

The bath was a huge, sunken, square tub filled with steaming hot water. Gingerly they lowered Chamois into its depths, Stravros again supporting him, until he became aware of his surroundings.

"Are you okay? Can we get you something to drink?"

They're clucking around me like a flock of old hens with only one chick between them. The uncomplimentary thought was in Chamois' head, and it caused him to start laughing almost uncontrollably.

"Hey, pull it together mate! You've given us all a shaking." Stravros could not understand what caused the outburst. Stonewall thought he was suffering from shock, and looked on with concern, though it was difficult to believe that Chamois had any nerves.

Brian's bleak heart sank even lower than before. Chamois had stared right through him when he told him he was his father. Now he was laughing at him!

Turning to climb out of the gigantic bath, Chamois hauled him back by his ankle. "You're not getting away as easily as that!" The tug had brought Brian back into the bath, causing a tidal wave that swamped them all.

"How about giving us some kind of reason as to why you've kept us all in the dark for so long, about something that I, for one, find more than just a bit intriguing, hmmm?" The question, asked in a joking manner, masked Chamois' real thoughts. He could no longer hold back the tears…of what? He was glad the splashing water hid them from his friends, including his father… especially his father, not knowing whether to laugh or cry.

He felt so overwhelmed that he was Brian's son, and had a living relative. His father was Professor Brian Dangerfield. Dear God, what did it matter why they had been separated all his life? When he had needed help most, his father had come to his aid.

Eventually his laughter was reduced to a wide grin, with no bitterness, proving he bore no animosity toward Brian, who was trying to explain his activities after saying goodbye to Crispin and Luke Denning in prison, all those years ago.

Suddenly they all became aware of the four scantily clad young men and women who had entered the bath, and had started to wash them. They laughed happily as they gently pushed Chamois down into the water, where they could wash his silvery hair. All the travellers were thoroughly scrubbed and shampooed before they were allowed out of the tub, to be patted dry with huge, soft towels, and then wrapped up in long, loose fitting, cotton rich, towelling kimonos.

The aroma of the food that wafted toward them made their stomachs growl like angry dogs. Again, they were treated like emperors of old, and served by several young people, who plied them with tasty morsels.

As they finished their meal, a special bottle of slightly warm Fire Dragon rice wine was poured for them by a young man, intent on making certain they had enough to drink. Alcohol was something that none of them had tasted for a very long time, and the effect was almost instantaneous.

Brian was the first to totter to his feet. "I think the time has come for all of us to get our heads down. I can't keep my eyes open." And he turned to where a young lady held open the door to a room with a huge bed.

"Yeah, I would never have thought that a few sips of that rice water would send me to my bunk, but like you Brian, my eyelids are being glued together. G'night." Stonewall drifted out through a door held open for him, to a room with a bed the size of a Martian water cistern. "This all for me?" he asked, then flopped on top of the futon that was covering it, and was asleep instantly.

Stravros was asleep on his feet, as two exceptionally beautiful women took him into yet another room with its wide comfortable bed.

Chamois was also shown to a room. His brain was too tired to notice anything other than a place to lay his weary head. The doors were closed quietly, allowing the men to sleep.

While the sun had yet to dim the golden lights of the Dragon Dancers, Chamois dreamed of Maria. She had visited him in his dreams whenever he slept. Now however, she felt so real, her soft sweet arms around his neck and her lips teasing him. If only the dream could go on forever. The lithe arms and thighs were wrapped around him like a hungry octopus. A galaxy of stars burst in his groin as he whispered her name…. Maria. Then he descended into a deeper, refreshing sleep.

Warm, clean clothing awaited them when they woke next morning, and over breakfast, Brian tried to explain why he had not claimed Chamois for his son as soon as he knew of his escape from the meteor storm over northern Europe, with its devastation in the Helsinki area. Then he tried to explain to them what happened when he and Jacob returned to Earth. "I resented you being alive when Astrid was dead," Brian told Chamois, "and I suppose I should say I'm sorry, but that sounds too limp and futile. I can't tell you what I've really felt these past twenty years or so." He looked at Chamois to try to assess what the younger man was thinking. He was met by a puzzled frown. "When I realised that your mother was dead, I felt as though the whole world had turned to ashes." Brian had said all he could, and now he had to let his son make up his own mind whether to reject him or not, as he had once rejected him.

There was a wrinkle between Chamois' eyes as he tried to puzzle out this anomaly. He began to realise that his father had been to hell and back, yet had been able to supervise his instruction with Stonewall and get him primed for the job of skipper on a space ship built especially for him. The man must be made of some incredibly stern stuff, he surmised.

"You want *me* to recognise *you* as my father, right?" The frown was even more pronounced as he continued, "Well *that* isn't good enough for me! I've been without a father all my life! What I need now is a reliable friend whom I can not only refer to, but also look up to as well. Someone I can tell *exactly* what it is that I experience and see, without him or her thinking I've lost all my marbles! Now if you think that you could fill *that* situation, then you have a deal!"

Chamois waited a few moments to give Brian a chance to reply. "Face the fact, Brian, I'm over twenty five years old. I no longer need someone to wipe my nose for me. But if you can accept me as a friend and an equal, then I'd say we'd make a great team. There's another thing you have to bear in mind. I could have the answers to questions you haven't been able to answer or understand yet, like, why did the camouflage of the Chameleon not fool me the way it did everyone else? What do you say?"

The quirky lifted eyebrow and half grin were too much for Brian, who swung his head from side to side in disbelief. Mute. Looked at his son and then went to him and hugged him like a bear.

" Is that okay then Brian?" They were both grinning like baby grand pianos.

Later Chamois asked Brian, "My mother's name was Astrid, yes? Am I wrong in thinking that she looked like me, tall, slim and blonde?" Chamois took a sip from the cup of bitter tea. He had eaten his breakfast the way Brookman had taught him, slowly and chewing each morsel to gain every drop of benefit from it, and had only just finished his meal.

Then it dawned on Brian that Chamois did not resemble him in any feature. "Of course; we don't exactly look like each other, do we?"

" True, but apart from that, last night when I made a brief and sudden exit from the land of the living, I saw just about the most beautiful woman ever born, standing by your side, Brian. She was so lovely, and she seemed to be full of love for both of us. Sorry if I'm upsetting you, but having seen her, I know something of what you must have felt when she died. So please don't apologise to me; we both lost someone wonderful."

The room fell silent as Chamois and his father came to terms with their present circumstances. Chamois and Brian looked at each other, a slight nod passing between them. They were friends as well as father and son as Chamois had suggested, with no secrets separating them.

Stonewall tapped on the table with a spoon. "It's about time we all decided that whatever the past has held, it's nowhere near as important as to what comes next. There are a lot of good people on our side, and if my guess is right, President Wong wants us on his side too. We have more vital intelligence than the rest of the Space Navy put together," he concluded.

"I wonder what he wants from *us* for our freedom? Something tells me he's going in for the kill next time we meet," Stravros remarked to his friends.

When President Wong summoned them to his study near midday, the heavy curtains in the room had been drawn, displaying a visage of the harsh winter outside, of lowering skies with the threat of a heavy snowfall. Even as he stood looking out at the mid-February weather, Chamois saw the huge snowflakes start to descend in a gust of icy wind that sent them into drifts, to pile up in the frozen gullies on the hillside.

The glow from the lanterns and living fire, reflecting from the unique, translucent amber walls, illuminating the room, had a restful and comforting ambience.

Somewhere, not far away, a woman was singing Turandot's lament…

In this place, two thousand years ago
A desperate cry rang out…

The voice was diamond clear, and echoed throughout the old building.

"My granddaughter, Celestial Joy, sings a very sad song, yet I know that she is very happy today," President Wong said as he sat waiting for them behind his enormous desk. He looked like the cat that had not only stolen the cream, but the caviar too. His almond shaped eyes slid to where Brian waited for him to give the ultimatum that he knew was to be the gateway to their freedom.

"Let us find a means of resolving your problem, Professor Dangerfield, and that of your companions!" He glanced up, and waited.

When no one tried to offer excuses, or tell him of their plans, he knew he had the right men and just where he wanted them - in his private sanctuary, away from the prying eyes of the Federation.

"You realise, of course that I know about the Orion, and the remarkable attributes of the Chameleon. I also believe that they are in some way connected. Am I correct?"

Brian stared at the President for a full minute, his brain twisting and turning, trying to understand what he was implying.

Without taking his eyes from Wong, Brian started to talk his way through what this Machiavellian man had said. "Orion and Chameleon had something in common? ...Hmmm. Both were built after Lucanite was discovered...only by those who had access to Lucanite...I know something of the capabilities of Orion, and I'm beginning to suspect those of Chameleon. Can the Lucanite be the common denominator?"

"Well done, sir!" Wong beamed a smile on Brian as if he were a schoolboy who had got all his sums right. "The question is, are you prepared to co-operate with me personally, to develop and explore the uses of this magical crystal you call Lucanite?" The half smile on Wong's face and the glitter in his, black eyes indicated he had an unquenchable thirst for knowledge and was avid for the secrets of Orion and Lucanite. This was the lever they could use to bargain for their freedom.

Brian had summed up the situation and was quite willing to tell President Wong about the Orion's capabilities regarding the use of the Lucanite, but that was all. Orion was his and Crispin's brainchild, a hybrid of The Black Swan, a space ship that Crispin Avery and he had built all those years ago and forfeited to Randolph Woods.

"If you allow us to proceed to the Orion, I will give you the formula for the drive I have installed, which it is hoped will take it out of our Solar system as far as Denebe in Cygnus. Yes, I have developed the drive from the Lucanite, and the person to thank is Luke Denning." Brian had the initiative; he would use it as far as it could take them. "Luke Denning's freedom will have to be part of our agreement." Have I beaten the old mastermind? Brian wondered.

Again, going by the half-smile that Wong was having great difficulty in hiding, Chamois reasoned that Wong must have a secret all of his own, and of course there was the premonition that the President had everything worked out even before they had arrived at Hami.

"Denning is waiting for you at Mars Way Station, or else, if you wish, I could arrange for him to be transported to Camber Park." Wong had known that Luke would not be left to rot on Mars while Brian Dangerfield had the means to rescue him. It would be a waste of valuable time for the Orion to be diverted to Mars, when the prime factor was to take the spaceship on its maiden voyage and trial run beyond Pluto, to test this new energy system. Wong wanted to know if Orion really could reach Cygnus in a reasonable period of time and the sooner the drive was activated to the limit, the better, as far as he was concerned.

"We have a deal then?" Brian asked, and then recounted all that he wanted from his side of the bargain. "Luke Denning is reunited with his property, namely the Lucan asteroid, and joins Crispin Avery at Camber Park. The Black Swan is returned also. I take my son and his crew out to Orion, and once they are familiar with the workings and set for the trials, I will return to you with the formula for the Stella drive." Brian waited, wondering, if Wong would really keep his word and let them all go free.

Wong sized up the man before him and decided that a man capable of bargaining like him, must have Jewish blood in him somewhere, or better still, Chinese. It was good that he had considered everything being asked, or rather taken, like the valuable asteroid!

Chamois, standing by the window, had missed nothing of the by-play. Brian had pushed the deal as far as he dared to get everything they needed. Wong, on the other hand, was definitely playing another game.

Chapter 17

Chamois still had the feeling that the President was actually gloating over something. I guess we'll just have to wait for that little piece of data to rear its ugly head. I only hope the crafty old buzzard doesn't take us too much by surprise. With that thought, he turned his attention to the woman who was singing Calaf's confident aria…

> *None shall sleep tonight!*
> *Neither will you, my Princess,*
> *Watching the stars from your cold chamber.*

He felt as though he wanted to join in. However he had never had much time to study music and the words evaded him. He knew only that a prince in disguise had managed to answer a riddle put by a proud and haughty princess, and now she in turn had to find the answer to the prince's riddle. Turandot had to discover the prince's name. Intuition was chewing at him; the plot of the opera was something to do with Wong's secret joy.

"I trust that I shall see you on your return, Professor Dangerfield?" Wong was visibly rubbing his hands. "I must leave now for the Federation meeting in Madrid. We are lucky that Spain is capable of producing so much rice and grain. The distribution is a problem. Few of the countries outside the Federation are able to contribute anything, yet somehow we must feed them!"

"Mr President, it amazes me that you trust me to return with the information from our side of the bargain." Brian too felt he was missing something…something overlooked that could eventually prove very expensive.

"Ahhh yes. You wonder why I have no qualms about you keeping your appointment. I suppose I should apologise. First, you are a man I would trust with my life any time; you are a man of integrity and honour. Next your son…Chamois, I believe is what he is called? Chamois was a Space cadet and in our custody for quite a long time before he went to Red Hero. It was considered a wise thing for him to be tagged; therefore a trace was included in his identity data without his knowledge when he was given his number at Red hero. Any attempt to dislodge it will cause his death. I can and will, at any time, kill him!"

"You wouldn't!" Brian was aghast, his face one of complete incredulity.

Wong made no reply. He simply bowed to Chamois, one fist enclosed within his other hand.

"There is one other concession I ask of you. A granddaughter has a great desire to go with you. She wishes particularly to travel beyond our solar system."

Wong touched a place on his desk, and a young woman came into the room, bowed to her grandfather and then to the group of European men.

"This is Celestial Hope. Her sister you heard singing is Celestial Joy."

Stonewall knew they had a full compliment of crew. Sean was waiting with a few other friends Chamois had made, and all useful people they were too.

"I think our crew is complete, sir, and where the Professor is planning on sending us would not be suitable for a female, especially one with no knowledge of the workings of our kind of transport."

"I should have mentioned that Hope is fully qualified in various sciences including metallurgy, a useful occupation, you will agree?" Wong was not to be put off from getting a member of his family in with the crew on such a trip as the professor had laid out.

Hope had stood quietly to one side, finding this political bickering a bore. She knew exactly what was wanted of her and she relished the idea. The way the men were arguing did not please this young woman who had very strong views of her own.

"Perhaps it is not the fact that you have a full crew that is concerning you Mr Stonewall. Maybe it is that I am female?" Hope's voice went from that of a sweet-natured woman, to that of a woman who had fought hard for her place in the world. "I have my Professorship in mathematics and space engineering. Then there is the little matter of having had four years with the College of Space and Time studies, which I found most interesting!" Hope was smiling as charmingly as only a young woman trying to defeat men at their own game, can. "I think you should also consider the probability that my grandfather will think several times before he terminates anyone's life, with my safety at risk."

Chamois had been watching and listening openly and subliminally, to all that was being said. Relaxing and casually stepping back into the shadow, he observed closer still what his gift of clairvoyance told him. He felt that there was indeed a secret here; more than one message was being given. Most important of all though, was that he would indeed be safer with Hope on board with them. She carried a message for him. There was only love and kindness in the room, no threat of death, either his, or anyone else's.

"I think it would be a good idea if we did have a back up with us, just in case some of us are needed to be in more than one place at a time."

It dawned on Brian that Chamois knew more than he did about the real reason for Wong wanting Hope to go with them. "Okay. I'll admit supplies are more than adequate for yet another crew member but there is one thing you must realise, Mr President, I guarantee nothing; not the safe return of Orion, her crew, nor your granddaughter!" The two older men faced each other.

As Wong bowed to Brian, with a look of great compassion he said, "You are sending your only son into something about which little is known. I am risking the life of a favourite grandchild. Even then, we have more in common than you think, Professor." With that, he touched yet another place on his desk and the guards appeared as if from nowhere. "Please go with the guards. They will escort you to your craft. You will have no difficulty leaving." Then, as if adding an afterthought, he said, "There have been some changes made at Red Hero. Mr Brookman is now in control of the personnel, and Mr Bristow has taken his place as a labourer. He was charged with the murder of a labourer and attempted murder." Wong allowed a smile to show in his eyes as he continued, "And there never has been a person by the name of Charles Dangerfield held in the camp!"

"Bristow in Brookman's care?" Chamois could not credit what he had heard. Wong only nodded, indicating that the conversation was closed. They were dismissed.

Brian, Stravros and Stonewall were shocked by Wong's revelation. They were even more shocked when Chamois thumped Stravros on the back, laughing. "Isn't it great to be free again?" he chortled.

"If you say so, but I really do wish you'd let us all in on the secret of your hilarity."

Stravros was definitely feeling ill at ease. It was bad enough knowing that Chamois had a tag in him, which the Federation keyed into, and knew all their plans at the exact time they did, but Wong also held the "Kill" button. Then to cap it all, they had been lumbered with a pet granddaughter of the President. The only good news as far as he could see, was the elevation of Brookman, and Chamois' name being cleared, even if it was in the most convoluted manner Stravros had ever known.

"Fuss not! The Federation won't want the jockey of their favourite horse dead. Remember, they will get all the kudos for space exploration, and once again everyone will forget all the everyday hardships they suffer, thinking that they were a part of it. They'll celebrate our conquest over outer space, and the fact that they are alive to see it."

"I still get the feeling that you have beaten us to the beer bar again, Chamois. I wonder why that is?" Stravros queried in a grim voice. He knew his friend a lot better than to be taken in by the superficial reason for his exuberance.

Bending over, he started to manufacture the weapon that had been used for thousands of years against a friendly foe…a snowball. He threw it at Stonewall, catching him in the back of the neck, which was well wrapped up against the bitter cold wind that chased them on their way to the shuttle.

"Oy! What d'y think you're doing? Just because I can't put you on a charge any more don't mean to say I can't sort you out!" and Stonewall proceeded to make his own ammunition, throwing the soft cannon balls at every one in range, including the guards.

Hope had taken refuge behind the bulk of one of the guards, and Chamois noticed there was a decidedly pink glow around the two Orientals. "So, that's the way the land lies, yet she's coming with us. Curiouser and curiouser! I need some answers ...*soon,*" he decided.

Brian led them to the small earth-to-space shuttle, the guards turned to go, and Hope cast only a slight sidelong glance at the huge guard she had gone to for protection. He, in turn, just stared at her, as if to bury in his heart the memory of someone he held more precious than life.

Orion seemed to hover in the dark void like a huge extinct bird about to come in to land, gull-winged, with the control cabin in the head of the thick outstretched neck, matt black, with an aura of deep purple. The logo of a hunter, with his club and net about to snare a bull, was picked out in luminous green on the main fuselage.

Chamois could feel the tremendous energy emanating from this fantastic bird and was convinced that anyone could see the power-aura but he realised his mistake when Brian said, "I hope Sean has the power up, and ready to go. Grant should have made it here too." Obviously he had not seen the glow that surrounded Orion. He was only looking for things to run smoothly. The run-in with the President had not been such a bad thing ultimately, for now he was aware of how much the Federation knew. His talk with Wong had given him the answers to the questions he knew Crispin and Luke would be asking. He looked over to where Chamois stood at the viewer, entranced. Wait till I sit you in the comm chair my son, and then you'll have a real reason to be impressed, he thought to himself.

Hope had sat quietly throughout the journey, but even she gave a slight gasp of astonishment at the sight of the vessel, shaped more like a gigantic, half bird and half lizard, a legendary fire dragon, no less.

"Welcome aboard, captain!" It was Sean; and Chamois, already overwhelmed with the sight of Orion, felt a lump of his heart was in his throat at seeing his old companion.

"This makes everything perfect! President Wong must have had a lot to do with so many of our mates being released from the Space Navy for service on Orion," he observed to Brian.

"Yes, I should have realised that things were running far too smoothly for there to have been no kind of divine intervention," was the chagrined reply. "Now I want to introduce you to Orion…. the computer-spaceship!"

Smells redolent of Dionysus came to Chamois, plus the feeling of belonging. He was home!

A safe free-fall had been installed in the main fuselage of Orion to the control cabin situated at the end of Orion's neck; this facilitated all-round vision. Multi-coloured stars quivered on a backdrop of indigo; nearby planets glowed and shimmered, moons and asteroids swung on their allotted paths. All this could be seen directly on the view-screen that made up three parts of the control-room, a window overlooking eternity.

Computer terminals were banked on the backing wall, their coloured lights winking on and off to indicate their operational readiness. The captain's chair with its comm-helmet suspended ready for use was prominent in the centre of this array.

Then the enormity of the project hit Chamois, making him see phantoms again. *No, not now! I've got to keep all my senses about me.* He admonished himself for his weakness, allowing irrelevancies to sidetrack him.

He also had to control his breathing. Brian had said that Orion recognised only his DNA, and would obey only his commands. He must keep all his wits about him, no matter what he felt, and what he felt just at that moment, mere words could not describe.

Brian was standing behind him and placed his hands on his shoulders. "Yes, it's quite an adventure just putting the helmet on, but don't worry, Orion knows that this is your first contact with him." His voice was low enough for only his son to hear. "Come, let me help you."

Turning, he called to Stonewall. "Perhaps you would like to help your captain into his chair. There is very little difference between this helmet and the one on the Dionysus, except that Orion has no visible connecting leads, not even micro-filters."

Stonewall and Brian were hovering over him once again like mother hens. Chamois' face then split into a wide grin. Memories of his command of Dionysus came flooding back. "Okay, lower away, boss. Let me get the feel of this firecracker and then I'll be able to tell you if you've made the right choice in picking *me* as your Skipper.

Chamois experienced no thunderstorms in his stomach this time. The journey to the chair above which the comm helmet floated, had been easy, confident and assured that whatever his father had designed for him, would work perfectly.

"Come now, sir. Mustn't keep the Professor waiting to find out how we are going to manage without him, must we?" Stonewall was chattering to cover the silence in which Chamois and Brian were both facing up to the moment when years of hard work and research would be put to the test. They would also discover if Stonewall had made a good job of training Chamois for the post of command. This was the undertaking that Brian had given him years ago, when they had discussed Chamois' capabilities. Brian had wanted his son to succeed him as a space research test pilot, knowing that by the time he had Orion ready for exploring a system beyond that of the Solar, he would be too old to react fast enough in cases of emergency. Orion needed a young man's touch and Brian. Chamois was to sit in the comm chair; it was his responsibility to command The Orion.

The puzzled look in Chamois' eyes marred the glow of excitement that surrounded him. "Stonewall, since when have you found it necessary to call me *sir*?" he asked his number one. "Ever since you came of age *sir*, and that was when you *didn't* nearly pass out with fright at the sight of the comm helmet." Stonewall had dug up the time when he had been commanded to take the comm on the Dionysus. Stonewall's sardonic grin had been softened by a gleam of pleasure. He had felt a real pride in Chamois' ramrod straight spine, as he walked towards his father and the comm.

Stonewall, standing tall, took up his place to stand at the back of Chamois' chair. His eyes and nose that would have done an eagle proud were alert and defying any who opposed his edict. This was the highest position of trust that any person could have, to be the shield for the back of a reigning monarch.

Brian stood beside Stonewall. He still had a hand on his son's shoulder and gave it a paternal pat as he said, "Stonewall's right! You've come a long way since you sat in the chair of Dionysus. There is also the power of command to consider. Whatever good friends you have among the crew, you will have to place yourself above them in terms of control—*you* have the control and it needs to be felt by everyone who serves you." Brian stopped to give Chamois a chance to think over what he had just told him, and then continued. "Knowing you are in control is all very well but the crew must at all times *feel* that you have the upper hand in order to respect your orders and be prepared to carry them out without question. Remember, the very top of the pyramid can be a lonely place but when you ask for input from these men, *I* believe you are going to get the best they can offer. Do I make myself clear?"

Chapter 18

"Yes s*ir!*" Chamois understood what his father was telling him and knew he was right to get the situation appreciated by his friends too. "Thank you, Brian. I'm certain we all agree on that point." Chamois turned to the rest of the crew and friends for confirmation.

Sean, Stravros and Grant nodded their heads to confirm Brian's statement. "We count ourselves lucky that you've chosen us to be Orion's crew, Brian," Stravros said. "I think we would all lay our lives on the line for Chamois. He's proven to be a great friend and able to make some appallingly difficult decisions, when a person of a lesser breed would have run away."

Grant and Sean agreed with Stravros. "Too true *sir.* It's everyone's greatest wish to have an officer they like and trust," were Sean's words.

Brian, without facing in any particular direction said, "Okay, Orion, it's time to interface with Chamois. And *you*, my son, remember, 'Softly, softly, catchee monkey'." The helmet floated, hovered, and then settled on Chamois' head, and gently moulded itself to fit his cranium.

Chamois closed his eyes as the visor came down to shut out the visions of his surroundings, then the mighty power of this firebird surged through him. There was a warm feeling, like being welcomed back home, which permeated every fibre of his being.

"Wow! Dionysus was wonderful, but this is beyond everything...I'm speechless!" Chamois muttered, as his senses became attuned to those of Orion.

Could it be Orion sensing the exuberance? Chamois wondered, or was it an echo of what *he* was experiencing? Whatever it was that he felt at that precise moment, and wherever it came from, was a mystery. All his mind would admit was that an outside agent, someone or something, was ecstatic because of his achievement!

Sean and Grant wondered what Chamois was experiencing, and whispered to each other, but Chamois' mind was too full of what all the sensors were telling him. It was if he *was* Orion, Orion's outer skin was *his;* the power generators, all these were his too. He was able to see Peter and Gabby, friends from his space navy days, at the controls, deep in the main body of the ship.

With the exterior sensors, he looked around outside the immediate area of space that Orion occupied, seeing the thick debris of minor asteroids of high-density iron pyrites that camouflaged their hiding place. Then he set his sights to the stars that were startlingly brilliant, pinpricks of light. The star system after which he was named swam into view, with Betelgeuse a scintillating red.

"There we are! There's Orion." Chamois' heart went out to the distant configuration of stars…and so did the ship! Slowly at first, then gathering momentum, Orion sped out of the solar system and towards his namesake.

"Whoa——haaaa—steady there! Orion felt your desire to be in the constellation of Orion and now we are on our way!" Brian gripped his son's hand to give him something warm-blooded to hold on to, and then advised him to concentrate on Earth.

Orion lazily, almost reluctantly, came about and returned to its moorings again. The trip had not taken long, but President Wong's team of watchers would log it and it would appear that Brian was not going to keep his word.

As Chamois hastily removed the control helmet, Brian asked, "I wonder what the ears and eyes of the Federation will make of that?"

"Don't worry Brian, they've got to expect some hiccups, but it looks as though I'll have to use a much more delicate touch with our friend Orion. It seems as if it's a case of my wish is his command!" Chamois observed.

"Yeah, I'd no idea he would respond so abruptly, "Brian agreed. "Take it slowly; you have plenty of time, the rest of your life in fact, to get to know him."

Chamois noticed that Brian had given Orion a masculine personality. "It's only right I suppose," he thought. "After all, Orion *is* the Mighty Hunter!"

Celestial Hope had watched everything intently that had occurred. "Perhaps it would be a good idea if Professor Dangerfield did accompany us on our very first manoeuvres beyond Pluto. With his knowledge of the vessel, he should be on hand in case he is needed. I am certain my father would approve." Hope spoke directly to Brian.

Brian was watching with admiration tinged with envy, as his son handled the craft. He became aware of Hope who was still trying to catch his attention.

"Yes, Hope. You have something further to say?" he asked, the gleam of mischief in her deep brown eyes completely lost on him.

"I think it would be wise to tell you now, that while we are inside Orion, Chamois' implants are not capable of receiving or transmitting anything to Earth!"

The incredible realisation that they were free from eavesdroppers made Brian's spirit soar, causing a bubble of mirth to rise from his stomach and burst forth and gurgle like the hot springs in New Zealand. All the nervous anticipation of uncertainty concerning Orion's test run, fear of being a failure, of his son rejecting him and so much more, were released in the laughter that shook and convulsed him.

He considered that President Wong and his granddaughter, Celestial Hope, were a pair well matched. She was right of course. Orion's outer shell, a mixture of Feuralium and Lucanite, would have masked any miniature radio waves. Something much more powerful was required to make Ship-to-Earth contact.

"We still have our friend Hope here though," Chamois pointed out to Brian, "and my guess is, that Grand-daddy had it all worked out while we were still breaking our way out of Red Hero."

Everyone turned to look at Hope. "What you say is quite true. My grandfather realised that *if* Orion had Lucanite as part of its outer casing, the same as The Chameleon did, then the same principle would also apply - no radio waves in or out, unless they went through the proper channels, in this case, through Orion himself!" Hope's intelligent eyes still sparkled with mischief. She was enjoying this situation, knowing it would now be possible for her to integrate with the rest of the crew in a friendlier manner.

"How did the President reach the conclusion that I would use Lucanite in the hull? It had to be an educated guess at best!" Brian felt as though a man whose job was primarily that of government had outsmarted him, and here he was sassing out spatial physics!

"To be honest, he asked my opinion and if you recall you were told about my qualifications." Hope could not contain the giggle of merriment any longer. "I am sorry if I cause you embarrassment, Brian, but I was asked how would I construct a space ship capable of travelling at speeds faster than light, what materials and fuel would I use. The answer was simple - the best available! And I had been part of the team who experimented with Lucanite. It proved to be very light yet dense, absorbing light waves that enabled it to blend in naturally with its surroundings. Experimentation is still being done. You are responsible for Lucanite being developed as a fuel and, of course, the Federation needs the formula to fuel future space vessels. Without it, the rest of our galaxy is lost to us." Hope stood before Brian, hands outstretched and palms up, as a person asking for help.

"You know Hope, you and your Grandfather are the very limit. No wonder we were caught. Remind me *never* to play poker with him." Then he turned abruptly to Chamois. "You knew this didn't you?" he accused his son. "You were not a bit put out when he threatened you with death!"

Chamois stood up to face Brian, his eyes glaring with suppressed temper. "Now hold on there! I didn't know anything about how Orion was constructed. I knew nothing about Lucanite until you mentioned it, and all I knew was, I was safe from President Wong. Stravros would have known too. Cast your mind back, old man, and try to remember. What did Wong do after his so-called threat, huh? He saluted me, that's what, the salute of honour given between the Knights of Martial Arts. It was a message that the Federation wouldn't realise had even been given. He warned me about the implant and what *it could* do, not what *he would* do."

His anger melted when he saw the look of dismay on his father's face. "Sorry Dad, you should know about my temper. It always did have a short fuse."

Brian was stunned! I must stop thinking of him as a boy, he reflected. Chamois had stood his ground and put him right back where he belonged. But miracle of miracles, he had called him 'Dad'. Brian's wry grin hid so much feeling, only Stonewall suspected the truth.

Trying to be the peacemaker, Grant came up to Brian and said, "He's right of course. Mito Iwaki taught you, him and me, and the very first thing we learn is to honour your opponent!" Grant's hand on Brian's arm conveyed the message that although he had made a glaring mistake, no one thought any the worse of him. "But of course it's our Chamois who correctly interpreted Wong's message. I must admit I didn't see it coming though. Did you Stravros?"

"Nah, can't say that I did. A bit out of my league. Sorry Chamois, I felt the same way as Brian, that you were hiding information from us, and *that* was why you were quite chipper when we left Mr President and gleefully played snowballs with us and the guards. I feel as wet as a can of 'addock water!"

Sean, giving Stravros a friendly punch, stirred up even more anguish for him. "It's not the first time Chamois has made *you* look an idiot though, is it?" and swiftly got out of Stravros' reach.

The bantering continued over Chamois' head. He was looking at Hope. The woman still had secrets that she was hugging closer to her chest than that of knowing he was safe from the Federation once he boarded Orion, so what were they? He decided not pursue the subject just then, because she had posed yet another question for him.

"Now you've given me more food for thought, Hope, I still harbour the suspicion that there might be a listening post nearby that the Federation could be using."

Chamois told the company of his feeling that someone was watching when he took the comm and the watchers were *very* pleased. "So if it wasn't the Federation, who else was it, apart from us, because I think it came from outside the ship. Who or what would be excited enough for me to be able to get an impression of it?"

"Could our security have been blown?" Stonewall asked of anyone.

"No, we tested Lucanite thoroughly with the information we had and I can assure you that Orion is invisible when it comes to the 'Search and Detect' facilities controlled by the Federation. Also, they have no outposts in this sector of the Solar System." The rest of the crew accepted Hope's sincere explanation.

"We'll have to put it down as another of those questions that will have to stay unanswered for the moment. Let's be grateful that whoever they are, they are pleased with our results!" Grant, who had said very little since their arrival on board Orion, had got to know Chamois better than any other member and realised that the man was a mystery in himself.

"Stop messing about. We've work to do, clear the decks for action!" Stonewall was using his post as Buffer to get everyone to their operational positions.

Brian realised that a lot of time had been used just getting the air cleared regarding how much Chamois knew and had kept secret. "Right, let's get things started again. We've a lot to get through before I return to President Wong with our part of the bargain. Now first, the engines must be stressed and strained to find out how well Orion would stand up to any difficult situation that might arise." Brian felt enough time had been spent in getting them accustomed to being aboard Orion. He added, "As the co-designer on board, I can make any necessary adjustments and that's a *real* bonus. I'll show everyone their stations, Sean. Stravros, Grant, with me. Chamois get to know Orion's data-banks." There was no doubt about Brian's power of command.

Meanwhile, Stonewall continued to stand beside Chamois' chair, like a guardian angel.

"Orion, you and I are going to have to get to know each other and it's going to be most important for you to be able to differentiate between what I would *like* to do and what I *must* do. There are going to be times when these thoughts are going to conflict, so you are going to use some of the intelligence that Brian installed in you and develop the ability to tell the difference." Chamois directed his thoughts immediately into the computer cum spaceship and waited while Orion's data banks analysed this piece of information.

"I will do as you command, Chamois, and not what your mind thinks. I am at this moment downloading all the relevant information and experience from your brain that could at some time in the future prove useful. That was an unusual use of a photon drive and weighing all the valuable information that has been derived from it, I would consider disobeying a direct order from a superior officer vindicated." Chamois wondered if Orion was trying to give him a hard time with reference to the occasion when he had disobeyed Stonewall. "Nah, he hasn't got the marbles," he decided. Later he was to wonder if he might have to give Orion's abilities much more careful consideration.

With everyone at their designated posts, Chamois gave Orion the mental command to take them five thousand kliks beyond Pluto, toward Alpha Centuri, a star which was reckoned to be over four and a quarter light years away. He watched, as Orion seemed to tilt and turn to get a clear run out of the asteroid belt and beyond the orbits of the planets that inhabit the Solar System.

This was every young person's dream. All the reading he had done at school about the early pioneers of the internal combustion engine, of hedge hopping over the oceans of Earth, which was the beginning of mechanical flying, the extreme dangers of the first space flights, nothing, nothing at all prepared him for this, the thrill of being hurtled through space with the feeling that there was nothing between him and the universe. He could almost feel the wind burning his ears as the craft ploughed through the everlasting night.

While he used his augmented eyes to survey the scene ahead, Chamois could hear Sean reading out the data from his screens - time taken, distance and velocity. He gazed at stars in their millions, galaxies spinning away in the far distance, sending out clouds of diffused light. "One day," Chamois thought, "one day soon… and that's not a command, Orion!"

"I'll give the engines a chance to prove themselves by running them at half power for ten thousand kliks, then we'd better take them up gradually to full power to see just what they can do." Chamois spoke out loud, knowing that Stonewall and Brian were at his side and would want to know what he was attempting.

The fathomless void presented no resistance to Orion, as, like a valiant bird of the incomprehensive infinity that he was, he glided effortlessly through the intangible vastness of space, reaching the speed of half a million kliks an hour, well beyond the speed of light.

"Now that's what I call moving, in *every* sense of the word!" Grant expressed everyone's heartfelt opinion.

"How right you are. This console is a bit more complicated than old Dionysus but I can see where the improvements help," Sean commented.

Chapter 19

Orion, at Chamois' directions, did the normal slowing and turning exercises, then carried out several manoeuvres that would be useful in the event of an attack.

"He moves like a ballet dancer," Chamois said, as he brought Orion into trajectory parallel to Pluto.

"I think you'll have tremendous pleasure getting to know Orion, but *do* take it slowly,"

Brian admonished Chamois. "Now head back to our rendezvous point and I'll take the shuttle back to Hami and give Mr President the fuel formula the Federation wants. Then I'll continue to Camber Park and find out how Luke and Crispin are. I'm hoping that they've responded to the anti-ageing drugs. They could both help me a lot, if their memories have been restored."

Chamois brought Orion to his moorings with a gentle glide. Brian was standing ready to disembark, with only a bag full of bliss for his load. The space ship had proven successful on his first real engine trials, Chamois, his son had called him first an old man, then Dad, after an argument, where he, Brian, had been proven right out of order! All things considered, a very successful experiment, he thought.

Chamois came to his father's side. He wanted to say thank you. In fact he wanted to say such a lot, but his mind just was not capable of putting into actual speech what he wanted to convey. Instead, father and son embraced, choking back all the unsaid words that would come more easily at a much later date.

"Go with God, my son. You've fuel enough for a good twenty light years of travelling, but come home safe before then, huh?"

"Yeah, sure Dad. I think I'll make for the Alpha Centuri star system first, then come back and report to you. Give our regards to Luke. Tell him, no *more mining*, and the very best to Crispin. I'm glad he is a friend of yours; I liked his spirit while he was in Red Hero. I'll look forward to seeing them too, when we return. And by the way, watch our friends, Wong and Hope. They're hiding something. I don't think they intend harm, but they definitely have something up their sleeves!"

"Yes, I did wonder if they have a little surprise waiting for me when I get back."

With that Brian waved a farewell hand to the crew and left them for Hami. He had known what his son was feeling, not wishing to say 'goodbye' yet anxiously waiting to be away.

The excitement of having Orion to control could not dispel the sense of despondency that engulfed Chamois as he watched the shuttle take his father back to Hami. He remembered meeting his father for the first time only a brief few weeks ago and almost immediately they had fought over the stupidest of things. He should have known that Brian would be feeling wound up tighter than a clock spring after so much hassle from the Federation and President Wong. He had slept very little during the journey across the frozen desert on a camel, and obviously had not thought too much about what he was saying. Yet, thought Chamois, Brian had risked his life when he broke into the labour camp to rescue him from Red Hero. It was something that only a person who cared very much whether he lived or died, would do and something that only he could have done. Somehow or other, Chamois was determined to make up for losing his temper with his father. The old man didn't deserve the backlash of his tongue! For now, he must go and see how Gabby and Peter were.

Turning to Stonewall, he said, "I'll just go below and have a word with the hired help in the kitchen." Stravros, who was standing nearby, laughed at the inference that the two engineers were slaving over a hot stove. "That's a joke, that is. Those two have got it made. You should see what Brian has fixed up for them, floating stools so that they can access any part of the engine no matter how awkwardly placed it may be. There's no need for them to wear heavy lead shielding when they examine the core because it's not atomic; a cool air system, and should they get thirsty there's even a cold water dispenser in there for them!" Then giving a slightly mocking bow, he said, "Allow me sir, to escort you to the dungeons."

"It's okay, Stravros, I do know the way. Orion has implanted all the information I need about his layout. It's all there, quite pat," said Chamois, tapping his head. Then he beckoned Stravros,

"Come with me anyway. I want you at action stations. I'll be bringing Orion up to full power soon."

"Yeah! And I need to know how the engines operate at optimum capacity over a long period," Stravros agreed.

As he made his way down to the engine room, Chamois wondered how long it had been since Stravros, Peter, Gabby and he had all been together. It seemed more like a decade since he had last been aboard the Dionysus and had got into all kinds of scrapes with them.

After the back slapping reunion and the usual 'do you remembers', Chamois felt more at peace with himself and returned to the main deck to take command of the comm.

The helmet was firmly wrapped around Chamois' head. His thoughts were still about the run-in with his father as he surveyed the star system where he would take Orion and his crew. "I wonder what would please the old man most?" he speculated.

"Get home in one piece!" Orion's answer was spontaneous and the most obvious one. However, Chamois wanted to do something more for his father, to help give back some of the happiness lost while he had mourned for Astrid. He wanted to thank Brian for having so much faith in him, giving him Orion to control and explore outside the Solar system. There must be something that would mean a lot to Brian, the impossible dream…just as Orion was to him.

"Take notice Orion, search your data-banks, and come up with an even more acceptable answer." Chamois probed his own memory for what he thought his father would appreciate most. "I don't know him well enough. In fact I don't know him at all!" he decided.

Using his gift of extraordinary psychic ability, Chamois reached out with his mind to Orion's data banks to find the core of intelligence, searching to discover if there was anything of his father's emotion deployed in the myriad of megabytes. Was it possible, that during the programming of Orion, Brian had left a trace of his own deep-seated wishes and longings?

Chamois waited and allowed his heart to slow down to a steady rhythm, his own needs laid to one side. Gradually a picture began to form in his mind's eye, of a man, dirty and sweaty, with a smear of blood over the back of his hand, crawling along a narrow metal tunnel. He was dragging a spool of microfilament optics, unwinding it as he went. It was Brian, lying in a homing device in Orion's nervous system of sight and touch, enabling the ship to return to the Solar system if ever Chamois and his crew were in difficulties. He was muttering under his breath, "You're gonna be one of the best, a phoenix! I'll give you the best of the Swan and then the best of," …a gasp of breath…" Crispin's intelligence and mine…You'll bring my boy back alive. Even if you go to the last place God made, you'll return to Sol." Another grunt for breath…

So Orion had been right. His father's dearest wish *was* to see him safe, yet even as he had watched him from a distance, he hadn't prevented him from joining the Space Academy and graduating. In fact he'd gone as far as designing this vessel just for him, making his life as safe as he could without standing in his way. Did Brian *know* he felt only half alive when he wasn't in space? Possibly. He'd been a Spacer too, and most likely understood and knew of the piercing ache in his heart when he had been denied the one job that satisfied within himself the reason for his existence. Chamois thought of the time when he waited to be sent to the labour camp and he gritted his teeth with resolution. He was determined he would do everything in his power to make this trip a success, get his ship back home safe with all his crew, his friends, as well as himself. *That* would give Brian all he needed to make his autumn years happy, even though it would take Chamois at least nine or ten years to achieve it!

A green light showing on the engine control panel claimed his attention. Sean was signalling for permission to start the recordings of velocity, time and distance.

Were they all at their workstations? Did Grant understand the complexities of the cybernetics of this incredible computer where all of the most delicate information was held? And would he be able to act fast enough to control it if necessary? Chamois laughed to himself. Of course Grant could. That climbing axe swing in time to save Sean's life proved that.

Information being given and asked for, left no time for Chamois to ponder over any more problems just now. He attended to all queries and asked for engine status. The adrenaline surged through his veins and a feeling of elation overtook him. Nothing else mattered, and they were on their way.

"Okay, Orion, take us out of the Solar System, then set the chart for Alpha Centuri sector."

Chamois turned his sights toward Earth, taking a last look at the Solar System, the scintillating sparkles of emerald, sapphire and ruby. There was Sol, the kingpin of the planets, holding his attendants enthralled. Then Chamois cast his vision around toward Proxima in the Alpha Centuri Sector where they were heading… he held his breath…was he going completely mad?

He could see that the twinkling stars were laced with a fine filament like a huge spider's web, with the stars for dewdrops. Several lines were connecting them together. Each brilliant point of light on every heavenly body had a thread of light trailing from it, making them look as though the points went on forever until they reached another pinpoint of luminosity.

"Orion, can you see the anomaly between the stars?"

"Calibrating…are you referring to the web of light linking them?"

"Yes. Get it on record and on the main screen. I want everyone else to see this."

Remembering to breathe again, and speaking directly to Stonewall with the comm helmet still in place, he asked, "Well what do you make of that, Number One?"

"What is it, sir?" asked Stonewall.

"Don't know yet. I'll get Orion's data banks onto it, though I doubt if there is a reference to anything like it there. If you don't know it, then no one does: I think we're going to have a bit of surmising to do. Perhaps you'd like to reflect on it yourself?"

"Yes, sir."

"Orion, why did you not see the filament immediately. Why did you have to calibrate?"

"What you call the filament, could only be recorded by calibrating my sensors higher than the normal human vision, up to three trillion vibrations per second, because your vision had been enhanced by the amount of adrenaline and other chemicals in your blood stream at the moment when you had been looking at Earth for the last time. Your normal vision registers light at five hundred million vibrations per second, and this is way beyond that."

"That would explain why it's not usual for anyone to see it, Orion. But why me?"

"Chamois, there is the anomaly within yourself, that of having the Pituitary Body and the Pineal Gland fully developed. Their vibrations have fused, making it possible for you to see the other complexities of life that are not available to normal sighted humans."

"Huh! I think you have just answered a mystery that has been bugging us for some time, like why I could see the Chameleon and no one else. I saw through the Lucanite, something no one else did. Well thanks Orion. What you have just told me helps the bits of the puzzle fall into place."

Chamois was fascinated by what he was seeing and felt that if he blinked, the vision of the web of light beams would disappear. Then as he surveyed the constellations of stars and saw that they all seemed to be linked by the cobweb of light, he was appalled at the apparent implication. There was a highway connecting all the galaxies!

Silence greeted him when he relinquished the comm to Grant. Stonewall and Sean looked as stunned as he felt. "Well, that's a turn up for the records," Stonewall said, knowing that whatever they had just viewed was because of Chamois' unusual gifts. That meant he had the ability to see and so pass it on, through Orion's lenses.

"We're going to have a lot of explaining to do and I for one don't know where to start. Do you, sir?" Sean was at a complete loss at the inference of what he had seen and hardly knew how to describe it.

Chapter 20

"The connotations are infinite and at the moment I would describe it like something out of someone's dream, a gossamer of gold and jewels." Chamois could not bring himself to speak of what he knew almost with certainty, what the vision represented.

Sean waited until Chamois had rested and seemed more in control of his thoughts and Orion was well clear of Pluto before he asked him the question uppermost in his mind. "What are we going to amuse ourselves with in the next four years?"

"Good one Sean! Every person on board this vessel will learn how to operate it. Orion will be given instructions to accept your orders. Everyone will learn astro-navigation so that we will all be capable of taking over at a second's notice any station in Orion." His grin was very much the same as the one they had all seen on Stonewall.

"Also, I want you to come up with some ideas about what was on the main screen just now. That should keep everyone from feeling bored for a year or three!"

Sean and Grant glanced at each other. A raised eyebrow by Sean asked if their new skipper realise what he was asking of himself and the other members of the crew.

"Excuse me Captain." Grant looked down at his shoes, this was going to be difficult. "The maths involved in Sean's post and mine - do you think perhaps some of Stravros' men might find them a bit out of their league?"

Grant let the question hang in mid air, not finishing it to query Chamois' ability to handle the high complexities of cybernetics and spatial maths although he had graduated along with every other candidate in pure maths.

Stonewall felt a wave of relief cascade through his body as if he were standing below a freezing cold shower of water. That was as close as I need to come to suicide, he thought. The idea of mastering modern technology, of understanding how these new computers worked, was not at the top of the list of things that he loved best!

It was Hope who came to everyone's rescue. "Captain Dangerfield, sir, I think that I informed you that I had a masters' degree in the fields that Mr Darnley works and I think that I would find cybernetics interesting."

Chamois looked down at her. The bright eyes were wide and spoke only of sincere desire to be of use.

Everyone turned to look at the diminutive figure of Hope. Grant broke the ensuing silence. "Yes, I think that you would find it interesting, and also it will stop you from being bored." His smile was that of a person who had found a kindred spirit.

"Well, I think that the rest of you can handle my job with adequate training and suitable back-up. Don't you agree number one?"

"Yes, sir." Stonewall's relief that he was no longer expected to understand how Orion's brain worked, was obvious to the crew and Chamois, so much so, that laughter echoed around the control deck and lingered while they went to their stations.

True to his word, Chamois set about having everyone taught to handle the comm helmet after Orion had been reprogrammed to accept their DNA. The finer points of handling the ship were left to those who were capable of doing so.

Hope worked harder than any man and spent long hours with Sean and Grant. She had put forward the theory that the web was indeed that, a web connecting all the stars, making them one huge body of...what? Chamois had a secret admiration for her. She had reached the same conclusion as he had, but not taken it to its final rationalisation. He would have also liked to ask her what was the hidden information she kept to herself, but decided that whatever it was, it did not concern the running of Orion. Therefore it could wait until they returned to Earth.

With everyone taking a turn at the comm every twenty-four hours, Chamois found time to study the star charts on the wide display screen.

He was interested in the distances between the stars and the time it would take to get from one to another. "More than a couple of lifetimes, even *with* the anti-ageing medication!" he said as he discussed the problem with Stonewall when they stood and gazed at the panorama before them.

"Yes, maybe," Stonewall agreed, "but don't forget that while we're away, Brian and Crispin are putting their mental powers together and I think there'll be some exciting news waiting for us. Also sir, you have to give some thought to that light web we saw."

"You could be right. Only God above knows for certain what that is, and Lucanite may reveal even more astounding factors than we've ever dreamed of." Chamois still felt there was something waiting just beyond his intelligence, hiding from him and felt distracted when he was unable to grasp it.

Taking his turn at the comm, he searched around the limitless space. There was no sign of the light web. Orion seemed to be floating motionless in the void with no indication of movement, yet the speed was now drive six, six hundred thousand kliks. The engines were running very smoothly. Stravros, Peter and Gabby were happy with their jobs and took delight in instructing Sean, Grant, Stonewall and him into the intricacies of the *"perfect beauties"* that Brian had built, while Hope stood in for whose turn it was.

Discussions regarding the light web were frequent. Once again, when Chamois and Stonewall were alone, his Number One had given him one of his unnerving glares, as if to intimidate him into telling him what he had deduced.

"If I tell you what I think Stonewall, you'll want to relieve me of command."

"I don't believe so sir. I know you've come up with some odd ideas from time to time, but they always paid off. I mean, remember when you told us that a chap who had been dead for centuries, and took us to a hidden cave was leading us? That saved our lives. I've started to have reservations about your so-called flights of fancy.

"If at the end of the day you save all our lives again, then I'm prepared to listen to anything you have to say. I can speak for the rest of the men too. Of course I don't know about the young lady, sir. She lives in her own world, does her job well mind, and can be spoken to when needed." In other words, Stonewall approved of Hope as a crew member and no matter how far fetched his deductions were concerning the star paths, Stonewall wanted to know what Chamois believed.

"You're not going to accept this all in one go, Stonewall. I couldn't. If what I think is true, then space travellers are going to have a lot of figuring out to do. Lucanite may get us out of the solar system, but is that the right course to take? What if there is a connecting link between all the stars, leading from one star to another by that web of light we saw? The hardest question to answer will be, how do we get into, or onto that path?"

As Stonewall digested what Chamois had told him, there was a silence as deep as a bottomless mine shaft. The older man exhaled the long breath he had held while the implacable young man had been speaking. He tried to remember what Chamois had appeared like when he had first arrived on Dionysus as a raw recruit…. a gangling ignorant youth, who looked as though a puff of wind would blow him over… and now?

"You don't pull your punches do you, sir? You've just put us back hundreds of years. Here we are, happily skimming along at drive six, thinking that we had space conquered and now you come up with the idea that we are on a dead ended road that will take us over nine years to travel. You know something - I believe you could be right!" Stonewall had pushed his cap back from his eyes and surveyed his protégé. His hard face even grimmer now than it had ever been, his eyes were ice cold and bleak.

"Any chance of contacting Brian and telling him what you think?" he asked.

"Stonewall, if I thought there was a remote chance of letting Brian and Crispin know without the Federation intercepting our transmission, I would send them a message on the emergency frequency Brian installed. However, we both know they have ears and eyes just about everywhere and I'll be *blessed* if I'll let them steal what is Brian's and Crispin's reward from all the hard work they've put in."

Chamois bit his lip as his anger started to simmer inside him. "It's like having an itchy place while on parade and not being able to scratch."

Stonewall gave a wry smile as he agreed with Chamois. "You're right there, but what do we do about it?"

"Log it. I'll put Orion on automatic, call a conference, with Hope included and after I've evaluated all the input, I'll make a final decision, but to tell the truth, I honestly don't think there is much we can do until we have more information."

"Yeah, I guess you're right there too! But do you really think it wise to have Wong's granddaughter along at a talk concerning something he'd give his anti-ageing ration for fifty years for?"

There was a definite gleam of amusement in Chamois' eyes as he replied, "Oh yes. Whatever Wong and Co. are cooking up, they have no intention of jeopardising their toe-hold in the Dangerfield household. Trust me with that one."

"Can I ask what is the estimated date of arrival at Proxima in the Alpha Centuri sector, or is that still a difficult question to answer?" Stonewall wanted to know.

"Strange you should ask that just now. It seems as if we are going to be well ahead of schedule. We are only three months away, in fact, from the Alpha System…. what do you make of that? We've maintained a constant speed of drive six, yet we are arriving at a place that was supposed to be well over four light years from Earth, and we have, by Orion's calendar, been travelling less than two years!"

Stonewall's already slightly lined face was screwed up like a used wet tissue, with puzzlement. "I'm sure there's a logical explanation. Have you asked Orion yet?"

"No, but it's on the agenda of a list of questions that I intend to put to him as soon as Grant has finished his stint. I'm glad I'm not tied to the comm all the time I'm awake, and Grant is proving a natural at handling Orion."

"You're not jealous of his ability to get along with your dream machine?"

"Nah, Orion can be a bit like you were when I was under your command. No disrespect Stonewall, but you did give me a lot of stick at times. Sean said that you were getting me ready for an officer's badge. I wish *Grant* had been a bit more helpful. He knew what was going on…though perhaps not; it might have made me negligent and some people wouldn't be here today."

"No, sir, I can't agree with that! Whatever you are, big-headed, quick-tempered, and all the other attributes of a young man of your age, never have I known you to be unmindful, not only of your duty, but of anyone who needs your help." The wolfish grin was back on Stonewall's face and all Chamois could do was to turn his back so that his Number One could not see his face reddening at the first and only compliment that he had ever heard Stonewall give to anyone.

The conference proved Chamois correct in his assumptions. They all thought that the paths or filaments could be a means of getting from one star system to another and the real problem was, how to access them. The final decision was that Orion's data banks would need to be analysed by Crispin and Brian before any tangible sense could be gleaned from them.

Chamois came out of a deep and untroubled sleep. The vibrations permeating through his sleeping quarters, told him that all was well with Orion, but a quick look at his chronometer indicated that he had been asleep for only three hours, so what had awakened him? Sitting up and listening more carefully, he still could detect nothing wrong with Orion. Yet there had been something amiss mocking his sleep laden brain. He thought of calling on the intercom, but he was intrigued and until he found out for certain what had awakened him, he would not be able to rest.

There was nothing else for it but to get dressed, go to the bridge and find out if there was anything unusual in Orion's sights. Sean was taking this watch with Grant and Hope as his backup.

As he entered the main deck, Stonewall came from the day rest room. "What woke you, sir?" he asked Chamois, as they converged toward the comm chair together.

"Don't know yet, but there's something out there that's trying to claim our attention, I think." Chamois still felt the remnants of sleep fogging his mind. "Relieve Sean of the comm and I'll take a look around. We're only eight mill kliks away from Alpha Centuri now. If it is inhabited by sentient life, perhaps they have a listening outpost."

Sean scrubbed his face with his hands as he left the comm chair. "I'm glad you came, Sir. For some reason the sights kept going blurred. Couldn't see why." Sean was far more than glad that Chamois had taken over. Having the responsibility of the comm was not his favourite job.

Allowing the comm helmet to embrace his head, Chamois settled his mind to accept Orion's input. "There is an incoming message on a far higher frequency than we have ever used before, Chamois. I am attempting to calibrate. However it is still too high for my sensors to read coherently."

"Stop trying for a moment or two. Wait until I instruct you, then very slowly open the channel again." Chamois gave himself thinking time to try to analyse this phenomenon. Would any intelligence have a transmitter powerful enough to stretch out into space to reach them?

Maybe…. wait, go back a bit…I saw the star paths when I was pumped full of adrenaline…. I felt there was something going on while I was still asleep…how do I go back to sleep yet be able to control a situation?

"You will not be asleep in the accepted sense, Chamois. Carry out the same procedures you followed when you were searching for remnants of Professor Daingerfield's thoughts in my data-banks."

Orion had the answer! "You really are a smart cart, Orion. O K, let's give it a buzz, and get everything possible on record. I also want whatever happens, to be displayed on the main screen. I'll want input from all the crew."

It would have been a very simple thing to go back to sleep. The chair was comfortable enough and the helmet supported his head and stopped it from falling to one side as he relaxed, but uppermost in his mind was the niggling thought that there was something to discover here that could be exceptionally interesting. Letting his muscles go limp and laying aside what the transmission could, or could not be, he settled down.

He did not have long to wait. First there was a sense of floating down through a green atmosphere, or was it water? Then came the knowledge that he was not alone. Chamois felt he that he had come to rest, his back supported by a wall.

He was sitting on a floor, and sitting opposite was a jovial little fellow…no, he looked more fish-like than a man! He handed Chamois a flask. Thinking it was meant to be oxygen, he took a deep pull on the straw that was protruding from the neck of it, and was shocked to discover that he had been given a drink of what tasted like fruit juice!

Communication was by telepathy, which, to Chamois' astonishment, came as if they had been doing it for years. "You do not need to concern yourself about breathing. You are here in your mind only. I must let you know how happy I am that you have visited me."

"Where are we? What's happening?" Not very scientific questions, but that was all Chamois could think of at that moment.

"We are on what you would call a water world that circles Proxima and you have come in answer to my plea for company. Now enjoy your short visit here, for you cannot stay away from your physical body for long."

"How do you know that?" Chamois found his companion most intriguing.

"You are not the first Earth being to visit me. Many centuries ago Earth people visited me regularly. They even came after they had given up their physical bodies, but of course, in time, they had to leave me forever. That is why I am so glad to see you!"

Things were getting out of hand. As far as Chamois was aware, Orion was the only manned space vessel ever to leave the Solar System successfully and reach another star. So how could someone else get here? His thoughts were answered by the little fish-man.

"There have been on Earth, people who were never satisfied by what they could see and touch. They knew that there was far more in the universe than the material things. Some looked at the stars and longed to be here. Their longing gave their thoughts wing and the power to travel here."

"But that's not possible!"

"If you did not believe it, then it would never have been and you would not be here yourself," came the enigmatic reply. "You are here, your carrier is recording our transmissions, and so you can take your time and think about this experience and come back on another occasion."

The next thing Chamois realised was that he was sitting in the comm chair and what had just happened seemed like a dream.

"Did anything come through to be recorded, Number One?"

"Yes sir. We have some rather hazy film of you sitting with a being that was half fish and half man. You sat there for a few seconds only, then became aware of where you really were." Stonewall did not fully understand what had actually taken place, but knew that Chamois had communicated with the being he had seen him with, and was at odds as to how to ask what had been said.

"Stonewall, I thought that this trip was going to be about as interesting as last week's laundry where the travelling part was concerned. How wrong I've been! We've seen highways in the sky that no one else even knew about. Now I've just been in touch with someone who says that we are not the first people from Earth to visit him! What next?" Chamois leaned back in the comm chair, helmet at the ready. "He said that he's been visited by Earth people in thought form, years ago, but that's beyond belief."

"Is it, sir? As far as I'm concerned it's beyond belief that *you* made contact with him, from Orion too." Stonewall walked away a few steps, then looked back at his Superior Officer, a youth still, in his eyes, but a youth with physical as well as mental powers that he hardly knew how to use or control.

He believed that his Commanding Officer's life was going to get tougher for him as he brought his abilities into use. His answer to Chamois' question was, "Take my word for it, sir. There really are more things in the Heavens than we have yet dreamed about."

Later, while resting with a cup of tea, Chamois wondered why he felt so sad. He should be elated about his latest discovery. Still the intuition that something was not quite right persisted, and perhaps it was something to do with the Proxima being.

Chapter 21

The group of people, who sat around the table they shared with Chamois, glanced at each other with wary eyes. They knew he was going to ask for input. Hope was the last to arrive. Like a shadow along a dimly lit wall, she slid into the room, and stood in a far corner, waiting to hear what the rest of the crew would put forward.

When some minutes had elapsed, she raised her hand to claim Chamois' attention. "The character you communicated with was pleased to have you visit. Would that indicate that he does not get company very often?"

"Could be, Hope. He gave me the impression that he was resigned to his way of life, anyway. Anything else?"

"Yes, sir. If he said that Earth people visited him centuries ago, how old do you think he can be and how intelligent is he?" Hope did not like the sensation that everyone was looking at her, but no one seemed to have grasped the import of what the presence of this ancient being meant.

"Hope, I think I'm going to have another talk with our friend before I can answer questions like that. Thank you for bringing them to my notice. Anyone else have anything to add? Any further questions? No? Meeting adjourned," Chamois said as he slapped the table and stood up to leave.

Grant stopped Hope as she tried to slide out of the conference room as silently as she had entered.

"You don't have to try to make yourself invisible. We all think you're O K. I'm sure you'd like someone to talk to occasionally apart from work, so why don't you join Gabby and me over a brew?"

"I would like that very much and you can tell me about Chamois when you were on the Dionysus together. I'm sure I would be interested in what you have to say."

And so Grant told Hope everything he knew about the man he was determined to protect.

There's something not quite right, Stonewall." Chamois sat forward in his chair, with an elbow on the desk and his head propped up by his open palm. They were in the officer's day cabin. Stonewall was lounging in a chair opposite, waiting, knowing that his Commanding Officer was still trying to come to terms with the conundrum that puzzled him.

"This man with gills who resembled a fish with legs appeared to be alone when I saw him. He seemed happy enough, yet I had such a feeling of despair after talking to him." Chamois shook his head, attempting to think the problem through.

"Go and talk to him again," Stonewall suggested. "You told Hope that you would."

"Yeah. But keep a sharp weather eye on what happens. I'll be at the comm. You take up the auxiliary command station, because I want you to see and hear as much of the exchange as conditions will permit… Oh, and watch our stern!"

Chamois' return journey to the water world was easier than his first trip. He found himself comfortably seated with his back against a wall again. With the telepathic link established, he told the Being who sat opposite him, that he was called Chamois, and asked why he seemed to have no companions, and what name was *he* known by?

As they exchanged thoughts, another man with black, heavy boots kicked and smashed the flagon of fruit juice. Chamois was shocked and asked his companion, "What did he do that for?"

"Not everyone thinks the way you do, Chamois, and some can be vicious in their attitude towards me. It doesn't matter. Please, forget it. I am known as Voki. I've been here longer than the Earth has had a moon." He raised the lids from his downcast eyes slightly, as a man with eyebrows would have done. "Those who have committed crimes, such as giving away sophisticated secrets to a race of undeveloped people are sent here." Voki hung his head in weary sadness.

The shock of this statement almost sent Chamois' mind back to his body on Orion. "But surely it would have been kinder to put you to death?"

Voki's reply was emphatic. "Yes it would, but then it is the belief of those who condemned me that if I were executed, my spirit would be free, free to wreak the same damage on another world not yet ready to plunge into the iniquity of absolute power."

Chamois felt that there could be no justification for the horrendous sentence that had been passed on Voki. "Was it so terrible, this information? Did it cause so much trouble?"

"I'll be truthful with you, young Earth-man. I do deserve the justice that has been meted out to me, also the vilification I receive from my fellow men. Even you will hate me when I tell you. I gave the wisdom of atomic power to a world that had only just climbed out of using paddles and sails to move their ships. I meddled in something I should not have, because I wanted to have domination over this beautiful, innocent world. Instead I destroyed it. The inhabitants blew themselves apart and made their planet radioactive where nothing could live. It became a place of desolation, with no oxygen or water. I gave them all kinds of knowledge in the hope that they would adore me for giving such gifts, but they grew to hate and fear me." A sigh of remorse gurgled from his lips in the dim green shadows. "A few survivors were taken to a neighbouring planet in the same system, by the Guardians. But it was a harsh and hostile place and they had to build what they could without the aid of atomic technology right from the very beginning." Voki gave a wry grin. "So now you understand why I was so glad to see you Chamois, and have a visitor who does not insult me, for I am to live in solitude for ever, or until the Prime Co-ordinators release me."

"Voki, what you've just told me makes this a whole new ball game. I'll admit that what you did and your reasons for doing so are appalling. However, I also believe enough is enough. I don't know when the Earth didn't have a moon, it must have been before records were kept, and that's just too long for a man to be kept in solitary. And solitary is something I do know something about!"

Chamois' recollections of his own conviction to the labour camps gave him authority to view Voki's predicament with the understanding of experience. He added, "I haven't met any Prime Co-ordinators, but if I do, then I'll have something to say to them about forgiveness."

Voki laughed… more bubbles in the green haze. "My dear fellow! You are the first Being ever to feel compassion toward me, but I must warn you, that for you to meet a Prime Co-ordinator, then you will have given up your Earthly flesh. You will be dead, Chamois!"

Frowning, he asked, "These Prime Co-ordinators, they're not what we of Earth refer to as God, surely?" This incredible mystery bewildered Chamois.

"Oho no, the Prime Co-ordinators are just that, all they do is carry out the directions given to them by the entity you call God!" Voki gave Chamois a distressed, furtive look. "The thought of being brought into the presence of a Prime Co-ordinator makes me freeze with terror. I'd rather not even contemplate going where that other particular Entity dwells."

It seemed to Chamois, that Voki's voice had lowered to a harsh whisper, as dread gripped him in its vice. He paused, as a shudder of apprehension trembled through him. "Goodbye, Earth-man, and thank you for all the understanding you have shown me. I won't forget." The memory of Voki's pitiful smile was to stay with him for a long time.

He suddenly became aware that he was sitting at the comm and Stonewall was signalling for his attention. "We have bogies on the port beam, sir." Chamois turned his attention to the position that Stonewall indicated. A craft, its outlines blurred by the extreme speed at which it was travelling, was approaching. It was surrounded by an aura of deep, angry, fiery red.

"Orion," Chamois addressed the computer-ship, "they're looking for trouble. We carry no weaponry. What do you suggest?"

"Engage an evasive manoeuvre pattern, and implement the Lucanite camouflage skin." As Orion gave this input, the stratagem was carried out.

Chamois brought Orion about and flipped over to take up a position just behind and above the colossal alien ship. It was like a mobile city. Then he sent out and easy-link message to ask them. "Why are you preparing to be aggressive towards an unarmed vessel?"

The response was slow and deliberate. It demanded that they leave the area immediately, the message being printed on the main screen.

Not satisfied with this reply, Chamois decided to augment his telepathic abilities by using Orion's power coils to boost his talent. Then, using every ounce of will power, he projected the message to where he considered the bridge to be on the alien ship. "You have not answered my question! Why are you so aggressive towards us, an unarmed vessel, and who gave you the authority to attempt to evict us?"

The result was anything but what he had been expecting. He found himself aboard the huge, threatening, unknown spaceship!

Going to see Voki was one thing; this situation felt altogether different. While he had been with Voki, he always felt as if he were still sitting in the comm chair, but now he felt as if he really was standing aboard the alien vessel.

Stunned though he was, Chamois stood as tall and commanding as he could. The Entities facing him were uncommonly taller and even more imperious looking. They scrutinised him with dismay. They had not been expecting a house call either.

He was impressed by the familiarity of the people he stared at; it was like looking in a full-length mirror. They were all over two metres tall, with white blonde hair and deep blue eyes. They could have been his clones or siblings.

There was a long silence lasting several seconds before one of them, who appeared to be in command, stepped forward and answered him. "This is a restricted area, a place of internment for the most dangerous criminals in this star sector. Prime Co-ordinator, Nazaire commands us to expel all who venture here, by force if necessary. Leave peaceably and no harm will come to you." The voice was not unpleasant, but very authoritative. The lines of his face were hard planes and angles; his eyes were flint, almost as gritty as Stonewall's, Chamois thought. He seized the information, the name of Nazaire! He could use it to make further communications with these guardians.

"Pass a message on to Nazaire for me, will you? Tell him, that I have always been led to believe …among other things, in the forgiveness of sin." Chamois gave his listeners a profound glare. "Does that apply to everyone including Voki, or just the favoured few?…Chamois, Captain of the Research and Survey Vessel, Orion…Out." As he bowed slightly, unable to resist the beaming smile of equals greeting, he noticed that the leader's face had also softened slightly from its grim lines.

Making himself aware of his surroundings on Orion, he commanded the ship to execute a graceful, stately manoeuvre and then instructed Orion to plot a course to head back home to Earth.

The stunned silence that greeted him as he emerged from the comm helmet was almost total. Hope was weeping silently into her handkerchief. Sean and Grant were holding onto their workstations as if their very lives depended on it. Stonewall's forehead was beaded with perspiration. Stravros, Gabby and Peter stood transfixed. Everyone was holding their breath and staring at him. "O K, what happened? What's everyone gawking at?" Chamois demanded. "Anyone would think that I'd ceased to exist."

Chapter 22

"You did, sir," Grant said. "We can't believe our eyes. But you did vanish!"

"Yes sir, you went from Orion to the other ship. We saw you on the screen with those men, all of them looking like you. We watched you back answering them!" Sean, who had known Chamois for years, felt the fear of the bizarre grip his heart. This was his old buddy doing a fairground trick; this was no deception; this was fact.

Stravros and his engineers let out the air trapped in their lungs from their gaping mouths as they relaxed. "You're safely back, sir, so me and the lads'll return to the engine-room," Stravros said, as they beat a hasty retreat, leaving the Buffer to explain what had happened, if he could.

Stonewall heaved a noisy sigh of relief. "Sir, we were out-manned and out manoeuvred there. They could have taken us out any time they chose, and they could have taken you along with them." He mopped his brow and face, and then pulled his uniform jacket straight as he replaced his handkerchief.

"Yeah, I suppose you're right, Stonewall. However, friend or foe, no one walks all over us to wipe their muddy boots on us…and who ever *they* are, the sooner they get to know this the better. They probably wonder where I got the balls from to talk to them like that." Chamois raised a quizzical eyebrow, as he commented, "and if they come after me, I'll blame you!" which caused Stonewall to explode with laughter as he replied, "And you, sir, want to watch they don't skewer those said balls for a kebab!" Chamois nodded and agreed. "Yeah, touché." Giving his Number One a mischievous grin, he asked, "Did I really flip?" then without waiting for a reply, he made his way to his cabin.

He leaned with his back against the inside of the closed door, his breath coming in deep gasps. Letting slip the mask of nonchalance that had fooled everyone, he wiped away the tears that had gathered inside his nostrils; glad they had not formed in his eyes, where every single member of the crew would have seen them.

It wouldn't do for them to see that he had been frightened witless!

Pacing the confines of his cabin, he tried to rationalise what had occurred. But it was too soon after the event. All his brain could register was the fact that these Guardians and he were somehow related. They had to be. It was too much of a coincidence that they were almost identical to him. The only difference that Chamois could detect was that he was much broader in the shoulder and a couple of centimetres shorter, which came from hard work and eating slowly, the way Brookman had shown him when he was in the labour camp. Also the genes he had inherited from his father must have played a large part in his structure. Brian was broad shouldered too and well under two metres in height.

The man who had spoken to him had eventually relaxed. Chamois had said something, which had made him unwind a bit…but what? All he had done was state Voki's case and ask for clemency. What on Earth had happened? He forced his mind to remember. He had been sitting at the comm, the helmet in place, wanting to know who or what the newcomers were. Intentionally drawing on Orion's power to get a boost, he had then projected his demands at the alien. He had not been aware of moving through space or of leaving Orion; he just had! What his father would make of it when the records were downloaded, he could not even begin to guess.

He had promised the old man that he would be careful and bring everyone back safely. "You nearly made a muck-up of that one, Chamois, old mate!" he admonished himself.

Later, as Chamois and Sean shared a pot of coffee, Sean asked, "Are we really going home?"

"Yeah, we've been away for nearly four years, according to Orion's chronometer, but with distortion of time in space, it could be much longer. I don't know, Sean. The journey has not been uneventful, and I think we've learned more than anyone could hope on a first trip outside the Solar System."

Chamois leaned back in his chair and stretched his long arms and legs, yawning. "I, for one, will be glad to see my father, Crispin Avery and Luke Denning. Do you realise, I've never even seen my father's home, Camber Park?" he asked.

"You're right about having learned a lot, far more than many spacers learn in two lifetimes patrolling the Solar, and I still can't grasp what has happened from time to time." Sean raised a mocking eyebrow, but Chamois ignored the half query. Sean then volunteered the suggestion, "Grant's been to Camber Park, why don't you ask him what it's like?"

"Nah, I'll wait until Brian takes me, *if* he takes me." Chamois took a long pull at his coffee, and then said, "Talking about Grant, he seems to be in Hope's company a lot lately. I'm not being a spoiler of paradise, but I think he ought to know that she is more than friendly towards one of the guards who escorted us to the space shuttle. Grant needs to be careful where he leaves his boots at night."

"If you mean that huge mountain of a Korean, then I would say you're quite right." Sean could imagine what kind of fight would occur if Grant convoyed Hope around, once they reached Earth.

For a while, Chamois and his companion thought about Earth and what they would wish to do when they returned. Visions of rolling green hills, still blue lakes, and the feeling of raindrops sploshing on upturned faces, causing eyes to be shut tight, only to open their mouths to taste the clear water as it fell. They fantasised about the thunderous nights and lightning slicing the heavens with daggers of searing, incandescent light. These and other daydreams haunted their vivid imaginations.

Eventually, Chamois stood up. He was tired to his bones and his face felt numb with fatigue as he scrubbed it with his hands. His eyes were prickly raw and his kneecaps were on fire. He needed sleep.

I'll go through the ship's log. I want to refresh my memory of what has happened since we left home." He tried to sound casual, but his mind was on the time when he had inadvertently visited the alien vessel. He wanted to see what had really happened on Orion. He felt that once he had seen that, he could sleep, but not before. In his cabin, Chamois looked into Orion's vacant monitor screen. He could call up everything that had occurred, but would it tell him what he really to know?

Chapter 22

Seeing the reflection of his grey, weary face echoing back at him, it was clear exhaustion and responsibility had taken their toll. He reasoned that no smart-arsed piece of machinery was going to be able to calm the anxiety that was gnawing at him. He turned away from the computer, allowed himself the luxury of a cold-water shower and slipped between the covers of his bunk.

Sleep was evasive; he felt too tired to relax, and anyway he could hear someone whispering outside his cabin door. He listened carefully in the hope he would be able to understand what was being said. It could be a conspiracy. However, try as hard as he could, the words seemed to be in a language he did not know or understand.

The door was opening cautiously, and someone was creeping craftily into his cabin on softly shod feet. There came again the soft murmur of conversation he did not understand… a woman singing far away, in a clear sharp voice, but the words making no sense.

The light tap on the cabin door brought him from a deep sleep, with Grant asking if he would like a brew of tea.

"Yeah, sure, come in Grant. I've been having a bad dream…I think." Chamois took the proffered mug of tea. "Thanks," he said. "I dreamed that someone was outside the door, then came in, too quietly to be up to any good. It gave me the creeps." Taking a swallow of the hot liquid, he asked Grant, "How long have I been in my cabin, do you know?"

Grant grinned at him as he pointed to the chronometer. "Sean said that you left him ten hours ago, and seeing that no-one had heard a peep out of you in all that time, Stonewall sent me to make sure that you were okay." Refilling Chamois' mug, he turned to leave, and then added, "Stonewall said, Orion won't fall apart if you take another couple of hours off. Orion has set the course for home, and we are on automatic."

After the two mugs of tea, Chamois felt fit to face the crew of Orion again with some semblance of normality.

As he entered the command deck, Grant was manning the comm, with Stonewall at his side. Didn't that man ever sleep? Sean and Stravros were at the controls that governed speed and fuel consumption. Gabby and Peter would be with their beloved engines. Hope had been taking samples of the gasses and fine particles they were journeying through. She was now analysing them.

"Number One, anything to report?" he asked, as he studied the map laid out in the star tank, an enclosed sphere that gave a three dimensional panorama of all known star systems.

"No, sir," Stonewall glanced at Chamois; he could detect no sign of the mental conflict he knew his commanding officer had suffered several hours earlier.

Everyone had furtively sneaked a look at him. Smiling to himself, he gave the command, "Carry on, as you were."

Routine and constant exercises, with classes studying maths, space-physics and metallurgy, occupied the time as they headed for the blue planet, Earth.

Chamois had found enough fortitude to peruse the situation of his disappearance from the bridge; he had learned little more than what his crew had told him. Orion offered no further explanation other than it was part of the development of the pituitary body and pineal gland. But as a rejoinder, Orion added that, that there was a surprising amount of adrenaline in his bloodstream. Would Chamois have been disturbed by the cavalier way the aliens had dismissed him? If he had, then, because he had not been in complete control of his emotions, he had lost control of the situation.

So, this computer *did* have the marbles to be acerbic, and fathom out when he was in a fury! Orion had more or less told him to master himself and keep his temper under control if he wanted to dominate any situation he was in.

The only consolation he had was that if such an occurrence took place again, he wouldn't be quite so alarmed as he had been during his encounter with the Guardians, and he'd keep his irritation at petty injustice shackled. With the Solar System only a few short days away, Chamois decided that it would be advantageous to send a coded easylink message to Brian. 'Cygnet'. That was all that would be needed to alert him that his space vessel Orion and the crew were on their way home, safe.

Hope had been silent, not even talking to Grant when they shared off-duty times. Chamois considered that she was thinking of the Korean guard, and was possibly feeling anxious in case he objected to her being on such close terms with Grant, and paid no attention to her reserved attitude. Pluto swam into long-range view, and then it could be seen filling the main screen, with its moon in attendance. Gradually the whole system could be seen like a strand of pearls carelessly scattered across the deep blue velvet of the heavens.

"We'll anchor where Brian had Orion stashed away while he assembled him, away from prying eyes," Chamois told Stonewall. "Brian will know where to look for us."

Sean was at the comm and before Chamois could give him the command. Sean said, "We have company…dead ahead."

"Very well, Sean, I'll take over from here, "Chamois said as he placed a hand on the other's shoulder.

There was a full flotilla of spacecraft waiting for them. "Orion, search their weaponry. Do they have anything aimed at us?" he asked the computer.

"No, Chamois, they are only expecting us. I detect no warlike attitude."

"No, neither do I. Hmmm, well, until I hear from Brian, we'll keep a low profile. Orion, augment the Lucanite skin. We will head for the junk yard in the asteroid belt." Chamois also gave Orion another command, to which the computer replied, "An excellent move, Chamois. My data-banks will be altered accordingly."

Whatever the welcoming committee had in mind, Chamois would rather wait until he had a chance to talk to Brian, before he let anyone else on board. No one but Brian and Crispin were going to get their hands on Orion's logs.

Causing his craft to do a smart about flip-over, Chamois took Orion on a trajectory on a parallel to Saturn, then slid to starboard to Jupiter and kept to the shadow of a large moon. Timing the leap to the asteroid belt to align with the spot where all the debris from former space stations and satellites had been abandoned, Chamois brought Orion to a steady pace, deep among the larger fragments of the rubbish collected there.

With enough abandoned refuse to confuse the probing scans, the distraction would give Brian the chance to reach them first. He was positive that there would be a homing device loaded into Orion's hardware, which would have been activated by the 'Cygnet' code.

Stonewall, at his usual station just behind Chamois' chair, asked, "What do we do now, sir?"

"We wait, keep our heads down and pray that Brian beats everyone else to the honey pot. If you can think of some other way of diverting attention from us, now is the time to tell me." Chamois turned and gave his Buffer a knowing smile. "You gave me a rough time when I was a raw recruit and as a subby, but I think if I needed to, I could switch these engines off, so that no one could trace us, and row the boat home." The grin widened as Chamois added, "Thank you, Number One!"

"Yes, sir, that I did, and it's paid off. And I honestly can't think of anything else that you can do to keep the brigands away," he replied.

With all the facilities, except life-support closed down, Chamois and his crew waited in the rare silence.

Chamois stood staring dejectedly out of a forward facing, large, square porthole. Looking past his own reflection, he saw the junk that made up their immediate neighbourhood. Fragments nudged against them as they nestled among the debris. Scavengers had been at work, making the old hulks complete wrecks. The twenty-first space stations, destined for an early retirement even before they had been completed, had been made obsolete by the out-dated components they were built with. It had taken the politicians many decades to realise that the way to the near planets and now finally to the stars, was to build a town-sized establishment on the Moon.

Orion had travelled millions of kliks, keeping his crew safe, and had returned home to have the rejected scraps of refuse for company.

"Stonewall, I'd like you and Hope to man the engine room while there's not much happening there. Pass my respects to our Chief Engineer, and tell him I would like him to accompany Sean and me to that interesting wreck on our port bow. I'm sure that they will appreciate the divergence. Sean has always had this fascination for antiquated machinery, like that two-wheeled item that he was repairing on Moon base when we were on the exam course for our subbies' badge, and I'm sure there is bound to be something to take his interest there. Also Stravros, as an engineer, should see what his predecessors had to work with," Chamois explained. He noticed the dawning, knowing look on the craggy features of his Number One. *He* knew that Hope was to be got out of the way while Chamois made a trip to the wreck with two of his most trusted companions.

The trio were out of Orion for a only few minutes. Stravros came back with a trophy, an old implement that had been used to tighten bolts and screws that held the ancient craft together. Sean was ecstatic with the treasure he had found, an abandoned plasti-kit envelope, with some real paper that still had some writing on it.

Once back on Orion, Chamois returned to his vigil by the porthole. Deep in his preoccupation and despondent mood, he gazed past his own image at the strewn rubbish, not noticing the small shuttle until it was bumping gently against a large fragment alongside Orion. Startled, he spun toward the communication control panel.

"Orion to shuttle, identify yourself!"

"Professor Brian Dangerfield, at your service, sir." Brian's familiar face overflowed the main screen. The grin filled his face, his eyes crinkled up and a row of startling white teeth showed how pleased Brian was to see his son and the crew of Orion, safe.

"Dad, are we happy to see you!" Chamois could not help but notice the streaks of grey in his father's hair, nor the extra lines running from the corners of his eyes.

"Everything's ok son. President Wong still controls the Federation and they obey his commands." All the crew had joined Chamois at the screen. Stonewall had his jaw clamped so tight, the knotted muscles threatened to burst.

Hope was glancing guiltily from Brian to Chamois, and then back to Brian. Her eyes appealed to him not to divulge a secret.

"Follow me to Moon Base. There's a welcome waiting for all of you, and some rather exciting news for Stonewall." Brian then turned towards Chamois, and with a mysterious grin said, "I don't know what you will think of the not so little surprise waiting for you, son." he then looked directly at Hope. He waved and then beckoned for them to accompany him.

Orion was led to the fore of the Federation Space Fleet. Brian had gone aboard his old space ship The Black Swan, which lay along side Dionysus. The two ships had taken up position in front of the great flotilla.

Then Black Swan's shuttlecraft came to Orion's entry port. While Stravros activated the opening device, Chamois and Stonewall waited on the control deck for their first human visitors for eight space years.

The diminutive form of President Wong was the first to enter the control deck. He made a slight bow to Chamois, giving him the greeting of a low bow from the waist. He also gave Stonewall a similar bow as he said, "Welcome home, sir, Commander-in-Chief of the Federation Solar Fleet, Admiral Jackson!" Turning his attention away from the shocked Stonewall, and back to Chamois, he announced, "Let me introduce you to my great-grandson, Wong Dangerfield Charles, but he likes to be called Dang!"

Chamois reckoned the youth to be about eleven or twelve years old. He stood nearly as tall as Chamois, with flaxen hair, deep blue eyes and an engaging smile.

Wong Dangerfield Charles bowed deeply to Chamois. "Welcome home, sir."

The laughter in the younger man's defiant eyes, dared Chamois not to recognise him as his son.

President Wong had given the entire crew of Orion the shock of their lives. Chamois could only stand and stare at his son. It was Stonewall who broke the spell.

"Sir, I must protest!" Stonewall was in a fury, like something of his days of fighting drug-runners. "I resigned my commission before I joined Orion. I want to stay liberated!" Puce in face, he clenched his teeth in the effort of stop himself from using ancient Tudor oaths. It almost seemed as though there was steam emitting from his ears.

President Wong's face remained as impassive as ever. "Admiral, I fully appreciate your desire to remain free. However, you have a commitment to society as an officer…and a well-experienced one at that. It is time for you to lead from the front. Steering young people from the rear with a Lieutenant-commander's stars was most admirable." Wong waited to see if Stonewall's turmoil had subsided. There had been a slight lessening in the tightly gripped fists. Good! Wong thought, I can continue. "Most of the ships you see on the display panel are commanded by men who have been trained by you. It has been their vote that has put you in the Admiral's seat. The Federation is bound by its duty to obey the wishes of the Space Captains. Admiral Jackson, you are considered indispensable by these Captains!"

Stonewall knew when he was beaten. The breath held too long in his lungs, came out of his mouth as an angry growl. But what of Chamois? How could he let this young man travel millions of light years away without his back up? Stonewall's glance towards Chamois was that of a man in deep anguish.

Chamois had been too engrossed in the appearance of the youth who stood before him, without a doubt his son, Wong's great-grandson, to take much notice of the conflict between President Wong and Stonewall. He caught a fleeting look of distress on Stonewall's face, which cleared as soon as he realised that he had Chamois' attention.

"You look as though you've swallowed an anchor, Stonewall, what's the trouble?" To see his Number One in such a state of high irritation was slightly amusing, but Chamois needed to hide his desire to smile.

Chapter 23

"I've been Shanghaied, sir." The old habit of giving Chamois the superior address was going to be hard to break. "Mr President Wong has given me the information that I have been voted by my *ex-students* to the post of Admiral." Stonewall's angry tone of voice was belied by the straightening of his shoulders. He could not quite hide his pride at the honour bestowed on him by his ex-pupils.

"Oho! I don't wonder, if you gave *them* the same tutoring that you gave *me;* they're just getting their own back!" Then, extending his hand in warm-hearted friendship, Chamois said, "It's the most intelligent decision the Space Captains will ever make."

"Yes, but what are you going to do for a Number One, sir?" Stonewall asked.

"Well, that's a question I can't answer straight away." A look of recollection came into Chamois' eyes. Old and reliable friends had surrounded him, yet there was one certain person who had proven his trustworthiness, whom he had missed on the deep space voyage.

He needed Brookman's kind of common sense in his team and he would request Brian's opinion, when he asked the same question.

Although Stonewall was deep in thought, he was aware that Wong had played two trump cards at one go. Why? He felt that there was more at stake here than his promotion and the surprise package in the form of Chamois' unexpected son. He decided to use the old ploy of playing the waiting game. Wong would reveal his true intentions soon enough. That little minx, Hope, must have known about Chamois' fatherhood. What else did she know? A careful question or two put to Grant might expose something of interest but for now, while the situation was still one of shock tactics, he would wait until he had Grant on his own, and as Admiral of the Federation Solar Fleet, he would use his authority to have that young man standing in front of him in his official office!

Brian broke the tension as he said, "I'm sorry to have to break up such a happy home-coming, but there is much to be done and these voyagers need some time on Earth to get their land legs back again." His statement carried enough authority to make it an order that even President Wong, of the Federated States of China, was obliged to obey. Professor Brian Dangerfield was owner of the Research and Survey Vessel Orion, and he felt it was vital to tell his son privately about Dang as the young man chose to be called.

Dang wasn't just Wong's great-grandson, he was *his* grandson too. Chamois had a right to know exactly the underhanded way that Dang had been conceived.

"Might I suggest that we meet for a conference at Camber Park? Chamois and his crew all deserve a break and I would like to offer you, Mr President, and certain members of your family, hospitality at my home in New South Wales." He spoke with as much coolness as he could without making it sound like a command.

"Thank you, that is most kind of you and I would gratefully accept for myself and on behalf of my granddaughters. However, the World Press and TV companies have arranged a welcome home for the crew of Orion at Hami." President Wong's busy brain was working at mega-drive. He wanted to manipulate Dang and Chamois, just as he did his granddaughters; and Brian had to admit to himself that for the time being he was beaten in his attempts to get Chamois alone.

Keeping his face urbane, he smiled and said, "Of course, that would be the only appropriate destination, and I am so pleased that the media have thought of it. I'll ask Stravros and Sean to stand duty watch keeping, then we can get underway."

"There is no need to post watch-keepers, Professor. I have arranged for a squad of Space marines to police Orion." As Wong said this, six men, all heavily armed came through the entry port.

Chamois stood rooted to the deck. How dare anyone, other than Brian, make such an arrangement? His ears turned the usual dark crimson when his ire was provoked. Then a whisper from the officer leading them stopped him from exploding into yet another blast of anger. "Beckett's Bar!" barely audible and without so much as a half-flicker of an eyelid. Chamois' memory shifted into the days when…yes! He had it. The Marines Stravros, Sean and he had put down one day in Beckett's Bar. Then they'd another fight a couple of days later that week attended by old Admiral Blake. Chamois' team had won the contest, then he had taught the Marine sergeant, -what was his name… Brad? - and his friends, the gentle art of Hapikido and other martial art movements. So Brad was now the senior officer, and in charge of Orion's security. Consequently Orion was safe!

Brian had been watching Chamois for his reaction to Wong's order. He had seen the boiling rage come, then evaporate! There was even a glint of amusement in his eyes. Obviously, his son had a friend here.

The exodus to Hami had been preceded by a flight of fast tenders, whose normal work would have consisted of taking senior officers from one major spacecraft to another. Today they were flying in an arrow formation, saluting Orion and its crew, each craft with its identifying beacon oscillating, blazing, and flashing lights overall! A fantastic view from any angle, from Orion's deck it was no less a noteworthy scene than that of the fleet of sea-going ships dressed in brave, joyful bunting, giving a 'Welcome Home' to a reigning monarch.

Most ship-to-ship communiqués were for Admiral Stonewall Jackson, to welcome him to his new post. Stonewall took each salute with his usual grim face, also a shadow of a diabolical sparkle in his eyes. Those space captains were going to pay for this.

Hami had put on its early summer dress of wild daffodils and blossoming trees. Military personnel, as well as civilians, smiled a greeting at the returning heroes, and a guard of honour led the way to the ancient building favoured by President Wong for his headquarters. "My family and I will be dressed in our national costume for the reception and dinner given for you this evening. The Press and T V companies would warmly appreciate your appearance in full dress uniform, Admiral, Captain Dangerfield, and that of your crew."

Chamois and Stonewall looked at each other in alarm! Full dress uniform? A hoary Tudor oath finally exploded from Stonewall. Neither man had even *considered* such a hideous idea. The man had the effrontery to promote him up to Admiral and Chamois up to Space Captain, without even consulting anyone. Then he expected them to dress up like stuffed dummies.

The steaming bathing room, with its female attendants, was the most agreeable sight since they had left Orion. Unashamedly, all the crew stripped naked and dived in, wallowing in the luxury that only a bath of foaming hot water can give.

Brian whispered a word of warning to Chamois. "Watch out for more surprises. Wong still has some tricks up his ample sleeves that he has not yet told you about."

"Don't worry, I too have a little deception or two that he'd never thought of. Though I must admit, being the father of a young man Dang's age did unsettle me a for a moment or two, but I've known all along that old man Wong was planning something that would give him the squeeze on us." Chamois gave Brian a friendly slap on the back. "It's a trick that may back-fire on him yet. I sensed no danger from Dang, and in fact the lad gave me the impression that he felt great loyalty towards us. By the way, how does it feel to be a grandfather?" For a reply, Chamois was ducked under the warm milky water, to surface spluttering with glee. It was wonderful, just to be in Brian's company again.

Later, wrapped up in the opulence of the dressing jackets that had been placed on them by the girls who had scrubbed and shampooed them, Chamois and his crew were escorted by more young ladies to huge bedrooms, where they found their dress uniforms waiting for them. It would appear that a tailor had made them to measure, for each fitted without a crease or tight seam daring to show anywhere.

Chamois glanced at himself in the full-length mirror. It was a different man from the one he had seen reflected on the port window of Orion only a few short hours ago.

Gone were the bruising shadows beneath his eyes and grim down turned mouth. His grey skin was now a healthy pink. His hair, now shoulder length, tied back with a length of black cord, had regained its pearly-white sheen. He wore his captain's uniform of white with deep blue trim, decorated with the insignia of a Space Captain's badge and stars, with pride. Shoulders back, head up, he went to join his comrades.

Stonewall was magnificent in his uniform, the Admiral's stars on his epaulets and the starburst medal on his chest.

Stravros Bertolozzte looked every inch a 'Spacer' in his deep blue uniform, chevrons of service on his cuff and his rank insignia on his breast.

Peter and Gabby in the same colours, but without any decoration except their service chevrons and workstation badges, were grinning at the unaccustomed neatness imposed by their smart dress uniforms.

The rest of the crew, including Hope, all freshly scrubbed, were equally unrecognisable from the tired people they had been a short time ago.

Tentatively Chamois opened the door from where they could hear the murmur of voices, and poked his head in. The handle was then tugged out of his fingers. Welcome, sir, please come in. We have been waiting for you." The gravel rolling voice belonged to none other than the

Korean guard, dressed in a resplendent uniform of Colonel of the Guard, Hope's lover! Chamois knew it was too late to try to warn Grant about these two being an item.

The noise from the room where the public reception was to be held sounded like a busy waterfall. Voices murmured, some rising to become a trill of laughter, but underneath were the gurgles of intense conversation.

As Chamois and his crew entered, all sound stopped, to be replaced by the tinkling of fingernails tapping on the crystal wineglasses.

President Wong and members of the Federation waited for this sign of respect to abate. Then stepping forward, dressed in a magnificent, deep green brocade Chinese robe he spoke to the assembled guests.

"The Federated States of China has decided to honour the officers and crew of Orion by awarding each of them the Order of Orion's Belt."

There were eight Sam Browne belts of real tanned leather. The waist belt carried three bright stars of gold and diamond. The shoulder strap carried one large, brilliant gold and ruby sunburst to depict Betelgeuse.

"Admiral Jackson, please accept this token of gratitude that every person on Earth feels for you. You have given the Earth something to be proud of. A man dedicated to the education of our future space fleet, going into an unknown and possibly a very dangerous situation; thereby making a role model for all aspiring young people who would follow in your footsteps. "Wong bowed slightly to Stonewall, who in turn had to lower his head to allow the belt with the attached shoulder strap to pass over his shoulders, which were almost half a metre higher than Wong's, the tinging tapping of wineglasses sounding like the clamouring of tiny bells.

To Chamois, Wong bowed much more deeply, and then the dark brown eyes were looked directly into Chamois' azure blue ones. They still held a hint of mystery, yet there was also fear!

The Sam Browne was placed on him as he, in turn, bowed to the president. The buckled belt clasped his waist, accentuating the broad shoulders. The smile he gave the President held the untold message, "You've been too cunning." Chamois, like Stonewall, turned and thanked the assembly, then stood and waited while the rest of Orion's crew was equally honoured.

It was as he made his way through the throng and spoke to each person he passed, that he noticed a woman who could have been Hope's twin, except that she looked as dainty and elegant as the finest bone china. She wore a sam-shong of pale primrose, trimmed with a slightly deeper yellow.

Unable to resist the pull of such ethereal beauty, Chamois made his way towards her only to be intercepted by the Korean Colonel. "Allow me to introduce you to my sister-in-law, Wong Celestial Joy. Joy, I think you already know Captain Chamois Dangerfield?" The exquisite young woman blushed delicate pink and showed tiny pearly teeth. Her almond shaped, topaz eyes sparkled as she smiled her welcome.

"Yes, I have met the Captain before, but I hardly expect him to remember me." Joy turned to face Chamois directly. "You had traversed a part of the Gobi desert and came to the bathing room here."

It was Chamois' turn to blush. "You were in the bath?"

"I had the honour of shampooing your hair." Joy was having difficulty restraining the giggle that she controlled in her throat. She wanted to laugh at his discomfort, yet there was another secret that she should share with him. Looking down, to hide it from those inquisitive eyes, a tear started to form on the lashes.

Sensing her turmoil, Chamois asked, "Would you like to show me the garden, Joy? The Spring night is very warm." He nodded to the Colonel as he led her out onto a paved terrace. Chamois steered Joy away from the prying eyes and into the soft, gentle light of the lanterns that were strung from trees and posts.

As Joy looked up at him, he caught a glimpse of the tear; it hung like a diamond on her lash and threatened to spill down her cheek.

"I don't know what is making you so unhappy, but if I am in any way responsible, please tell me. I promise you that if it is within my power to put your mind at ease, then I will!" Chamois held the child-sized hands as he spoke.

"My grandfather says that you will be very angry." Her jewel bright eyes were now swimming with unshed tears.

"Your grandfather thinks himself very clever. *He is,* make no mistake, but he is not infallible. He can make mistakes and this is most likely one of them. Tell me what is troubling you and let me be the judge whether or not I am to be cross with you." There was already an idea of the reason for Joy's dilemma forming in Chamois' mind, but he had to get Joy to admit to it herself.

There was a slight rustling of twigs. The shadows of a tree parted and Wong stepped forward.

"What my dearest granddaughter is hiding from you is the knowledge that she is Dang's mother." Wong came into the pool of light cast by the overhanging lantern. He took Joy's hand from Chamois' and held it in both of his. "I love my granddaughters dearly. They were all that was left alive of my family after the volcanic eruptions and earthquakes. My son and his wife, who died too, had already spoken to the Han family about possible marriages when they were old enough, but *they too*, perished. I wanted only the best for my grandchildren, and their happiness of course."

Wong walked away a few paces; his face was once again in shadow. "Joy, and other high-born young ladies in a similar situation, pass some of their free time entertaining my most important visitors, but they never shared their beds with them. This time however, they decided that an opportunity to have children by men with courage and intelligence, such as yours, could not be ignored. There was the possibility of you not returning. Joy and her friends took advantage of your exhaustion. That is their only crime against you, because I, too, saw the chance to continue the Wong dynasty with great improvements and agreed to allow them to carry out their plans of seducing you and your companions when you could not reject them. Your father also was a subject for their attentions... you have a half-sister, Chamois."

Chamois felt his wits slide from his control, like quicksilver scattered across his consciousness. Speechless, he attempted to make sense in his mind of what Wong had told him. First he had a son, now also a sister. What else did the crafty old fox have up his sleeve, Chamois wanted to know?

Joy was standing in a pose of utter misery, her shoulders drooped and her head hung down. The tears were no longer restrained; she was shaking and sobbing as though her soul was in torment.

"Oh, dear God! Joy, someone had to be Dang's mother. This is a normal biological procedure and something scientists could never improve upon; and Dang seems to be a normal, happy young man. If I had been fully conscious when you visited me that night, I don't, by any stretch of the imagination think that I would have turned you out of my bed. I have never seen anyone as lovely as you!" Chamois placed an arm around her shoulders and stroked her hair.

Joy searched his face. "What about Maria? You called her name as I loved you."

Chamois gave a snorting laugh as he recalled the voluptuous Maria. "I doubt very much if Maria waited twelve months for me, and certainly not twelve years." He looked down at Joy. "Why did *you* wait twelve years for me? There must have been other men who saw you as a beautiful woman, and don't tell me your grandfather stood in your way. Somehow I can't believe that."

Chamois now held her face in his hands. Wong had disappeared back into the night.

"I couldn't get the thought of you out of my mind, and when Dang was born, he resembled you so much it was as if you were still with me. I have never wanted another man in my life. Your son and the memory of you were enough." Joy had said more than she intended. If Chamois was half the man she thought he was, then he would get the message very loud and clear that she loved him dearly.

"Tell me, Joy, as we left early next morning on our way to Orion, I heard you singing. Why were you so sad?" he asked.

"You were leaving and the chances of your not returning were almost absolute. It was only the fact that I was to have your child that saved my sanity."

Chapter 24

Chamois felt as though his heart would burst. His regard for Maria had never felt like this. He wanted to take Joy in his arms, away from everything that could possibly cause her a moment of unhappiness, to caress and cherish her. But he was a Space Captain, and that was where his dilemma lay.

"Joy, Joy, what can I say? I love your sweetness and loyalty. I love you! But I have my commitment to the Space Navy; it is my lifeblood. I would have to leave you at the flash of a red chip as soon as the trouble started. I will be going to places only yet dreamed about. Joy I can give you no promise of a permanent commitment." He felt he would be lying if he let Joy believe that she would come before his quest for new adventures with Orion.

"I want no pledge of love for eternity, Chamois. All I need is for the three of us to spend a little time together, like a real family." Chamois saw only uncomplicated truth in her eyes.

Wong suddenly appeared. "The media are waiting to take more photos of you and your crew. Will you come in now and face them?" Wong's attitude had undergone a subtle change.

The music and chatter hushed as Chamois, escorted by the president and Joy, came back into the room. Questions were asked of him, to which he gave smiling reassuring answers.

"Did you meet any aliens?" One sweaty, red-faced journalist asked.

Thinking for a moment, finding a way to answer without telling deliberate lies, Chamois said, "We did not directly meet anyone. When the ship's log is released later by the Space Authority, everyone will be able to view it and see for themselves, and then all your questions will be answered."

Tiredness was creeping up through his nervous system threatening to overcome him;

the unaccustomed wine was making his eyelids heavy. He thought of the last time he had tasted wine and had to suppress a smile of regret that he had been oblivious to the sweet nectar of love that had been bestowed upon him.

A light meal and sleep…alone, for eight hours, would give him the strength to parry the difficult questions these people were asking, but not now.

Sweaty face was asking another question. "Did you know that you had a son before you left for deep space, Captain?"

"I knew as soon as I saw him. There was no mistaking the fact. As for knowing before I left, well, sir, he was conceived the night before we left. No fertilisation specialist in this world can tell you the sex of your child in such a short space of time! My lady waited twelve years for me. No man could ask for more, and I would have been just as pleased to see a daughter waiting for me. Any more questions?"

President Wong realised that his guests needed to eat and rest, and called the conference to a close. The questions were spoiling the tranquillity of the gathering that he had hoped would endure for the evening. He made a note of who had asked such baseless questions and would see to it that he was not invited to his official residence again.

"That was a close one." Stonewall was walking towards the dining room with Chamois. "And where did you and that luscious lady disappear to hmm?"

"You don't want to know, Stonewall! Believe me, leave it till you've had some food and sleep, and lock your door!"

As Chamois reached Grant's side he asked him about Hope and her escort. "How did you get on with Hope and her companion?" he enquired.

"Oh, you mean Max? Great! He's a big pussycat where Hope and their two children are concerned...why?"

"You seemed to be more than close buddies while we were on Orion. That's all." Chamois was perplexed. If they were not having an affair, what was it that was so interesting that held them together? He wanted to know.

"Errr, yes, well you see, Hope has a sister who's taken a tumble for you like a tonne of rocks, and she wanted to know all about you, and I mean *all!* I had to tell Hope everything I knew about you, so that she could pass it on."

Grant was having difficulty meeting Chamois' eyes. Shuffling his feet as they walked, he continued, "I told her about the fights you got into when you were a cadet, how you like your tea, what to watch out for when you are about to lose your temper, you know, things like that."

"So now, Dang's mother knows more about me than I do!"

"Dang's mother, is she Hope's sister? How do you know?"

"I was talking to her and her grand-daddy out on the terrace, that's how. Now my little guardian

Grant, stand down! And that's an order. I don't want you looking over my shoulder any more." A magnanimous grin took away any animosity that Grant might be feeling.

For the rest of the evening, Chamois was deep in thought, and refused to tell anyone what caused him to be so evasive.

Dang had gone back to the academy where he was studying a course on astro-navigation. Chamois missed him and wondered how his own father must have felt when he could not even identify himself to him.

The meal after the reception had been a tremendous success. Members of the Federation, who were the only guests invited to stay for supper, did not ask awkward questions, but kept the conversation on the future of the Space Academy, and how the training would have to be altered to give the young people an opportunity to experience deep space at some time during their apprenticeship.

Stonewall suggested that five or six of the somewhat more promising ones should be allowed to go with the most experienced officers and crew, to a point outside the Solar System, not necessarily as far as another star system.

This, everyone agreed, would be considered in the next debate to be held concerning the problem.

Later, as they made their way to the sleeping quarters, Brian said to president Wong, "I think some time away from the attentions of the media would be a good idea. I'm taking my son and his crew to Camber Park. If you, or any member of your household, would like to join us, you will be most welcome." He was not taking any other answer except agreement. The level blacks on black eyes were grim. Chamois, his son, had been placed on the executioner's block to answer an offensive question for which Wong was partly responsible.

"I am not able, due to the summit meeting in Lima, which I must attend. I would like to join you as soon as it is ended though." Wong was standing on very dangerous ground, and if he were not careful, he would spoil everything he had planned these past years.

Camber Park was everything Chamois had dreamed it would be and more. Stonewall had taken a month's leave to be with them. He too felt the need for rest and fresh air, before taking up the demanding post of Admiral of the Space Fleet. At least that was the excuse that he had given. In truth he just wanted to make certain that Chamois had his replacement before he left him.

As Brian told the computer in the crowded land vehicle to slow down, two pale grey, mottled horses galloped towards them on feet that did not seem to touch the ground. The men from Orion, with Hope and her sister Joy were entranced. The greys nimbly trotted along side the coach, tossing their long manes and occasionally kicking out with their back hooves.

"The big brute is Skybolt, the other is Calypso. He flies and she dances. You can watch them later if you like when we put them through their paces." Brian turned to Chamois. "Tomorrow morning, you can ride him if you like."

"Huh, me? I've never been in any kind of saddle, let alone perched on top of a giant like that." Chamois' face was a picture of dismay. "Dad, you can't do this to me." His eyes were wide with an unnamed terror.

"You'll be all right. I'll tell him that you are my son," Brian said, as he patted Chamois' back in an attempt to reassure him.

Brian was mocking him, wasn't he?

While the vehicle was still stationary, Brian turned to speak to Stonewall and Stravros. "Stonewall, my old friend, Stravros, there is something that President Wong has not disclosed to either of you." There was a gleam of speculation in Brian's pitch-black eyes as he continued. "You know that Chamois has a son, Dang; well you too have a son, Stonewall, a boy the same age as Dang. He's called Glen. And you Stravros, you have a daughter, Melody, and I have a daughter, Lucy!" The look of astonishment on the old spacers' faces was classic. "But I don't know any women that well," Stravros blurted out.

"And I'm sure as God made little fishes that *I* certainly don't!" Stonewall was dumbfounded. His look of wonderment was exquisite.

Brian was now openly grinning. "Remember coming in to Hami, being questioned by President Wong, then going for a bath, having a meal and a drink of rice wine, wine that you, Stonewall, thought was rather weak? Then we each fell into a bed big enough to sleep the lot of us? Well, we all had a visitor that night. Celestial Joy, Hope's sister, is Dang's mother, and we have some rather classy ladies for the mothers of our progeny. I'm telling you this because you are going to meet the mothers when we have supper tonight. The young people are away at school in Gouldburn. They'll be home at the end of the school period next week."

Stonewall and Stravros were staring at each other. Each expected the other to have the answer to this situation. Stonewall growled through his teeth, "I knew it, that crafty old… old…man had something else tucked up his sleeve. He aims to control us through our sprogs. Well it won't work. These brats and their mothers can be as pleasant as you like, but I'm assuring you now, Wong will not have *me* in his pocket!" Stonewall had voiced what Brian and Chamois suspected.

Then Stravros asked Chamois, "Do you think Dang and these children are a ploy in Wong's plan to control us and the Admiral and therefore the Space Navy and its development?"

"Yes, I do, but he may have underestimated how our children and their mothers would feel about us. I think he has shot himself in the foot!" He turned to Joy. "Dang has accepted me as his father and you, my wonderful lady," Chamois' twinkling blue eyes met Joy's enigmatic ones with a loving kiss in his glance, "have waited twelve years for my return. That tells me everything I need to know. The three of us will be sharing our lives together whenever possible. Do you think grandfather Wong even considered things would turn out this way?"

"You are probably correct in your assumptions concerning my grandfather's original intentions. Yes, he would want to control the Space Program the same as he controls the Earth, and as you say, he feels responsibility as well as Chamois. They wrapped themselves well and truly around his power crazed heart as soon as they were born."

She laughed at the recollection. "Dang, as a little boy, would argue with him for hours about the need to have an effective Sea and Space Navy if anarchy were not to gain control and spoil the lives of peace-loving people. My grandfather loved every moment he spent with the child. Then when Dang wanted to bring his friends Glen, Melody and Lucy into the discussions, Grandfather could not say no. I've watched him when he thought that no one was looking. He has definitely shot himself but not in the foot; straight through the heart. He loves all his great-grandchildren and the pull of a family has proven even stronger than the pull of absolute power."

"Joy is right." Hope was smiling broadly. "Grandfather dotes on my two children, and knowing how much he loves Joy, when she gave birth to Dang, another great-grandson, I would say the power hungry chains that held him in a strangle hold were undoubtedly smashed for good."

Joy took up the conversation again. "Grandfather Wong considers the children of Professor Brian Dangerfield, Admiral Jackson and Chief Engineer Stravros Bertolozzte to be his. He positively loves and cherishes those children and glows with pride."

Joy had a delighted smile on her face; she had shown another side of her grandfather to her lover and these impressive men. They all exuded a power of command, even the ones who had not stayed that fateful night in Hami. And what was more satisfying, she sensed that they all loved and were loyal to the man she adored. Joy wanted to live this moment forever.

"Dad, when you've got a minute, there's something I must tell you." Chamois needed to pass on the knowledge concerning the star-paths, what happened on the water-world and his trip to the alien vessel, to his father. But not in front of Hope, not yet anyway.

"Yes, I'm waiting to have a good long natter with you too, son." Brian was aware that Chamois was keeping something under wraps. He didn't trust Wong's change of heart too far, either.

A long, low white building had come into view at the curve of the extensive private drive. Its roof was scarlet in the brilliant sunshine;

windows stood open to the fresh, eucalyptus-laden breeze. Trees gave shade on the wide lawns. Chamois knew he had, at long last, come home, and felt as if he would choke on the mass in his throat.

There were some people running toward them. Crispin Avery… running? Luke Denning, lumbering after him and glory be, there was Brookman! Grant pinched Chamois' shoulder. "Welcome home, sir!" They were tumbling out of the vehicle as it stopped. Chamois did not know who to hug first of these men who, at one time or another, had played such an important part in his life.

Brookman had beaten Crispin and Luke in the race to greet the travellers. "White man, it's good to see you. You haven't been crawling down any mine shafts to give your poor old buddy a heart attack while you've been gone, have you?" Brookman had him in a vice-like hug; tears were coursing their way down his Nubian face.

"Brookman, am I pleased to see you! I'll have something to say to you after supper, okay?"

Crispin Avery, though still an old man, had much brighter eyes than when Chamois had left him all those years ago after their escape from Red Hero. Crispin had been on the point of death by the time they had reached Hami. He stood back and feasted his eyes on the men from Orion; he was unable to utter a word except, "Thank you for making our dream a reality!"

Chapter 25

Luke Denning waited, smiling. "You done it again, boy! If I know anything you've pulled off the prize of the Space Fleet." Turning to Stonewall he said, "So, you're the blue devil Mars Rescue told us about, who wanted to try and stop this young whippersnapper from rescuing a bunch of no good criminals, huh?

And if I had known what I know now, I'd have probably tried to snatched him out by the scruff of his scrawny neck too."

"Mr Denning, I am now Admiral of the Solar Fleet," Stonewall replied. "I am not a 'blue devil'; but I *will* be the devil incarnate if I catch Captain Dangerfield disobeying orders again!" Stonewall shook Luke's hand. "I'm glad he had the spunk to ignore me that time." Turning to Chamois, he added, "But don't try it again or I'll have you grounded."

A bath of warm water, a change into light clothing, then Brian and his guests sat down to a meal of fresh food, cooked over an open fire on the cobbled patio.

"I feel as though I've died and gone to heaven," Gabby said.

"Me too," Peter agreed, "but I miss the music of those sweet engines."

Stravros heard the conversation as he joined them, drinking a low alcohol beer. "Make the most of your chance to breathe air that hasn't been through the scrubbers a dozen times, and food that tastes the way nature intended it to."

"Hey, Stravros, have you met your sprog's mother yet?" Peter asked.

"No! And I don't intend to make a meal out of it when I do, so shut up!"

"Touchy…touchy." It was Gabby, risking Stravros' wrath.

Hope and Joy were assisting several women helpers by passing around the plates of food. Brian had yet to introduce the mothers of Lucy, Glen and Melody.

A woman dressed in a pure white silk, oriental robe, interrupted Stravros' display of bad temper. She was carrying a dish of savoury pastries.

"Would you like one of these, sir?" she asked.

Stravros looked at the charming creature. She was not a bit like Hope, whom he had never really trusted. Her almond shaped eyes held no guile and her smile was trembling on her lips as if she were afraid of him.

Stravros had to blink his eyes. This lovely woman should not be waiting on the men-folk. She should be taking her ease and sitting on cushions. Better still she should be propped up in a bed. What am I dreaming about, he wondered.

"You don't mind if I join you for a moment or two, Stravros? This seems to be the best time for me to introduce you to Melody's mother, Dulcie."

Brian had seen the effect Dulcie was having on Stravros. The recently returned spacer should be introduced to her before he went into a catatonic coma, and was completely overwhelmed by the woman.

Stravros snapped his mouth shut. He had been unaware that it was hanging open. He'd been drooling like a lovesick baby and thinking the unthinkable. "Yes, sir, Ma'am. Pleased to meet you." And as Stravros took the proffered tit-bit, he looked around for support, but Gabby and Peter had disappeared with Brian, like rats deserting a sinking ship, and Stravros felt completely out of depth.

Dulcie had placed the rest of the food before him; with it was a glass of sparkling white wine. Taking a careful sip, Stravros found it tasted like the sweetest fruit juice he had ever had at Beckett's, except it had a slight sharp tang as it went down his parched throat. Taking a longer pull at the nectar, he emptied the glass and glanced at the beautiful woman sitting opposite him. She didn't belong there; that had never been his luck. Some lucky brute would soon be coming along to claim her for his own.

"Dulcie, you don't have to waste your time with me. I know that you have a good man waiting for you who has been a worthy father for Melody." Stravros felt as though his heart would break, but better for it to be broken now before he fell even more deeply in love with Dulcie… Dulcie. The name would stay with him till he died.

"Stravros Bertolozzte, I have not left a discussion with a trade delegation at Moon Base just to have *you* give me the old heave-ho! I have waited like the seventh virgin, with oil in my lamp for twelve years just for you, and no man will be my daughter's father except you, do you hear?" The once limpid eyes were now ablaze with fire.

Stravros gasped. Boy, she was bold, beautiful, and she was his. The 'Yes my lovely Dulcie!' came out in a whisper. A smile of a mesmerised man, flitted across his face. He was afraid he would wake and spoil the dream.

Stonewall stood outside the party of assembled friends, watching their happy faces. Everything was changing. Chamois was now a grown man who no longer needed a buffer to watch his back and keep him out of trouble. Wong had manoeuvred him, the best training officer in the Space navy, into a desk job. He'd been lumbered with a woman and baby. Things couldn't get much worse, could they?

The wine, as he sipped it, tasted of bitter aloes. A newcomer had arrived, dressed in Spacer uniform. Another friend of Brian's, he thought. Stonewall watched as the person spoke to Brian, who nodded his head, then pointed towards him.

A tall, stately woman in Commander's uniform was now weaving her way sinuously through the crowd. A right battle-axe no doubt, was Stonewall's opinion. Coming to tell me I'm needed and my holiday is over.

"Admiral Jackson, sir?"

"Yes, Ma'am. What can I do for you?" Stonewall had, kept his voice low. Something was telling him that the Commander was not here connected with navy business, and she was not on a mission of mercy either. She reminded Stonewall of a deadly snake about to strike!

"I am Commander Greys, of the Training Ship, Excalibur." She had skin the colour of alabaster, and her hair was as black as the darkest, moonless night. Her cool turquoise eyes were speculative. "You are my son's father, but I see no reason to prolong that relationship. We both have our separate lives to live and I do not wish to be the consort of the reigning Admiral. When Orion left for deep space, very few people expected it to return. Anyway, you were already past your prime and I didn't want to be lumbered with a man who has lost his libido. Therefore I constructed my career in the Space Navy where I would have the opportunity to get promotion. I will admit that having your son gave me a certain amount of leverage when it came to enhancing my status.".

There was a half smile playing about her flawless, vermilion lips. "As the Admiral of the Space Fleet, I know that you could have me demoted if you wish but I can assure you that I rank about the best instructor when it comes to teaching astral-navigation. Once *I've* instructed a pupil to find their way around the Solar System, they never get lost." The smile was now as derisive as caustic soda.

"I agree with everything you say, Commander. Let's hope that your tutoring is equally rational when it extends to outer-space."

"What do you mean?" Her eyes flared open wide, the mouth hardened.

It was Stonewall's turn to be malicious. He could have been vindictive, but the woman standing before him didn't justify that much energy! "Cadets and junior officers will need special training if they are to be able to duplicate the route taken by Orion and his crew! Don't let me keep you from your star charts." He saluted her and asked her, "Will you excuse me? I can see a friend signalling for my attention. Good evening, Commander."

Stonewall wondered what kind of young man his son had turned out to be. *I can only hope to God he has more intelligence than his mother has just displayed,* was the thought in his aching heart?

Chamois and Crispin had taken a brief respite from the general company with Brian, in his private study.

"Now then, Chamois, what is it that you are breaking your neck to tell me? Something that Orion's logs won't divulge… huh?" Brian watched Chamois' face as at first astonishment, and then a wide grin appeared.

"Sure. How did you guess? But it's something that Crispin must know too. Wait a moment and I'll get Stravros over here." Opening the door wide enough to poke his head out and looking around to where several of the Orion's crew and friends still stood chatting, Chamois saw Stravros talking to Dulcie. He called his chief's name, and Stravros sauntered into the study, carefully closing the door behind him.

"Yes, boss, what can I get you?" Stravros had a glass in his hand and looked at peace with the world. He was beaming all over his face.

"I know you have enjoyable ways of passing your time now, but be a good mate and go and get that item that you picked up on that old spacecraft we went to while waiting for Brian, will you?"

"Sure boss." With his grin still in place, Stravros went and did as Chamois had asked.

Carrying his trophy carefully protected in a metal case he had made for it, Stravros produced the implement. "Don't look much, but without it there would be no space program today. It's a screwdriver, used to tighten the bolts that held the inside of the craft together…can you believe it? I sweat at the thought of relying on such a primitive outer casing as the plastic tiles glued on to a frame, instead of the spray moulded Lucanite-carbon we have. With Brian making a Lucanite sub-shell too, our safety is as perfect as our technology can make it. A set of these and a few other equally primitive tools was all they had to rely on if things went wrong," Stravros said, as he handed the implement to Chamois.

"You're right Stravros, those days were a bit hazardous, but they too thought they had the best technology and safety margins." Carefully Chamois began to unscrew the shaft of the driver from its handle. Holding the shaft over the desk, he tipped it up. A fine spool of computer wire fell out.

"Now that's what I call a crafty move." Stravros' amused face radiated delighted indulgence.

"Crispin, I'd like you and Brian to look at this carefully and tell me what you think it means," Chamois said.

Gingerly the old man picked the spool up and placed it in a tissue. "If I know you Chamois, you have stumbled across yet another anomaly, yes?" Crispin's eyes crinkled with happiness. He might be ancient, but his brain was still in command, and that made life really worth living. "Thanks Chamois. You know I love nothing better than a brain-teaser." Crispin's smile was sublime.

"Can you give us a clue what's on it?" Brian's curiosity had been whetted.

"We called them Star-paths. That's the first anomaly. Then, well, I'm not certain what happened, but Orion said that I'd lost my temper again and therefore lost control of the situation." Chamois gave Brian the benefit of a shamed-faced expression. "But it's interesting as you'll see. Needless to say, Naval Intelligence does not have access to this wire."

Brian looked at his son. A huge enlightened grin started to spread across his face. "I don't know how you plan keeping the N I ignorant of the situation, or how you edited Orion's data-banks and I don't want to know. If anyone comes here asking questions, none of us will know what they're talking about."

"Here, here." Crispin approved. He was increasingly enjoying the situation. A light tap at the door made him wrap the booty and put it in a pocket.

"Yes, who is it? Come in," Brian called.

"I'm sorry to trouble you just now Brian, but most of our guests are retiring and I wondered if you have anything to say to them before they disappear for the night?" The speaker was an elegantly dressed Eurasian. She had the perfect face of an oriental and the figure of a Caucasian woman.

"Come in, my dear. I've been so overwhelmed that I have neglected my good manners. Victoria, come and meet my son, Chamois, and his chief engineer, Stravros. This is my wife, Victoria. She's been working in the background making certain that all my guests are well fed and comfortable."

Victoria sidled into the study as if she were unsure of her welcome.

Chamois guessed that she, too, must feel guilty at trapping Brian when he was asleep. Now she had to face his adult son and answer for her activities. Brian had come from behind the huge writing desk and held his hand out to her.

Chamois saw the uncertainty in her face and the slight tremble in her body. She was afraid of what he was going to say about being foisted with a young sister, he thought, and wondered if that was the real reason why she had kept out of sight all evening.

"I believe that you have made my father a proud and happy man, Victoria. When do I get to meet Lucy?" Chamois had moved forward and kissed Victoria on the cheek and then placed an arm about his father. "You were getting to be an old man, Dad, but a young daughter should keep you on your toes for quite some time to come. Well done, Victoria. I hope Dang and Lucy are friends?"

Victoria was visibly relieved. "Yes, all four children are great pals and when they get home at the end of the week you will meet them. It's like having an extended family, Brian and I love them all." Her glowing smile was like the sun trapped and scintillating from raindrops on a rose petal.

"Chamois, I hope you're not thinking these youngsters are children in the accepted sense. They're not. They really are young adults with ideas and aspirations of their own. I have done my best to guide them along the accepted paths of good behaviour, though none of them caused much trouble. Dang does have a sharp temper however, and had to be corrected from time to time. I hope you don't mind?"

"Mind? Dad, if he's anything like I was at that age, you have my sympathy! Has he said what he plans to do when he graduates?"

"I think that is something he had better discuss with you himself. All I can tell you is that he is very strong willed!" Taking Victoria's arm, Brian turned to leave. "I wish you all a good night's sleep, and don't forget Chamois, you have a riding lesson in the morning. That puzzle you brought us has taken up too much time and prevented Brookman giving you a display of horsemanship with the greys, but we'll make up for it tomorrow."

CHAMOIS

A pearly dawn had barely lightened the morning sky, when Chamois was awakened by the sound of hooves on the cobbles below the window of the room he had shared with Joy. Stealthily sliding out of bed so as not to waken her, he looked out of the window to see Brian and Brookman walking three horses.

Brookman's face broke into the happy smile that seldom left it now that he was free and living with people he loved. As far as he was concerned, he would die a happy man now that he had seen Chamois return home.

"Come down! The morning is wasting!" called Brian. "There is too much to do just to laze in bed all day!" He felt as though he was the luckiest man alive. Chamois had shown his approval of Victoria in the kindest possible way and so now he could continue to live in harmony with his whole family. He was indeed a most fortunate man, with a wife, a son, a daughter and a grandson. The years of mourning for Astrid were over; he had finally laid her to rest.

Chamois had brought with him so many reliable friends too. Brian gazed at his house; it was a home that glowed with love and kindness.

"Come on, dad, what are you dreaming about now?" Chamois had stepped out onto the cobbled drive.

Skybolt, Calypso and a gelding that Brookman was going to ride called Cosmos, were anxious to be away. The call of a gallop across the green fields of Camber Park made them tug at their reins, their hot breath boiling out into the cool air.

"First, let's have a word with Skybolt. Let him smell you and above all do not let him think you are afraid of him," Brian encouraged Chamois.

Chapter 26

With nothing to lose but his dignity, Chamois came closer to Skybolt. The magnificent beast took all of his attention and thoughts, which were of deep admiration. Chamois gently offered Skybolt a hand to smell and then coming closer, sensitively rubbed the horse's neck, crooning softly, praising the animal for his beauty and fine muscular build.

Skybolt had lowered his head so that Chamois could scratch the place just behind his ears.

"You sure you've never ridden a horse before? I've never seen Skybolt bow his head for scratching to someone he didn't know and like. You might just as well see what he thinks of you sitting in his saddle." Brookman had cared for the horses ever since he had come to Camber Park after leaving Red Hero ten years before.

With Chamois cautiously lifted into the saddle, Skybolt raised his head, snorted, and then delicately clip-clopped toward the open field. There was a bouncing swing to his body as he moved.

"Grip with your knees Chamois, and hold the reins very slack. Go with his rhythm." Brian and

Brookman were riding either side of him. Fear at first had stifled the breath in his throat, and then slowly he felt himself relax. He was riding!

"Now watch him when we come to the hedge, gather the reins in just a little bit and grab a tuft of his mane." Brian could only hope that his faith in Chamois and Skybolt had not been misplaced.

The hedge loomed up in the early morning mist. Skybolt seemed to gain speed. Chamois gripped the tuft of mane, then before he realised, he and Skybolt were flying, up, over, and then Skybolt gave a mighty kick with his hindquarters in mid air. They had not just cleared the hedge but had sailed ten feet beyond.

"Wow! You might have warned me!" Chamois had instinctively gripped his knees tighter, bent low over the saddle and gone with his horse.

"How do you feel?" Brian asked.

"Like I've won an Olympic Gold." Chamois had never felt so exhilarated as he did at that moment.

"Skybolt likes you, otherwise you would have ended up landing on your crown. He'd have thrown you clear over that hedge, head first," Brookman told him.

Relaxing with friends and relatives for the first time in years, discussing the section of Orion's log that he had edited out of the computer, and riding Skybolt had made the time fly. It was with amazement that Chamois discovered that he had been at Camber Park for over a week.

Dang had brought the small runabout to a halt by the back porch. Joy and the mothers of the other three young people rushed out to greet them.

Chamois gazed in wonderment at the youth who stood before him, the square set of his shoulders and splendid lift of his head. His heart felt fit to burst with pride. He wanted to hug him just as Joy had, but satisfied himself with a hearty handshake and a friendly slap on Dang's back and a grin that wreathed his face and eyes.

Dang passed a computer wire to his father. "This is what my tutors at the Space Academy have to say about my efforts, dad. We'll have to discuss whether or not the grades are good enough for me to apply for a post on the Excalibur!" Dang wasn't talking like a boy just twelve years old, bringing home his school report to his father. It was more like an adult telling him, like it or not, this is the situation!

Chamois looked to Brian for understanding, but he just shrugged his shoulders, indicating that Dang was now his responsibility.

"Okay, let's see what you've got here. Hmmm." Chamois punched the keys that would access the wire's information. There were 'A's with stars and comments of brilliant work. One tutor had written that Dang would do even better if he could control his quick response to a provoked insult.

"And what does that mean, Dang?"

"Oh, some moron said that you ran away from prison and raped my mother. I helped him to understand the situation a little clearer, that's all." Dang held his head up and at an angle. Oh, yes! Chamois thought. I know that feeling all too well.

"This person obviously has heard a garbled report of what really happened, son, and one of these days I'll tell you all about it, but for now, let's make the most of our free time. Huh?"

"Yeah sure, Dad. Mito Iwaki is arriving later. He's looking forward to seeing you again, and we'll have a few bouts. As you say, relax for a few days. Then I'm off to Moon Base for a meeting with some of the other guys who hope to be selected for Excalibur." The explosion of shock hit Chamois like a stray asteroid. Dang had no idea that he had taken his father by surprise. It seemed he thought nothing of travelling a quarter of a million miles to talk to some friends.

"Hang on there Dang. First, let us have an understanding. Going to Moon Base to chat to some mates at your age isn't on, you know. I can't have you chasing off like that. You'll have to have Brookman or Gabby or someone with you. You're not old enough to go so far from home on your own!"

"Dad, what are you saying? I'm nearly twelve. I've just completed my state cadet training facility. I was working on a space nodule near Jupiter last month and I only had Glen for back up. He's hoping to get Excalibur too." Astonishment and hurt strained his voice.

Brian decided that rather than see father and son at loggerheads, intervened. "Chamois, as I told you earlier, Dang's not a baby. He's an adult with his head screwed on just as firmly as yours was when you were eighteen. The age difference is due to his intelligence and the way young people have developed while you've been away. They are being taught basic maths by the time they are two years old." Brian then looked at Dang. "Supposing you give your father a break and invite your friends here. Let him get used to the idea that you're a responsible adult?"

Chamois and Dang looked at each other in the ensuing silence. Dang relented. "You're right, Brian. I've got a lot to tell you, Dad, and there are some questions that need answering that may take up some time…but I do want to get on the Excalibur!"

"That's easily sorted. Glen's mother Cassandra, Commander Grays, may be able to tell you what your chances are, if you ask her in a very diplomatic way. For instance you could ask how many new recruits she is expecting. But I wouldn't place too much hope on her giving you much in the way of help and advice, unless of course it helps her to get her foot on the next rung up of the ladder."

Brian rubbed the back of his neck. The next bit of advice needed all his tact and diplomacy. "You know you cannot expect always to get exactly what you want. Some things are not presented to us on a plate."

Dang tilted his head up and sideways. "Yes Brian, a few disappointments along the way, makes you appreciate the time when things *do* work out the way you want them, right?"

"Spoken like the true son of a Spacer!" Brian said.

Chamois had been following everything Brian and Dang had been saying. At the end he could only marvel at the way the young lad…no, no longer a child…young man, had reached a conclusion that had eluded so many of greater years.

As Brian and Chamois made their way out into the moonlit garden for a breath of fresh air, Chamois asked his father, "Tell me dad, how did a son of mine come to be called Dang? It's like nothing that I've heard before."

Chamois could see Brian's white teeth as his grin split his face. "You're right! The boy was about two years old, and grandfather, President Wong was besotted with him. He took him everywhere including to the conference hall. Can you imagine that? Anyway, as our beloved President is escorted into the hall, a lackey strikes a gong. Everyone stands up to acknowledge the President, right? Our little lad must have noticed this, and one day at an important meeting with heads of state and other bigwigs, he points to himself and says, Dang! No one understands what he is implying, so he grabs the gong hammer and gives the gong a mighty whack. 'Dang!' he says. President Wong, master of most of the world, laughs. He understood. When the gong is struck everyone stops talking and stands to attention. What Dang wanted was for everyone to take notice of him. He wanted to be boss too!"

"Nah, Dang? My boy? Putting one over the President? What did the old man do?"

"Do? He just about doubled up laughing. Thought his grandson showed initiative! I believe that his mother wanted him named Charley. Need I tell you more? Come on; let's go back inside. I've had enough fresh air and need to let my brain box do some work before our guests arrive. I do that best sitting down with a glass of Scotch in my hand."

President Wong and Mito Iwaki arrived at the party at the same time; they had known each other before, but by reputation only.

Mito showed his pleasure at seeing Chamois, his former pupil by saluting him with a well-honoured bow, with his clenched fist in his open palm, President Wong reserved this form of greeting for Chamois too.

Chamois saluted them in return. "I think this makes the party complete." He gestured for his companions to follow him into the garden where the rest of the guests were gathered.

All the younger members came and greeted the President and Mito, excited by the appearance of such honoured visitors. Then the young people brought refreshments to a shady table. When all the chattering had died down, Brian suggested that the younger members gave a demonstration of their prowess at karate.

The tournaments brought shouts of encouragement and claps of approval. Chamois glanced toward President Wong to see if he found the entertainment amusing, and discovered that he was being stared at with shrewd questioning eyes. "Uh, oh. He's found out about Orion's doctored computer log." The aura around Wong was a deep, reddish-brown. "Boy, is he in a temper." Chamois' intelligence raced to find a good excuse for the edited logs and thoughts scampered like squirrels around a nut bush through his mind. I wonder when he plans to tackle me about it?

He did not have long to wait to find out. After the bout of karate, the president suggested that Chamois and he walked in the flower garden.

"My daughter Hope told me before she came with you to Camber Park, that there were some unusual occurrences recorded in the ship's log. Yet on examination there seems to be little of interest apart from the fact that you did travelled where you said. There were no signs of any anomalies, such as she mentioned…star paths she called them, or your disappearance from the con. Can you tell me why my daughter should tell me one thing and the log another?" Wong had kept his voice low, his anger barely under control.

"Mr President, I am certain that Hope served me with all the care and help one could expect from a person who has never been off-world before. However you really should give her the benefit of not interpreting correctly everything she saw or thought she saw, and you must recognise the fact that the stars do create all kinds of unusual demonstrations for no reason at all. There were times when there was no one at the con when I considered it safe to leave it unattended. I think this is probably what Hope would be referring to." Chamois knew Wong did not believe him but, there was little that the wily old man could do about it just now.

"Very well Captain. I will accept that my daughter may have been mistaken, but remember this, it is a well-known saying that 'truth will out'".

So saying, Wong started to make his way back to where the young people sat around and discussed their ambitions. Mito stopped him. "Mr President, how pleased I am to have this opportunity to speak with you," deliberately guiding Wong away from the crowd. "You must be a very proud and pleased man to be blessed with such an enjoyable family." Mito gave Wong no chance to answer. "To have two intelligent and attractive grand-daughters, with handsome and noble lovers who have in turn presented you with these exquisite great-grandchildren!" Mito watched Wong's face. There was indeed the look of a man who was considering the treasures he had in his hands for the first time.

"I believe that Glen, Melody and Lucy, also look to you for wise council." The thin compressed lips were definitely relaxing and a smile dawning on the harsh features.

"If I had so much wealth I would guard it with my life. Treasure such as you have, needs careful nurturing, don't you agree?"

Wong listened to the tinkle of laughter that could be heard through the trees. He loved them, everyone, fiercely. It was torture to think that Brian or Chamois could take it away from him. "What you say is true, master Mito. My heart trembles when I think that I have to share them with Dangerfield. I would take them to Hami and keep them safe from any harm."

Mito now had to give Wong the anodyne for his fears. "You are surely much wiser than to think Dangerfield would deprive you of the love of those you hold dear? The man has lived in very interesting times and is not about to cause you grief, knowing it would only alienate his grandson Dang and his mother Joy. No, he loves them far too much to want to see them unhappy. Rest assured, the Dangerfields will do nothing to cause their loved ones misery." Mito took a chance and placed a consoling hand on Wong's shoulder. "Remember, a bird will lay quietly in your hand if you hold it gently. If you try to hold it too tightly, it will only fly away and never trust you again. Take the advice of a man who *did* lose *all* his family in the earthquakes. Cherish the loved ones you have while you can. Let those who would conquer the stars do so. You, sir, saved the earth from anarchy. You have every right to relax and let these young people have the cares and woes of governing the heavens." Mito bowed deeply to Wong and left him to meditate on the enlightenment he had given him.

A gale of laughter from Cassandra made Chamois take notice of what was being said. "Dang, if you aren't a chip off your father's block, I don't know what is. You and your friends all want to join Excalibur, right? Well take it from me, I don't know whom I'm getting in the way of new recruits, but I must admit I should be most gratified if I have you and your cronies. I will be taking on only six for the forthcoming trip. The destination has yet to be worked out with my Lords of the Space Navy, and that is where Admiral Jackson comes in. He will have most to say about that." Cassandra gave Stonewall a speculative, critical look. She had passed that particular buck with admirable dexterity.

"This is not a matter to be discussed lightly, though I have suggested to the members of the Federated States, that new members to the Space Navy need to be instructed as soon as possible in the ways of deep space exploration. I think a short foray on the route toward Sirius would be useful. What do you think, sir?" Stonewall had addressed this question to President Wong.

"What you suggest is right. Yes, the officers of tomorrow should be educated to the highest degree. There have already been some exploratory excursions out toward Sirius and Canis Major. The Lucanite engines have made that possible. But we must carry our expeditions further. There could be other worlds that may have intelligent life forms and we could benefit from them. There could also be more deposits of Lucanite waiting to be found." President Wong was pleased that he had been consulted. However Mito's words were repeating themselves in his mind and the more he thought about them the more he could see how right they were.

"You will have to plot and plan very carefully for the future Space Captain's education, Admiral. I feel certain you will do so with your usual perceptiveness."

Wong had an unusual feeling of satisfaction delegating so much responsibility. A shrewd thought passed through his active mind. "Jackson was well chosen for the Admirals stars and now he can start to earn them."

Chapter 27

Stonewall was in his bedroom and about to retire for the night when there came a light tap on his door. "Yes, who is it? Come in."

The youth, who stood before him, had his height and grey eyes. There was also the upright carriage. His smile was diffident.

"I trust that I am not too late to see you this evening, sir?" The young man had removed his student's uniform, and wore only a light cotton vest and pants. "I'm Glen, your son. Cassandra, is my mother, or should I have said Commander Greys?"

"Come in and sit down Glen. I was about to get some sleep. It's been a very long day, but I'm glad you looked in on me. As Admiral of the Fleet, I'm not going to get much chance to be with you, son, so let's make the most of what time we do have. I believe that you would like to join the Space Navy as an astro-navigator. I'll take a look at your results, then I'll be in a better position to tell you what your chances are."

"Yes, sir, I have them here with me. I was hoping that you would be interested." Glen's face was still set and serious. He would take nothing for granted. His mother, Cassandra, had been inclined to be sarcastic, saying that Jackson was an old fool who didn't know when to give up and make way for the younger generation. Yet others had spoken of his father as the very foundation of the new order of space travel. For a start it was Admiral Jackson's teaching that had made Captain Dangerfield into the formidable senior officer that he had become.

Glen looked carefully at Stonewall as he passed the computer wire to him. True the Admiral was an old man compared to him but he knew more about what the space navy required in a cadet than any other man alive.

"You seem to have all the qualifications to get the post you are aiming at. I'll have a word with Sean Darnley; he's the best man to guide you in that particular faculty. Who knows, you might even get Captain Dangerfield's permission to fly with the Orion." Stonewall gave his young son a friendly hug and bade him goodnight.

The time seemed to fly. The young people returned to Gouldburn, to be assigned to their new posts.

Admiral Jackson took the shuttle to Moon Base with Cassandra, who went on to Space Training Vessel, Excalibur, to await her new crewmembers.

Chamois found himself being sent out on rescue missions. Brookman said he would join him as soon as Brian found a replacement for him.

News came through to Chamois, that Dang and Melody had been assigned the Excalibur, but not Glen; it was considered that because his mother was the Commander, it would not be a suitable assignment for him. He was to join the Dryad, a survey vessel operating in the asteroid belt. Lucy had applied for a post in Quantum Physics and had been assigned a place at the university of Parramatta. To Chamois, it seemed as though the young people never had any childhood!

"Don't worry Grant," Dang said when the results were placed for all to see. "As I said to Brian, when we don't get everything we want, it makes us pleased when things do go right for us!" He had tried to cheer Glen up, but Glen's mind was far away on what his father had told him, and trusted that one-day the dream of navigating Orion would come true.

"You never know, one day you might be glad you didn't get the Excalibur. The Dryad is supposed to be working with Eurydice, and there's never a dull moment on *that* ship," Dang continued, not realising that his friend's heartfelt wish was far beyond Excalibur.

Chamois called Dang into Brian's study the day before he was due to join Excalibur. "We never got around to having that talk you wanted. Was there anything in particular you wanted to say?" Chamois asked.

"Well the thing is this…" How could he tell his father that he was more like him than the superficial looks portrayed? "Brian said that on the journey through the Gobi desert you often spoke to someone that no one else could see. I…. I too see and hear things no one else can. At first I thought I was going mad. I told Brian about it and he advised me to tell you." Dang's troubled look made Chamois smile.

"Yes. It's a troublesome, wonderful gift that we have son. But it carries its own responsibilities. You have to be able to know when to speak out, and when to keep a still tongue. I was with good friends in the Gobi and the knowledge that I shared with them saved our lives. It's not all care and worry though. You know that you can trust Brian, and me. You can also trust Admiral Jackson, and the rest of Orion's crew. Brookman would understand too. You are no longer alone. You won't feel so isolated now. Go and make the most of your training Dang. Have a good life. I'll see you in a couple of years' time." Half of Chamois' heart walked out of the door as Dang left.

Once the young people had left Camber Park to take up their various duties, their mothers left to resume their different workstations and the place seemed deserted.

Brian took Chamois out to Orion in his sharp-nosed runabout. They often spent time discussing the star paths. The question uppermost in their minds was how to get on to them.

"I don't think I've ever come across anything so tantalising!" Chamois said one day. "I saw them and so did the rest of the crew. We speculated on what they were and we all came to the same conclusion that they were the access paths between the stars; nothing less!"

"Yes, that's what Crispin and I think too, but it's like trying to grab a handful of moonbeams to find out how to use them." Brian was touching instrument panels and layout plates, caressing them like old friends.

"You miss going to deep space?" Chamois asked his father. It was a statement more than a question.

"Sure, he replied, but I had to let you have your head. Anyway sending you out on the trial run, got you from under Wong's feet."

As he spoke, a red light suddenly started to blink and wink on the main control panel. Orion's voice filled the cabin. "Major alert! Major alert! Training ship Excalibur missing from the tracking web."

Chamois smashed a hand down on to the controls governing the web site of Sirius. There was no telltale sign of the presence of Excalibur! His heart cried 'No!' But the web was completely devoid of the training ship's signal.

Already his hand had pressed the 'Call to arms' signal for his crew. They would arrive as he prepared Orion for his race to the path to Sirius Prime.

"Dad, you take Black Swan and search from the point they were last recorded. I'll start sweeping the area five hundred thousand kliks ahead. We've got to find something even if it's only wreckage." Chamois turned to Brad who had stayed on as chief security officer, and said, "Get Brookman from Camber Park to Stonewall's side. The man's a genius in a disaster."

Orion with a full crew minus Stonewall had his engines running as high as the safety speed would allow inside the Solar system. Then, with Stravros easing them up to maximum speed, he headed toward the Sirius sector.

"Sean, something tells me we're going in the wrong direction!" Chamois had felt distressed and confused once they had headed for the Dog Star.

"You take us to where you think we should be, Chamois. There's no sign of Excalibur anywhere near the last manifest reading. There's something strange happening here and weird is in your back yard." Sean's logic was sound. There was something unnatural happening.

With the command helmet in place, Chamois reached out to Orion's data banks, to try to assess where Excalibur could be. The computer-ship was searching through all his star charts. Chamois watched as sector after sector was examined.

Finally a faint blip, moving toward the giant dark orange-red sun of Betelgeuse in the Orion sector, was discovered. It had Excalibur's code.

Questions of how and why could wait until after the training ship was safe. For now Chamois gave Orion the order to set a course for his namesake at his top speed.

The stricken ship was being dragged into the gravitational pull of the huge star. Nothing could stop it from hurtling into the fiery hell.

Grant and Sean stood by Chamois' side, as they watched with horror the scene being enacted out on the main screen.

"Orion, plot a course to hit Excalibur just under and on the port wing. I want you to make contact in a way that will send Excalibur off at a tangent away from Betelgeuse."

"Yes, Chamois. I will do that. 'Brian's Law' is overridden by the need to save the young lives on the training vessel."

Orion's crew knew that their lives were forfeit, yet they relaxed as the command was carried out. The youngsters would now stand a chance.

Chamois removed the helmet and looked carefully at each of the men whom he had come to trust and love. "Thanks to all of you. We've been a great team!"

Impact and certain death! It was the only solution. Chamois had made the decision without really thinking about it. Survey and Research Vessel Orion would snooker the crippled training vessel away from its destruction.

Orion and his crew would be lost but the training vessel Excalibur with the group of high achieving officers, including Chamois' own son Dang, and Stravros' daughter Melody, would be saved from annihilation.

Oblivion for Chamois and his crew, as Orion headed into the giant sun, Betelgeuse. Chamois' memory badgered him about the time, over thirty years ago when he was just a kid, struggling through the Star Fleet Academy with old Stonewall as his mentor. Sean and Grant had been with him then. The rest of the crew were like burrs collected along the way...

Orion had carried out the instructions Chamois had issued, and as the two vessels collided, it had given an extra flip of his wing tip to toss Excalibur well clear of the Betelgeuse gravitational force field.

The impact had set Orion on a path directly in line toward the waiting furnace.

Chamois watched, as Betelgeuse grew ever closer; prominences geysered, arching into the shimmering, pulsating corona, shafts of burning gases of bronze, ruby, orange and yellow; white and violet at the heart of the fountain that seared Chamois eyes. He was appalled at the ferocity of Betelgeuse. Turning to Grant he asked, "Have you ever witnessed such anger?"

"Yes, Chamois, old friend. When Stravros tried to stop you from going down that photon shaft, I thought that you were going to bust a seam!"

Stravros, Gabby and Peter came onto the main control deck. The engines could not fight the merciless drag and Stravros had shut them down.

"We were just talking about you Stravros, about the one and only time you tried to stop me from doing anything."

"Oh yes, when did I not know, not to spit into the wind?"

"When Chamois rescued the miners, you tried to stand in his way."

"Hmp! Once again, our goat jumped into the fertiliser and came out smelling of violets. Even when he got sent to that penal work station, he meets up with an old friend, Brookman!" Stravros placed a hand on Chamois' shoulder and continued, "Thank God you did too. That was no place for a poor innocent Spacer like you. Most likely you would have had half of them learning karate and the rest of them keeping well out of your way." His laugh echoed his imagination of such a situation.

Chapter 28

There was no need to place any more strain on Orion. The ship deserved to die with dignity, not have his engines torn out of him by asking the impossible.

The heat soon rendered them breathless. Chamois watched as his crew succumbed to everlasting sleep, collapsing where they stood.

As the feeling of a jet-black night crept up his neck into his brain, Chamois felt an impression of elation, and he thought that surely death was meant to be frightening?

And then darkness.

His oxygen starved lungs forced him to take a deep breath of air laden with the scent of clover and new mown hay. Chamois detested the smell. It was the odour of betrayal. He had detected it in the courtroom at Alice Springs, when Sir Arthur Pelham had sentenced him to five years of penal servitude at Red Hero. Anger sent the adrenaline surging through him like a hot razor blade.

Through the haze that blurred his vision, he realised that he was lying on the deck of Orion, looking up at a person who had no right to be there.

"Welcome back, Chamois. I believe you know my name. I am Nazaire. No, you have not left your physical body behind; in fact you are very much alive. As soon as you feel that you can stand up again and understand what I have to tell you, then I will explain everything." Nazaire looked at him with deep compassion, then continued, "We have almost completed reprogramming Orion's data banks. When we have finished you will be able to access the Star Lanes that you are eager to explore. You must try to understand they are not just a means for getting from one place to the next. The Star Lanes are not of your normal three dimensions; they belong to the fifth, where time has no place. While you are in them, all time ceases. Do you know what I am telling you Chamois?"

Nazaire wasn't quite standing on the deck. Chamois could see a space between deck and the intruder's feet.

"And here was I thinking that I was dead!" he said as he examined his clothes for scorch marks. "You talk in riddles, Nazaire. If I were to believe you, then it would mean that my ship could go wherever I choose to take it and there would be no time to account for." Chamois heaved a huge sigh in an attempt to get more oxygen into his lungs to feed his brain. This information needed more intelligence than he was gifted with. Crispin Avery was the one who would understand the logic of this, if there were any.

"Now, let us discuss Voki. He suffered all the pangs of his idea of hell as long as he did because he could not absolve himself for the destruction of a populated peaceful planet. Once you showed him compassion, he saw a way to forgiveness and is now working to help others who made similar mistakes that he did." Nazaire gave Chamois a tender smile. "Yes, that is all Voki had to do, forgive himself! Everyone must face the mistakes they make while incarnate, and be truly repentant, then forgive him or herself. Some, like Voki find it almost impossible, yet all those who were involved forgave him once it was obvious that he was truly apologetic, even the entity that you label as God, had absolved him."

The smile broadened on Nazaire's face. "Now I come to what do I want." I want you to continue to have your desire for knowledge, to live a life that is as interesting as it is long! Come, there are people mourning your loss. Orion has been programmed to take you home by the short cut…through the Star Lanes. You only need to transfer your orders by thought control and Orion will carry them out."

Chamois still had so many questions of why and what for. How did Excalibur reach Betelgeuse in such a short time and why was it out of control, he wondered?

"Excalibur was brushed aside by the gamma rays emitted from a collapsing black hole.[1] We knew they would be safe once you arrived, but we had to prove it."

Another question pierced Chamois' foggy brain. Prove to whom and had Nazaire read his mind? But looking at Nazaire he could tell by the mysterious, almost sly smile that he would have to be content with the knowledge and help he had already received. As Chamois looked at him with the puzzles still unsolved, Nazaire seemed to shimmer then fade.

Stravros was the first to awaken. "What happened, boss? I thought we were a goner then."

"Stravros, let's just say that our guardian Gabriel was taking good care of us and leave it at that for now, eh?" Chamois' grin lit up his face with pure contentment.

They had been to hell and back. The fire god had spat them out, just as the old aborigine had predicted. And what had been learned would be kept under wraps until Brian and Crispin could evaluate it. No one was going to get at Orion's memory or workings until Brian said so.

"Home, Orion. Let's put everyone on Earth out of their misery."

The Prisoners' Association to the Star Fleet presented a jet-black plinth, bearing a carved silver, horned goat, standing rampant. Admiral Jackson had taken it into care, to be mounted in the Space Museum on Moon Base, along with Chamois' Order of Orion's Belt. The requiem mass was being sung for Orion and her crew in every major town and city.

It was almost too much to bear for the officer who had taught Chamois everything he knew. Stonewall's face was withered and drawn. Brian's heart felt like a dead weight in his chest. "My son. Thank God I got to know you!" He wanted to hug Dang, but the boy seemed to be in a world of his own.

"He's not dead, you know," Dang said, as the group of Star Fleet Officers and friends of Chamois gathered outside the church. Several people gasped, thinking Dang was out of his mind with grief.

Brian went to him and asked, "What do you know, Dang?"

"Chamois and his crew are safe. Orion is coming home!"

As Dang said this, Admiral Jackson's wrist communicator flashed a message. "Identified ship in the Jupiter section. Ship bearing the I. D. of Orion approaching Earth."

Jackson's voice rasped as he choked out the command. "Identify yourself before you approach Orion, then escort Orion to Moon Base. Do not attempt to board Orion. Give Captain Dangerfield and his crew the message from Earth, "Welcome home."

President Wong sat alone in his study. He should have gone to greet the valiant Captain Chamois Dangerfield who had rescued the Excalibur and the people aboard her, which included his great-grandson, Dang. Chamois would be a great hero to Joy and Dang… to the whole world. He, President Wong was in debt to the Dangerfields. It was an intolerable situation. A sigh escaped him. With his head in his hands he allowed the feeling of dejection to overtake him.

The slight tap at the door almost went unanswered, but Wong was an old statesman. Straightening his back and firming the harsh lines on his face, he bid the intruder enter. Joy, his beloved granddaughter entered, followed by Dang, then Chamois.

"Grandfather, we wanted to see you first, to share our happiness at the deliverance of Dang and Chamois." Joy's exuberance was infectious. Wong found himself smiling. Standing up to enfold Dang and Joy in his arms, he bowed low to Chamois then held him in an affectionate embrace too.

The "Dragon's teeth" had finally been drawn!

The company of friends and relatives at Camber Park had celebrated the safe return of Orion and Excalibur. Wong and Mito had found that they had much in common, discussing judicious theories and merits of unarmed combat tactics.

Brian surveyed his home as he had when Chamois had first arrived. Nothing would ever be the same. Too much had happened. He felt the enticement of space exploration tugging at him. Victoria and Lucy were more than mother and daughter to each other. At times he had felt as though he was an interloper. They loved him, of that he was certain but being a man had its drawbacks in female discussions.

Stonewall had congratulated Cassandra on her handling of the situation, when Excalibur had careered out of control. "I will have a word with your captain regarding promotion. Good-day Commander!"

"I suppose I should have realised that you couldn't even begin to be trivial in your judgement of people. But the fact remains, no one would have really missed me if Excalibur had collided with Betelgeuse, and I had died." Cassandra's face had a puzzled almost naïve look. There was the stirring of a sensation that was completely alien in her heart.

"Madam, for a very clever person you are also very foolish. You have so much to learn. Unfortunately, none of it is in books. It is something only caring and loving another person can teach you!" Then touching his cap, he saluted her and left for his office on Moon Base.

Gradually everyone had gone their separate ways. Even Orion's crew had dispersed to their homes. Only Chamois was left with Brian after Dang had joined the Eurydice with Glen, and Joy had taken up a post at the university again.

Luke Denning had taken advantage of the jewel-like properties of Lucanite and set up a thriving business, dealing in rare gems and expensive jewellery.

Crispin had been like a child with a new toy when Chamois had told him about the new program in Orion's data banks and wanted to go out to where the ship was moored. "No, old friend, Brian and I will go to Orion and download it to your computer in the stables. You'll have more fun being able to use all those gadgets that you've invented and remember this is even more classified than that spool of information I gave you," Chamois told him. "You agree, Brian?"

"Yeah, sure." Brian seemed absent minded. If he went out to Orion again, the chances were that he would not be able to restrain his desire to skim the Star Lanes himself.

"What's the matter, Dad? What's chewing at you?" Chamois could feel the apprehension in his father and would do anything he could to ease whatever it was that was upsetting him.

"Son...if I go on board Orion again with the new programme you've been telling us about, I'll not want to come back here without giving them a test. Do you understand?" Brian was almost pleading with Chamois. He so desperately wanted some action before finally he had to admit to time and old age.

A tingle of excitement fizzled in Chamois' brain as a germ of an idea was hatched. "Dad, let's have some prime time together to make up for those lost years. We can go and explore the Southern Cross in the Milky Way or even the Sagittarius Dwarf and be back before anyone notices us missing. Coming?"

Brian could not suppress the hunger of his excitement any longer. With a gleam of almost childish daring in his eyes and the broad grin, he said, "Okay, let's go, but I think that we will keep to our own galaxy. The Sagittarius Dwarf is 60,000 light years away and is reputed to be rather unstable, thanks to our galaxy pulling it apart and trouble on our first trip out would not be advisable. Remember we have wives and children to consider."

"Oh for heavens' sake, don't be such an old dodderer, dad, come on! Just think, we could watch the two galaxies merge, perhaps. I'm certain, that's what's happening. Our galaxy is pulling Sagittarius into our Milky Way."

Brian recognised the boiling acid of insatiable curiosity in the veins of his son. It was one of the reasons that he had chosen him to pilot Orion in the first place leaving this galaxy to explore beyond the confines of known space… "Chamois, you don't even know if the galaxies are linked in the way that the stars in this galaxy are. How do you plan to get out there and back without the star lanes?"

"Dad, it's only simple logic. If the mechanics who constructed the star lanes did anything, they did not do it by halves. Of course they are linked, each and every galaxy in this universe and every universe. Want to check it out?" Chamois stood level-eyed, facing his father…daring him.

Brian threw back his head, laughing. "You're my son all right! If we're not back in time for dinner, I'll blame you!"

"And if you think you're going anywhere without us, then you're seriously mistaken!" Stravros and the rest of Orion's crew stood in the entrance lock as Brian and Chamois boarded. "Orion warned Glen that you were making your way here, we guessed the rest. So what are we waiting for? As the man said, let's go!"

[1] Stravros Gribbin. "Death Rays from Space" Page 241 Focus." Science magazine number 114.

About the Author

Joyce Doŕe lives with her husband in a sea side village. Her writing is normally done in a converted garage that overlooks the rear garden with its variety of flowers, trees and emerald green lawn.

At night she would gaze at the stars and wonder if man could possibly be alone in such an incalculable depth of space; and she began to jot down ideas.

Joyce has travelled to many countries and seen the strangeness of some cultures listening to their beliefs. All she learned was remembered and written about in this book "Chamois".

Printed in the United Kingdom
by Lightning Source UK Ltd.
104278UKS00001B/31-102